PRAISE FOR MARI

"Frontlines is earnest, optimistic, and fun ... deals with subject matter that's intrinsically grim. It's a story that strikes the perfect balance between escapism and serious reflection, and it's the perfect military sci-fi series to escape into for a week or two."

—The Verge

"Powered armor, nuclear warfare, and [a] bit of grand theft auto combine for a thrilling tale of battle in space."

—*Booklist*

"Marko Kloos's military science fiction Frontlines series is quickly becoming one of our favorites . . . Kloos is well on his way to becoming one of the genre's best assets."

—*io9*

"There is nobody who does [military SF] better than Marko Kloos. His Frontlines series is a worthy successor to such classics as *Starship Troopers*, *The Forever War*, and *We All Died at Breakaway Station*."

—George R. R. Martin

"Military science fiction is tricky because it either intends to lampoon the military industrial complex or paints it in such a way that you must really have to love guns to enjoy the work. *Terms of Enlistment* walks that fine line by showing a world where the military is one of the few viable options off a shattered Earth and intermixes it with a knowledge of military tactics and weapons that doesn't turn off the casual reader."

—Buzzfeed

SCORPIO

ALSO BY MARKO KLOOS

Frontlines

Terms of Enlistment
Lines of Departure
Angles of Attack
Chains of Command
Fields of Fire
Points of Impact
Orders of Battle
Centers of Gravity
Measures of Absolution (A Frontlines Kindle novella)
"Lucky Thirteen" (A Frontlines Kindle short story)

The Palladium Wars

Aftershocks
Ballistic
Citadel

SCORPIO

MARKO KLOOS

47NORTH

This is a work of fiction. Names, characters, organizations, places, events, and incidents are either products of the author's imagination or are used fictitiously. Otherwise, any resemblance to actual persons, living or dead, is purely coincidental.

Published by 47North, Seattle

www.apub.com

ISBN-13: 9781542035491 (paperback)
ISBN-13: 9781542035507 (digital)

Cover design by Shasti O'Leary Soudant

Cover image: © David Paire, © Katrina Yu / ArcAngel; © Visual Unit, © DM7, © Welshea / Shutterstock

Printed in the United States of America

For Robin, always.

CHAPTER 1

Lanky-occupied colony planet, 18 Scorpii system
46.1 light-years from Earth
17NOV2124, 0000h Standard Colonial Time
Eight years, three months, and eleven days since the Lanky invasion

At the precise moment when Alex officially turns twenty-one years old, she is sitting in the back of a Spaceborne Infantry mule that's rolling across the gravel fields of the southern plateau, three hundred kilometers from home.

She touches her wrist computer to turn off the vibration alarm she had set for 0000 hours. It's an arbitrary marker, of course—she knows she was born at 0447 Standard Colonial Time, not at the stroke of midnight—but the law says that midnight marks the transition. And according to the law, she's a full-fledged colonial citizen now, with all the rights and responsibilities of that status.

Happy birthday to me, she thinks. *Wish you could be here, Mom and Dad.*

Alex looks around in the mission module of the mule. The armored eight-wheeler is a military machine and not designed for comfort. There are only four people in here with her, sharing a space that can hold a dozen SI troopers in battle armor, so there's room for them to spread out a little. Private Lopez is sleeping on the other side of the module, stretched out over four seats that he turned into a makeshift bunk with an insulated mat and a sleeping bag. Sergeant Frye is sitting in his seat in the space between the troop compartment and the cockpit, scanning the displays in front of him with bleary eyes and sipping from a plastic cup of long-cold instant coffee. Up front behind the forward armor bulkhead, Private Harris is driving the mule, leading their little two-vehicle column south at fifty klicks per hour. To the rear, a colonial all-terrain cargo tractor is following a few hundred meters behind, close enough to stay under the protection of the military transport's gun turret but far enough to get to safety if the mule runs into trouble.

Ash, who is curled up by Alex's feet, stirs from his snooze and looks up at her with dark, soulful eyes.

"Good boy," she says softly and rubs the top of the dog's head. Ash settles back down with a content little grunt. The black shepherd is the reason she's riding in the military vehicle instead of back in the tractor with the other civilian colonists on this expedition. He's small for his breed, the runt of his litter, and he's useless as a regular military dog because there isn't a gram of distrust or aggression in him. But out of the three dogs the colony has left, he's the best at sensing approaching Lankies. Ash is a biological early-warning system that works even in poor visibility, and he has never failed to detect a Lanky coming their way. People being what they are, not everyone in the colony really earns their calories every day. And dogs being what they are, Ash has proven his worth many times over.

"He's gotta be bored out of his mind," Sergeant Frye says from across the aisle. "I know I am."

"He's all right," Alex replies. "Napping is his default state anyway. But I'll need to let him out before too long."

"We're coming up on a waypoint marker in a few. Gonna have to stop anyway to send up a drone."

“What’s it look like out there?” she asks.

Sergeant Frye nods at the screens in front of him.

“Come see if you want.”

Alex unbuckles her harness and walks to the other side of the compartment on slightly unsteady feet. She takes the seat next to the sergeant’s command station and leans forward to look at the display panels. Outside, the world rolls by in various shades of gray, soot-colored clouds above windswept gravel and craggy rock formations. Sergeant Frye nudges his control stick and pans the view to give Alex a wide-angle perspective. Behind them, the cargo crawler is following in the tire tracks the mule made, kicking up little puffs of rock dust and stone chips with its large, knobby tires.

“Three hundred twelve kilometers out,” Sergeant Frye says. “Let’s hope the juice is worth the squeeze. I’ll be pissed if we come back with half a case of MREs and some wonky battery cells.”

“We picked everything clean that’s close to home. Pretty soon someone’s gotta figure out a way to get across the mountains and up north to the spaceport.”

“Not gonna happen,” Sergeant Frye says. “Not without wings. Mule would run out of juice halfway even with a spare energy pack. And that’s assuming you could get over those mountains in the first place.”

“I know, I know. I just keep imagining the haul we could get out of there. Nobody’s cracked those underground stores open in eight years. Imagine coming home with a half ton of sugar and a hundred brand-new filters for the air scrubbers.”

“And a working drop ship with half a million liters of fuel. Since we’re wishing for unicorns now,” Sergeant Frye says.

“Think there’s anyone alive over there?” Alex asks. “On the other side, I mean.”

“At the spaceport?” Sergeant Frye bites his lower lip while he thinks about her question. “Never say never. Their admin center is a Class IV unit. Tough as shit. Maybe it was enough. Maybe they holed up and rode things out like we did."

He drinks the last of his coffee and throws the cup into the recycling container that's strapped to the bulkhead lining next to the vehicle commander station.

"But there's no way for us to know for sure since comms went down with the satellites when the Lankies arrived. If they're still alive, they're in the same boat we're in."

"But you don't think so."

Frye shakes his head. "They don't have the hydroponic setups we have in the Vault. They didn't have food stores or water for eight years. And that spaceport is out on the coastal plains. Pretty far away from bedrock. I think they held out a month or two, maybe. Not that I would mind going out there and knocking on doors to find out for sure."

"Same here," Alex says. "I've started to forget what the place looked like. Before, I mean. We went once a year for the proctored school exams, and the medical checkups."

"Did you know anyone there?" Frye asks.

She nods.

"Micah and Aurora. Their dad got reassigned to the med center. They moved three months before the Lankies came. I thought they were the luckiest, to get to live out there by the spaceport. Micah was a smug little shit about it too. I told him, 'I hope your stupid puddle jumper crashes.'" She shakes her head with a sad smile.

"Hey, none of us had any idea. Our platoon was packing up to rotate out to Station 21. If the Lankies had shown up three days later, we would have been down there, all alone on that little peninsula. And that would have been that. It was the luck of the fucking draw, nothing more," Sergeant Frye says.

They ride in silence for a while, and Alex wishes she had broached a different subject because now she can't help thinking about what it must have been like out at the spaceport when Lanky pods started falling out of the sky without warning. None of the visuals her brain serves up are pleasant, so she tries to push the thoughts away by looking at the landscape outside again. A rainstorm passed across the plateau a little while ago, and the cargo crawler following in their tracks is splashing up water as it rolls through puddles left in the wake of the downpour. Overhead, dark clouds are roiling in an angry-looking sky. Her father used to say this place was *beautifully harsh*. Before the Lankies, when people could be outside without being in a vacsuit or a vehicle, Alex had agreed that there *was* a certain beauty to the planet. Now, however, their home world is just harsh, and getting harsher every year as their resources slowly dwindle and the Lankies keep undoing decades of human terraforming work.

"All right," Sergeant Frye says with a glance at the map display. "Two klicks to the waypoint. I could stand to stretch my legs a little. Harris, Bayliss, are you awake over there?"

"Depends on your definition of the term, Sergeant," Harris replies from her seat in the cockpit.

"We're coming up on marker 320. Let's make station for a little while and send out the bird. Pick us a cozy spot to park."

"Affirmative," Private Harris replies.

Frye looks past Alex to Private Lopez, who is still stretched out on his makeshift cot and snoring softly.

"Lopez," he says. "Hey, Lopez. Get up."

When Lopez shows no sign of having heard the sergeant, Frye fishes his cup out of the reclaim container.

"Duck," he tells Alex, and she gets up and out of the way. Sergeant Frye chucks the empty cup in Lopez's direction. It bounces off the infantry helmet the corporal is using for a pillow and lands on top of his sleeping bag.

"*Lopez*," Frye calls out. "Wake the fuck up."

Private Lopez stirs and turns his head.

"We're making a recon stop. Get your gear on and get ready."

Lopez lets out a muted little groan. He props himself up on one elbow and starts to unzip his sleeping bag.

"All right, all right," he mumbles and flicks the cup onto the floor. "I'm up. Where are we?"

"Marker 320."

"Shit," Lopez says. He checks his wrist computer with another groan. "Slept for four hours. Feels like it was ten minutes."

"You're rested so you get to take overwatch," Sergeant Frye says. "See if you can get some coffee going, and then we're trading seats. Dog's gotta go, and so do I."

"Copy that, Sergeant," Lopez says and sits up on his bench to pull the sleeping bag off his legs.

"Join the Spaceborne Infantry," he says. "See the galaxy. Visit exotic planets. Learn to sleep in a wide variety of uncomfortable circumstances."

He looks up at Alex and winks.

"Naturally, the recruiter left out that last bit."

"Of course he did, blockhead," Sergeant Frye says. "It's a recruiting office. You ever see one of those for jobs that are *fun*?"

Alex chuckles as she gets back to the other side of the compartment. She sits down by Ash, who is now paying attention to the sudden activity.

"Let's get you geared up, buddy," she says to the dog. Ash thumps his tail against the floor in response.

Ash has his own mission suit, a load-bearing vest with an independent oxygen supply and rebreather system rigged from an engineering vacsuit. His mask is stowed in a side pocket of the harness. Alex takes it out and straightens the straps before putting it on the dog's head. Ash is used to the procedure, and he sits patiently while she tightens the fasteners and checks for a good seal. He has a sturdier constitution than the human colonists, but even Ash can't breathe the air on this world for very long without a mask anymore, not with the levels of carbon dioxide introduced by the Lanky terraforming process. The mask muffles his sense of smell, but he doesn't seem to need his nose to know when a Lanky is coming their way. Alex adjusts the mask and connects it to the air supply in the dog's battle pack.

"Good boy," she tells him again when Ash is ready to step out. "You look fierce. Ferocious. Like a war dog."

The ferocious war dog gives her a dubious glance and taps his tail on the floor again in a decidedly unwarlike manner. She double-checks all the connectors and fasteners on his harness before checking her own.

"Dog team ready for dismount," she reports back to the commander's position and exchanges a thumbs-up with Sergeant Frye.

"All right," the sergeant says. "Masks on for dismount. Harris, let the civvies know we're making a stop. Lopez, get your ass on the gun. The remote station is all yours."

"With joy, Sergeant. With joy."

Frye climbs out of his chair and lets Lopez take his spot. Both SI troopers put on their helmets and lower the visors. Frye takes his rifle out of its storage bracket and checks the loading status of the weapon.

"All right," he says and swings himself over to the seat next to the mule's rear hatch. "Rest stop at marker 320, sixty minutes. Remember, always stay in sight of the tour bus. And don't buy souvenirs from the locals. It's all a rip-off."

CHAPTER 2

When the mule is stopped and the rear hatch opens, Sergeant Frye climbs out first, rifle at the ready. He scans the surroundings and waves Alex on.

"All clear. Come on out."

Alex leads Ash down the ramp and out onto the gravel field that stretches as far as she can see in the humid haze outside. It's warm and sticky, and she feels perspiration bead up on her temples almost instantly. She leads Ash away from the mule and out of the way of the cargo crawler that is now caught up and pulling alongside.

The dog team's task is to stand guard some distance away from the vehicles, to make sure that the noise and activity from the other team members doesn't distract the dog or interfere with his senses. Alex is fine with that because it gives her an excuse to keep avoiding Blake, the colony's assistant administrator and second in charge, who is riding in the cargo crawler with a five-person team of civilian salvage techs. Blake is a hard-ass when it comes to rules and regulations, and he's thorough and vigilant, character traits that combine with his authority to make him a natural nemesis of the colony's teenage and young adult population. What's worse, he is the rare kind of stickler who applies the book as strictly to himself as he does to everyone else. Not being able to fault him for abusing his authority makes her dislike of him almost entirely petty, and the awareness of that fact is an added annoyance to Alex whenever she has friction with Blake. She can't even fully hold his greatest character flaw against him—his dislike of dogs, the closest thing to heresy in Alex's catalogue of personal sins—because it means she doesn't run into Blake much anymore since she joined the dog team and started spending most of her working days at the kennel.

It feels good to be out of the mule and in the open, even if the air is toxic and the scenery isn't much to look at. The gravel flats in the middle of the main continent are hundreds of kilometers across, and everything always looks the same in every direction, a hard and sharp landscape that's constantly scoured by the sand and the wind. Alex walks out to a small rock cluster and lets Ash do his thing. She looks back at the vehicles and watches the civilian techs climb out of the crawler and meet up with the soldiers. The wind is swallowing what few sounds are drifting over from the group. Bad weather, quiet movement, and low talk have been a way of life for this colony for eight years. Alex can't remember the last time she ran around under a clear sky and made noise just for the fun of it.

She starts walking the perimeter with Ash. Each of their dogs has a unique patrol pattern, a preferred pace and movement to take in their surroundings. Ash likes to do a sort of overlapping figure-eight pattern that slowly shifts around the site he is guarding. As friendly as he is, he never wags his tail once he's on the job except as a trained all clear signal. Alex has often wondered whether he understands the seriousness of the danger, or whether he's just picking up on the anxiety of the humans around him.

A few minutes into their slow orbit of the rest stop site, one of the soldiers comes out of the vehicle circle and toward the spot where she is walking with Ash. Private Lopez is carrying the mule's recon drone high over his head with one arm. As Alex watches, he breaks into a trot, then a run. He flings the drone forward, and it soars up into the dark sky with the near-silent whirring of its electric propeller system. Alex follows the drone with her eyes until it disappears in the haze a few hundred meters away.

The launch run has taken Lopez halfway between the vehicles and the spot where Alex is standing with Ash. Instead of turning around and going back to the mule, he walks over to her.

"Thirty minutes until the drone gets back," he says.

"That's a really short flight," Alex replies. "Twenty, twenty-five klicks?"

"I don't want to stretch it. Stuff's getting old. I checked the cells in that bird before we loaded it up. That's a ten-year-old battery, and we've used the shit out of it. Almost three thousand cycles. We're supposed to junk those packs after a thousand."

"Got no spares coming in anytime soon," Alex says.

"Exactly. Gonna use 'em until they're totally dead."

"You're not supposed to chitchat with the dog handler, you know."

"I'm not distracting you, am I?" Lopez says.

Alex can see the smile underneath his mask. "It's not about distracting *me*. It's about distracting the dog. He needs to divide his attention now."

"But I'm not a threat."

"Like hell you aren't," she says, and Lopez's smile widens.

He reaches into a pouch on his leg armor and pulls out a small object.

"I brought you something. Hang on, gotta prep first."

She watches with amusement as he turns around and fidgets with the object. When he turns again, he holds it out on the palm of his armored glove, and she chuckles. It's a dessert pack from a military ration box, decorated with a chemical light he cracked in half to make it start glowing.

"Happy birthday," Lopez says.

"You remembered," Alex says and takes the offered package. "Despite me not saying shit to anyone about it."

Lopez shuffles his feet a little. "Kind of. I was off by two days. Blake told me it was today."

"Nothing that man doesn't know about anyone, I think."

Back by the vehicles, the subject of their exchange waves a flashlight in their direction.

"Don't look, but he's calling you back," Alex says. "Wait him out a little. It's not like he's going to walk over here to drag you away by the ear."

"That would be more civilian-military friction than I need today," Lopez says. He looks over his shoulder and responds to Blake's signal with a flash of his own helmet light.

"Gotta go," he says. "Shouldn't be talking to the dog handler anyway. Distracts the dog, you know." He winks at her again. "Enjoy your birthday cake."

She looks down at the writing on the package. The ration packs only get used in dire emergencies or out on overland missions, and there are six different dessert cookie flavors. It's serious trading currency in the colony, where sugar has become a rare commodity. With the odds of the draw and the rarity of the occurrence, she hasn't had a cookie bar in her favorite flavor in almost a year.

"Thank you, Lopez," she says. He nods and turns to start his walk back to the vehicles.

"Hey, did Blake tell you that I like the lemon bars best?" she calls after him.

He shakes his head and replies without turning around. "*Nah*. I remembered that one right, I guess."

Alex smiles as she watches him walk off. There are only a dozen people in the colony who are in her age bracket, a demographic so small and so awash in hormones that most of their possible relationship permutations have been mapped out among them over the last eight years. Lopez is too old to be in that group, but he's one of the youngest of the soldiers, barely thirty, and he's easily the best looking of his cohort. Most of the girls and at least one of the guys in Alex's little peer group have had a crush on Private Lopez at some point during their teenage years.

Amazing that our bodies still make us care about stuff like that, she thinks. *Nobody is starting a new family in this place ever again.*

Next to her, Ash is patiently standing by her side without tugging on his lead, but Alex imagines reproach in his gaze as he looks up at her: *Come on, lady. We have a job to do here.*

"Go on, Ash. Go seek, *go.*"

She tucks the lemon bar into the arm pocket of her jumpsuit and continues her round with Ash. A lemon cookie bar is something that needs to be saved for a very bad day, not scarfed in the back of a mule out in the middle of nowhere. And in this place, the next very bad day is always just around the corner.

—

The drone comes back a little over half an hour later. It drops out of the low-hanging clouds and glides in for a rough-looking landing on a flat spot in front of the colony vehicles. Alex watches Lopez retrieve the drone and haul it back to the mule, where he hooks it up to its console to download the recon data from the sensor suite. The other soldiers and the civilians start gathering at the rear of the mule until they're all standing around the console in a cluster to look at the results of the drone sweep. She can tell there's a low-key but animated discussion going on. Then the cluster of people breaks up again as the civilians return to the cargo crawler and the soldiers stay with the mule. Sergeant Frye walks a few meters away from the back hatch and starts looking around for her. When he spots Alex, he signals her with his helmet lamp: *return to the ride.*

Alex raises her flashlight and signals her acknowledgment.

"Come on, Ash," she tells the dog. "Back inside. Let's go."

Ash doesn't like having to climb back into a metal box after spending time outside, so she usually humors him with an off-leash race back to the vehicle, which he always wins with ease. They run across the gravel together, Ash circling her in what she imagines is a decidedly mocking commentary on her speed.

Back at the mule, Sergeant Frye and Private Lopez are packing up the drone and its control unit. The remote gun turret on top of the mule is whirring softly as it slowly turns left to right and back again, scanning the area for threats.

"What's going on?" Alex asks the sergeant when she stops behind the mule and clips the lead back onto Ash's harness.

"There's a Lanky path off to the southeast," Frye says. "Not super close, but not far enough to not have to worry about it. Drone spotted half a dozen Lankies on the move."

"We can't go around it?"

"It's not really cutting across our path. But we need to get within five klicks of it. There's only two ways off this flat. We either go that way or turn around and make a detour of a day and a half."

"And what does the boss say?"

Frye heaves the drone container into the back of the mule's cargo compartment with Lopez's help.

"The boss says we keep going the way we're going. We'll just have to be on our tippy-toes. We go parallel to the Lanky trail for about a klick and a half. If they spot us, it'll be a tight squeeze. But I agree with Blake. We don't have the range in the batteries to tack on a day and a half."

Alex isn't wild about getting close to Lankies on purpose but having to stay out for another day or more and potentially coming back with nothing to show for the effort is almost worse than the idea of an encounter.

"Hey, it's a five-klick gap," she says. "They get too close, you'll shoot 'em, right?"

"That's the idea," Sergeant Frye says. "But let's avoid making all that ruckus with the cannon if we can help it. It really pisses off the neighborhood. Now saddle up."

Frye shoos her and Ash up the ramp and into the back of the mule, where she takes her seat and straps in. Sergeant Frye follows her inside and closes the tail ramp.

"We're sealed up," he calls toward the front. "Ready to roll."

"Copy that," Corporal Bayliss says from the driver's station. "We are rolling."

The mule's environmental system hisses quietly as it restores the proper ratio of oxygen to carbon dioxide, which got thrown out of balance while the mule was parked with its rear hatch open. After a minute, the warning light on the forward bulkhead goes from red to orange, then to green. The soldiers start taking off their masks, and Alex follows suit. The half-hour patrol outside and the little run with Ash at the end made her sweat enough to leave her perspiration pooled at the bottom of her mask's rubber gasket seal, and she lets the sweat drip out before wiping down the interior of the mask with the sleeve of her jumpsuit. When she takes off Ash's mask, she cups the dog's muzzle in both hands and gives his snout a vigorous rub, which he rewards with a little grunt.

"Good boy," she says. "Ready to go down to where the dragons live?"

Ash licks his muzzle and puts his head down on his front paws. He looks up at her and huffs out another sigh.

"I'm with you there," she tells him.

This has always been his life, she thinks. Ash is only three years old, and he's been out on patrol with the overland salvage teams for less than a year. He has never known a world without Lankies, one where he hasn't done what he's doing now. Alex can't quite make up her mind whether that would be a blessing or a curse to her. She still remembers her life before the Lankies, but those memories are getting more and more abstract and fuzzy around the edges as the years go by. Maybe one day those memories will be something precious, but right now they're just high-water marks in her mind that remind her how much they all have lost.

Outside, one of the fast-moving local rainstorms is passing over the plateau, and just a few minutes after they start moving again, heavy raindrops are starting to ping off the mule's armor. The drumbeat of the rain quickly rises to a steady thrumming that's almost drowning out the whining from the mule's electric drivetrain.

"That's good," Sergeant Frye says. "Keeps 'em from sensing us. Lots of background clutter."

"I know. I just don't like the idea that it keeps us from sensing them as well," she says.

Frye shrugs with a smile.

"If we're all blind out here, it's our advantage, not theirs."

Alex knows, of course. This is her tenth overland patrol. The soldiers that are left are all smart and capable, and they have lots of experience with the Lankies after eight years of having to dodge them everywhere. But that knowledge doesn't keep her guts from doing that floaty, twisty thing they always do whenever she knows she's about to get close to those things.

Lopez gets out of his seat and climbs into the secondary command station up front next to Sergeant Frye. Both soldiers are now sitting with their backs toward Alex as they get on the controls for the sensor array and the remote gun turret. She never feels more like ballast than she does whenever everyone in the mule is busy with an immediate task to drive or protect it, and there's nothing for her to do except check her harness and pet the dog. But Ash doesn't mind the attention, and at least the action helps to keep her anxiety in check a little. She suspects that part of the reason why the soldiers bring their rifles on missions despite their very limited utility against Lankies is that the guns give them something to do with their hands when they're nervous.

By her feet, Ash has settled in for a nap, head resting on his paws, unconcerned by the noise of the rain and unaware of the dangerous route they are about to take.

Definitely a blessing, she decides.

CHAPTER 3

"Well, hello there," Sergeant Frye says in a low voice. "Got eyes on target. Two of 'em at three o'clock, eighty-eight degrees."

Alex can only make out half the screens at the command station because Frye is blocking her sight, and what she can see isn't terribly informative. She shifts in her seat to lean forward and get a better look.

"I only see one," Private Lopez replies from his own station. The gun mount above their heads swivels with a faint electric hum to track Lopez's view as he moves his control stick.

"The other one's trailing behind him. He's offset to the left and back fifty meters. Check on my mark."

Lopez rotates the mount back a few degrees and stops.

"Got him. Range twenty-one hundred, give or take a few. Moving northeast at thirty klicks per hour. Also give or take a few."

"They're not in a hurry," Frye says. "Just out for a walk. Keep moving, fellas. Nothing to see here."

Lopez glances back at Alex. When he notices that she is trying to get a better view, he motions for her to come up. She gets out of her seat, steps over the dozing Ash, and moves to the seat directly behind the gunner's station. He leans back a little to give her a better look at the targeting screen of the mule's automatic cannon. The gun is trained at a ridge to their right, where two vague shapes loom in the distance, almost invisible in the haze. Alex watches the screen and sees the faintest of outlines, the familiar shapes of Lanky cranial shields swaying slowly and steadily as the creatures make their way down the trail.

"They're skylining themselves on that ridge," Lopez says.

"They don't care," Sergeant Frye replies. "Got no ambush to fear from anyone around here. They own the place now."

Lopez slowly tracks the distant Lankies with the gun's targeting reticle as they move across the field of vision of his optics. The magnification is so high that the image on the screen is soft and blurry, AI algorithms trying to compensate for the lack of resolution. Alex watches the progress of the nightmare shapes on the screen, specters from another world, maybe even from a different galaxy altogether. Between all the scientists, the amateur xenobiologists in the colonies, and the civilian rumor mills on the public networks, there are probably as many theories about the origin of the Lankies out there as there are individual Lankies in the known galaxy. Alex doesn't have any idea where they came from or why they are taking over human colonies one by one. All that matters is that the Lankies are here now, and that they put an end to her old life when they arrived.

"Could you hit them from this far away?" Alex asks.

"Yeah," Lopez says. "Eventually. I'd need a few ranging shots to dial in the gun. Manual says the effective range on the twenty-five millimeter is three thousand meters. But the manual is full of shit. That's on a dry and sunny range, against a big static target, with something to bounce the targeting laser off of."

He taps the range readout in the corner of his targeting screen, which changes constantly as the Lankies move past on a reciprocal heading and open the range very slowly: 2100 . . . 2175 . . . 2210.

"In real life? Two thousand is pushing it. And you can hit 'em from here, but it won't do much. Those rounds lose a lot of steam by the time they get out past a klick and a half. With the twenty-five mil, you want to wait until they're inside of five hundred meters, or you're just pissing away most of your ammo."

"Noted," Alex says.

"You gonna train her as a gunner now or something?" Sergeant Frye says.

"I'm just a private first class," Lopez replies. "I ain't training nobody. That's outside the scope of my rank, Sergeant."

"You've been a PFC for half a decade, Lopez. You're probably the most experienced PFC in the entire Corps."

"Only because the promotion orders got lost in the mail. I probably made sergeant this year just on time in rank alone."

"God help us all," Sergeant Frye says. "If *you* made sergeant, I gotta be a fucking twenty-star general by now."

They watch the Lanky shapes move through the distant haze in silence for a few moments. The huge creatures are stomping down their trail at their measured, steady pace, without any sign that they're aware of the human presence. Alex knows not to ascribe human motivations to the Lankies, but their stride looks a bit arrogant to her, as if they agree with Sergeant Frye that they have nothing to fear. The salvage teams have killed a handful of them over the years whenever they couldn't avoid crossing paths, but it was always a desperate surprise encounter at close range. The Lankies don't seem to be actively looking for more humans, and the colonists and Corps troopers follow a strict avoidance policy, running and hiding whenever possible, and only using weapons as a last resort. There's something about the way they're strolling down the path leisurely that makes her angry. Three thousand colonists spent over twenty years setting up this planet for human habitation, and now all that work has been undone, and most of those colonists are dead and gone except for the less than two hundred who had the luck to be close to the admin center that day. Alex wants to reach over and pull the trigger for the cannon, but she also knows that it would be pointless. Killing one or two of these things won't make a difference, not when there are thousands more burrowing into the planet like monstrous termites.

"All right, they're moving off," Sergeant Frye says. "We're in the clear for a bit. Four minutes until the next one comes up the rabbit trail."

He reaches over and pats the bulkhead behind the driver's station.

"Bayliss, carry on. Slow and steady down the slope. Take your time."

"Copy that," Bayliss replies. A moment later, the mule starts rolling again.

"Twenty minutes to target," Sergeant Frye says. "We almost have this in the bag. Keep alert, everyone."

CHAPTER 4

Colonial Administration research outpost Victor-426
17NOV2124, 0838h Standard Colonial Time

Every one of the settlements and science stations they've raided has been a ghost town, empty and broken buildings overgrown with moss and blackened from years of acidic rain. But science outpost Victor-426 looks truly haunted to Alex, not just merely creepy and depressing like all the other facilities she has seen. The outpost is a compact cluster of multilevel buildings a few hundred meters from the base of a terraforming station. The Lankies seem to have a particular dislike for terraformers, and this one did not escape their attention. As the mule and its civilian companion vehicle roll down the sloped access ramp to the station, Alex is watching the targeting screen of the mule's gun. Private Lopez is using the mount's sensors to sweep the ruined station and the remains of the huge terraforming tower looming behind it.

The Lankies have torn down most of the atmosphere exchanger, and the remnants that are still standing look like a rotten tooth that's long past salvage or repair. Lopez cycles through all the targeting filters—infrared, thermal, low light, and a few that Alex doesn't recognize. As they roll into the central square formed by the wings of the main building, the only thing moving on the screen is a loose and tattered tarp that's hanging from a twisted steel frame in the rubble of a vehicle hangar and flapping madly in the wind. At the foot of the hillside slope a few hundred meters away, a giant excavator lies toppled over by unimaginable physical force, a hundred tons or more of heavy-duty engineering equipment knocked on its side and mangled like a child's beach toy.

"All clear," Sergeant Frye proclaims. "We are here, freakin' finally. Signal the civvies to move up and get next to us. Get ready to unmount. Lopez, you stay on the gun and cover. Something big comes out of the weather and heads down the hill toward us, don't ask for permission to hose it down."

"Affirmative," Lopez replies without taking his eyes off the targeting screen.

Alex puts on her mask and checks the airflow. She nudges Ash to get his attention, then takes his mask out of its harness pouch to put it on his muzzle.

"Does he ever just refuse to let you put that thing on?" Lopez asks, his eyes still glued to the gun's sensor display. "That's got to suck for a dog."

She shakes her head.

"It's just what he knows. He's never been outside without it. I think it gets him excited when I get it out because he knows he's going somewhere."

Lopez nods to acknowledge her reply. She looks down at Ash, patiently standing still to let her connect his breathing air again, and she feels a brief swell of sadness when she thinks about what she just told the private. Dogs weren't meant to be holed up in caves. Humans weren't either, but the colonists all accepted the possibility of world-ending dangers when they volunteered for the settlement. Ash did not give his consent to being born into this mess. But Alex knows without a doubt that her claustrophobic little world is better with him in it.

"Dog team ready for dismount," she tells Sergeant Frye, who replies with a thumbs-up.

Next to the mule, the colonial overland tractor pulls up and stops to the sounds of sighing hydraulic brakes and crunching gravel. The civilian utility transport is half again as high as the mule, and with its attached trailer it's twice as long, a clumsy articulated combo that's rolling on five pairs of immense knobby all-terrain tires. Sergeant Frye checks the cargo hold and crouch-steps across the compartment to the tail ramp.

"Let's go shopping, people," he says.

With the vehicles sheltered by the hill and the ruins of the station on three sides, there is only one approach to guard, the long uphill slope that leads back the way they came. Alex walks up the hill with Ash until she is out of earshot of the soldiers and colonist techs who are now busy unloading the heavy equipment they brought along—demolition tools and steel cables to pry apart the carcasses of mangled buildings to get at whatever treasures they may still hold. They can grow their own food in the hydroponic gardens in the cave and make their own breathing air, but before the Lankies came, Alex never realized just how much of their daily lives depended on things that had to be brought to the colony the hard way, by putting them on pallets and ferrying them across forty-six light-years on a spaceship because the colony lacks the ability to make them.

The 3-D printer in the colony workshop can make small parts, bolts and brackets and screwdriver bits, but it can't make things like high-density power cells, plastic explosives, or neural network circuit boards. In this new world, finding a universal battery pack with zero charge cycles is better than finding a chest full of gold, and infinitely more useful. As the dog handler, Alex does not have to do any of the hard salvage work, but she also doesn't get to go deep into the guts of the buildings they are strip-mining for a chance to experience the thrill of a big first discovery. There is plenty of tension and adrenaline in her life now, but precious few genuine thrills, no opportunities for joyous excitement. On the plus side, she gets to be out here with Ash all by herself, which is more solitude than she gets back at the Vault.

At the top of the access ramp, the only sound she hears is the wind, which has picked up since the last stop they made on the plateau a few hours ago. It's hot and humid as always, and Alex can tell from the weighty impact of the occasional raindrops sporadically splashing against her jumpsuit that a major downpour is imminent. Next to her, Ash pauses to take in their surroundings and listen to the distant thunder rolling across the landscape. She waits in silence until he looks at her and gives a furtive wag of the tail, his way of telling her that everything seems fine for now.

"Good boy," she says, and he wags his tail again at hearing the praise he craves. She ruffles the top of his head between the straps of his mask.

"You're filthy," she tells him. "It'll take me an hour to get you clean again." Ash's overcoat can hold astonishing amounts of sand and gravel dust after a weeklong patrol. At least there's never a shortage of hot water at home, not with their underground freshwater lake and their fusion reactor, the lifeblood and the beating heart of the Vault. She knows that she probably needs an hour under a hot water stream as well at this point. Whenever they are on an overland mission, they turn the environmental controls in the vehicles to the highest tolerable temperature to save precious power-cell capacity. By the time they come back in after a few days of sweating in a titanium alloy box in thirty degrees Celsius without changing clothes, salvage team members are invariably grimy and smelly, and their mission suits can practically stand upright on their own.

This all used to be ours, she thinks as she looks back at the ruined station. People used to live and work here and come and go at will. The outpost was a geologic research facility, and they tore into the nearby hillside with excavators and explosives to expose the local sediment layers, methods that would now draw Lankies from kilometers away. These days the surviving colonists must be sneaky foragers, vermin in someone else's house, always in danger of getting found and eradicated by the new owners.

Down at the main outpost building, a hundred meters from where Alex is now standing, the salvage team has started its work. She can see the spotlights from their headlamps dancing over the rubble of the building's front, which took the heaviest damage when the Lankies came and destroyed the facility. The debris of a big colony building is full of nasty ways to die—exposed wires that still carry live current from not-quite-depleted emergency batteries, the many sharp edges of mangled and twisted support frames, cavities in the debris that can swallow someone and drown them in deep pools of stagnant water from broken pipes. The colony has lost three people to salvage accidents in the last eight years, and no team ever returns without at least a few injuries.

Alex watches from her elevated vantage point as the crews gear up and start laying out safety ropes and spools of fiber-optic comms link. There are the three soldiers—Sergeant Frye, Corporal Bayliss, and Private Harris. They're working alongside Scott, Cheryl, and Andres, the three techs Administrator Blake brought with him. The first time Alex was out with a salvage team as the dog handler, she felt a bit like a slacker for not helping the team with the setup and recovery. But her presence here with Ash is much more helpful to the mission than just an extra pair of hands for hauling gear. It lets the soldiers focus on the task at hand without having to watch the perimeter for Lankies constantly.

As always, Ash determines the trajectory of their patrol. The access ramp down to the research station is the shape of a narrow wedge, with the wide end at the top of the hill and the tip ending at the U shape formed by the main facility and its auxiliary buildings. The dog leads her halfway down the slope until she can just barely hear the faint electric hum of the mule's utility winch as it slowly reels off its spool of cable. He stands still for a moment, ears perked, and she waits as he takes in the sights and sounds. Then he looks at her and turns to make his way back up the ramp.

"All right," Alex says to herself and follows him back up the incline.

The sad remnants of a few small buildings are lining the ramp on both sides, standard modular containers like the ones that serve as their individual shelters back at the Vault. They're rugged little boxes, capable of being stacked ten high even loaded up to their maximum gross weight, but they were not designed to withstand Lanky attention. Each of these has been smashed flat and compressed into piles of rubble that stand no taller than hip high. As she passes them on her way back up to the top of the ramp, Alex tries to imagine the force needed to crush the tough honeycomb structure of a shelter module like this. She walks over to one of the flattened containers and circles it to see if she can spot anything interesting in the wreckage. Everything in the stack is solidly compacted, and the whole mess is partially buried in the coarse soil. Alex picks at a few mangled wall sections and bits of broken gear, but she knows right away that digging deeper and properly peeling away all those layers of debris would take hours, and it would require far more powerful tools than the pocketknife she carries.

She drops the broken piece of circuit board she had plucked from the wreck and turns to follow Ash, who is now twenty meters ahead of her on the gravel ramp. He's in work mode again, the one thing he knows to do whenever he is outside of the Vault and not in the back of a vehicle. The two dogs that sired him, Max and Hera, were on the colony as the pets of the colonial constable and his family. Ash's sibling Cleo turned out too timid for the training, too eager to please her handlers with alerts, so she gets to stay at the Vault and do what she does best, which is to take naps, accept the adulation of the colony's young children, and beg for treats. Ash and his brother, Blitz, get to do the same when they are home, but whenever a team goes on a salvage mission, they morph into single-purpose specialist tools. She's always aware how his personality seems to change as soon as they are out of the Vault's airlock, as if he knows that he is no longer just a dog whenever he goes outside.

Up at the top of the ramp, Alex needs to stop to catch her breath. As always when she is exerting herself even moderately, the inside of her mask is slick with her sweat, and she pries it away from her chin to wipe the inside with her gloved fingers. The brief whiff of unfiltered air she breathes while cleaning her mask smells faintly of decay and old sweat, and she makes a face when she realizes that some of the smell is the stink of her clothes.

"Let's pick an elevation and stick with it, buddy," she tells Ash, who is trotting from one side of the ramp to the other. He looks at her and wags his tail once, then returns to his little patrol pattern. Beyond her vantage point at the crest of the incline, the rocky slope of the gravel field stretches as far as she can see in the humid haze.

A large raindrop splashes onto her head. The water runs down her temple past the straps for the mask and trickles into her collar. She reaches up to wipe the water from her skin, and another heavy drop lands on the sleeve of her jumpsuit, then another. The wind slacks off until the air is almost calm, a sign she knows well.

"Great," Alex murmurs and reaches for the collar of her jacket to unroll the rain hood.

When the rainstorm comes in, she can see its advance. The squall line is moving in from the direction of the gravel flats, rolling across the barren landscape like a semi-opaque curtain, drenching the rocks and leaving puddles and fast-flowing rivulets in its wake. Alex pulls her hood over her head and tightens it around the bulk of her mask. She whistles softly to get Ash's attention.

"Come here. Let's get you buttoned down."

The dog trots over to her obediently. She can hear his soft panting breaths underneath his mask. Alex ruffles the top of his head and opens the pouch on his mission vest that holds his rain poncho, tailored to his shape from a military-issue weather cover. It takes a few moments for her to latch the now rain-slick clasps, and she bends over Ash to shield him with her own rain cloak while she tightens the straps. She has to reach around him to take the slack out of the front strap of the harness, and she only realizes that the dog is growling softly when she feels the vibration resonating in his chest. Alex freezes, her arms still wrapped around Ash's muscular bulk. He's not paying attention to her. Instead, he stares at a point somewhere out on the gravel field, which is now shrouded in cascading bands of heavy rain.

Ash's growl increases in resonance until she can feel the vibration of it in her arms as she is holding him. She can't hear anything over the sound of the rain that's pelting her hood and the ground all around her, but the dog's focused concern fires up the primal alarm circuits in her brain. Suddenly, every wind-whipped ribbon of rain out on the plain in front of her takes the shape of a twenty-meter nightmare with long and oddly angled limbs, and the ground under her feet that felt inert just a moment ago seems to shake minutely with the impacts of slow and heavy steps in the distance.

The dog's growl morphs into a bark. It's not a loud noise, just a low and breathy huff that's muffled by the mask, but the knowledge of what it means makes Alex jump. Ash is trained to only ever bark for one reason.

"Shit," she says and jumps to her feet. "Shit, shit, *shit*."

Alex wheels around and starts running down the access ramp as fast as she can. A second later, Ash overtakes her, loping downhill in long, flying strides that make it look like his paws are barely touching the gravel. This time, it's not a contest. Even with her fear spurring her on, the dog beats her to the bottom of the ramp easily.

Down at the bottom of the hill, Lopez is in the open rear hatch of the mule. He's speaking into a hardwired handset that's connected to the external comms station next to the hatch. Ash sits down in front of him and barks again. Alex skids to a stop next to the dog.

"We may be getting visitors," she tells Lopez.

"I gathered," he says and toggles the transmit button of his handset.

"Incoming, incoming," he sends. There's a fiber-optic cable snaking its way from the comms station into the remains of the building where the rest of the team is combing the rubble for supplies. "I repeat, we have incoming."

A few moments later, Administrator Blake emerges from the rubble of the building's entrance vestibule, followed by Sergeant Frye and the rest of the infantry team.

"The techs are staying inside," Blake says. "They're in the basement already. They're better off holing up down there."

"We running or sheltering in place?" Private Lopez asks.

Sergeant Frye looks over to the top of the access ramp.

"We're staying put," he says. "Can't see shit out there in this weather. Only one way in and out. We roll up to the top, we may run right into one of those things. Lopez, deploy the camo. And then get on the gun."

"Copy that, Sergeant," Lopez says and disappears in the back of the mule.

The camouflage cover unfolds from its storage rack at the top of the mule and cascades down the sides of the vehicle until it touches the ground. When the cover is in place, Lopez activates the active camouflage, and the eight-wheeled armored war machine turns indistinct in front of Alex's eyes, a high-tech trick that never fails to impress her. The active camo uses the same technology as the bug suits of the Fleet's special operations troops, a polychromatic layer that suppresses the mule's already faint infrared signature and hides it from view by making it blend into the background. Next to the mule, Administrator Blake climbs into the cockpit of the civilian crawler and spins up the electric drive. He backs up the vehicle and drives it forward into the shelter of a demolished equipment shed.

The SI troopers disperse on the plaza and take up positions in the rubble, where they ready their weapons and aim them at the top of the access ramp. Next to Alex, the mule's turret whirrs softly as Lopez swivels the gun mount to point at the same spot. Alex looks around for a hiding spot, but Ash picks it for her by ducking underneath the mule's camo cover, which ripples with his passage as he vanishes from view. She follows him and walks up the tail ramp in a crouch, the heavy polychromatic cloak billowing above her head.

"Hit the switch," Lopez says when she's inside. Alex pushes the button to raise the tail ramp and moves up to take the seat next to the private, who is looking at his targeting screen unblinkingly.

"That didn't take long," he says. "We barely got started. I knew we were cutting it a little too close on the ingress."

"Blake and the sergeant both said we didn't have the range for a detour. See anything?" Alex asks.

Lopez shakes his head without taking his eyes off the display.

"Nothing but the rain. Did you see it coming when you were up there?"

She shakes her head.

"No, but the dog sure thinks something's off. I didn't want to wait around."

"I hope he's wrong this time," Lopez says. "We're kind of corralled in down here. Gonna be a big fucking mess in a hurry if we have to start shooting stuff."

Alex looks at Ash, who is now back in his spot underneath the jump seat where she usually sits. He's watching them intently, as if he knows there's something significant happening. As much as she doesn't want the dog to be wrong, she agrees with Lopez. If the soldiers have to fire their weapons, she knows that the mission is over. Even if they drop a

Lanky or two and get out of this place unscathed, they will all be clearing the area at top speed, and there won't be any salvage.

The air-quality indicator on the forward bulkhead of the mule switches from red to orange and then green to signal that it's safe to remove masks, but Alex takes her cue from Lopez and makes no move to take off Ash's or her own. She knows that if they have to leave the mule in a hurry, they may not be able to spare the extra ten seconds to put them on and connect the air hoses again.

Lopez wipes his forehead with the heel of his palm and blinks to clear the sweat from his eyes. The targeting screen shows the ridge a hundred meters uphill. The rain is coming down almost sideways now. Lopez's hand is on the control stick for the gun mount, and he lightly strokes the safety cover on the trigger with his index finger.

"Come on," he says softly. "Let's have another hour or two of boredom, please."

Across the aisle, Ash perks up his ears. Then he growls again, a low, ominous warning from deep inside his chest that Alex knows isn't directed at them.

This time, there's no doubt that the ground underneath the mule is moving just a little. She can feel the vibration beneath the soles of her boots. A few seconds later, it repeats, then again, a familiar pattern that makes her stomach twist. She exchanges a look with Lopez.

"So much for boredom," he says and flicks the safety cover away from the cannon's trigger.

For a few moments, the sensor screen in front of Lopez's eyes remains unchanged, showing just a barren patch of gravel whipped by bands of heavy rain. Then the sky beyond the top of the access ramp seems to be in motion as a gigantic shape materializes out of the squall. The Lanky's cranial shield comes into view first, a roughly triangular shape that's twenty meters above the ground, bobbing slowly with the cadence of the creature's walk. At this range, the Lanky's upper body fills out the entire screen of the targeting system. The sight of it so close to her is making the primitive part of Alex's brain attempt to short-circuit the rest of her gray matter by screaming at her to run away and find a deep hole to hide in, the reaction of a prey animal sensing that it's about to get eaten alive. She takes a deep breath and lets it out slowly to tamp down the panic that's flaring up in her chest. She has seen dozens of Lankies before, but most of those sightings were through high-powered optics from a prudently long distance. This one is so close that she can see the rainwater splashing off its head and dripping down the edge of its wide, toothless maw. The sheer size of it makes it look primal, irresistible, a force of nature like a storm or a landslide.

Lopez has his finger on the autocannon's trigger now. He nudges the control stick's hat switch with his thumb and lowers the magnification of the optics to keep the Lanky fully in sight as it walks to the top of the access ramp with slow and heavy steps that make the ground shake minutely. Alex's heart skips a beat or two as the creature pauses near the top of the ramp. It raises its head and turns it slowly from side to side. To Alex, it looks like Ash is trying to home in on an interesting scent from the galley.

"Keep moving," Lopez mutters. "Ain't nothing but trouble for you down here."

The Lanky shakes its head and sends water flying from the rim of its cranial shield. Then it resumes its slow, ambling gait. When it reaches the crest of the ridge, it turns slightly to its left and continues past the ramp, following the path toward the gravel flats. For a few moments, Alex and Lopez get a perfect profile shot of the creature as it stomps off without any hurry. The shield at the back of its head more than doubles the length of its enormous skull, and the mouth looks big enough to fit most of the cargo crawler into it. From just a little over a hundred meters away, Alex can see the texture of the Lanky's skin, a shallow and slightly wavy pattern that looks a bit like macerated human skin to her. Some of the soldiers think the Lankies look like prehistoric Earth dinosaurs, but Alex doesn't share that opinion. The head with its protective shield looks vaguely saurian, but the rest of the body has no resemblance to anything in the colony's repository of school textbooks. She has been around them for years, but they're too weird in both appearance and in the unsettling pattern of their movements to ever look natural to her.

Lopez huffs out the breath he had been holding once the Lanky is out of sight again. He removes his hand from the gun mount's control stick and flexes it slowly.

"Sit tight," he tells her. "There may be more behind this one."

"Oh, I'm not going anywhere for a while," she says. "Not until my legs stop shaking."

"Big sons of bitches, aren't they?"

She has to laugh at Lopez's understatement. The act relieves the tension a little, but she still feels like her nerves are tingling with faint electric current, and when she looks at her hands, she can see that they're shaking as well. She reaches into her leg pouch and takes out her pocketknife. Lopez is still focused on the screen, and his hand isn't far from the fire controls. The picture from the targeting sensors has returned to showing the top of the ramp and the stormy sky above. Alex folds out the utility blade of her pocketknife. She turns the knife slowly in her hands while she stares at the screen with Lopez.

The private notices her movement and glances at the knife with an amused little smirk.

"Those things won't even feel that, you know."

"It's not for them. I just like to feel the weight of it. Gives my hands something to do when I am nervous. Better than holding nothing."

He reaches out.

"Can I see?"

She gives him the knife, and he puts it up in front of the targeting screen to look at it in the light from the display.

"Look at all those tools. Blade, screwdriver, can opener. What's that one on the back?"

"Sewing awl," she replies.

"That's a neat little antique," he says. "It looks like it has seen some shit."

"My dad gave it to me. Before . . . you know. It's one of the few things he brought along from Earth. It used to be my grandfather's."

"That's gotta be a hundred years old," he says. He closes the blade and hands the knife back to her.

They watch the targeting screen together in silence for a while. Alex tries to concentrate on her breathing, but the stress-relief technique that usually works well in tense situations at the Vault isn't nearly as effective after coming face-to-face with a twenty-meter alien that makes the ground tremble when it walks. But then Ash comes over and lies down next to her. He nudges her hand very lightly with his head. She reaches down and pets him, and the presence of the dog manages to do what the slow and deliberate breathing didn't. Gradually, her tension ebbs away until there's only the primal alertness left that's always with her when she leaves the Vault, the constantly heightened senses and humming nerves of a prey animal venturing out of its safe burrow.

The mule's intercom comes to life with Blake's gruff voice.

"Give that thing five more minutes to gain some distance and then get the dog out here again. We're going back downstairs."

Lopez switches the setting on his auxiliary screen to the external view. Blake is standing underneath the camo cloak next to the closed rear hatch, talking into the handset of the mule's wired intercom system. Lopez punches the push-to-talk button on his own intercom panel.

"Shouldn't we send up the drone to make sure the coast is clear?"

"I don't want to spend the time to wait for the bird to get back. Weather's shit anyway. The dog will have to do. Let's get done with this as quickly as we can. I don't have a great feeling about this spot."

"That makes two of us," Lopez says to Alex. He toggles the intercom switch.

"Got it, boss," he tells the administrator.

On the auxiliary screen, Blake puts the intercom handset back in its protected little box next to the rear hatch without another word and trots off toward the research post's main entrance.

"Wish he'd learn that he needs stripes on his shoulder boards to give orders to me," Lopez grumbles.

"He was ordering me around, not you," Alex says. "I'm at the bottom of the ladder. Everyone gets to tell me what to do."

"There's only four handlers, and that dog likes you best. Blake needs to be more appreciative."

"He has a whole colony to run. Everyone comes to him to bitch when shit doesn't go right. And shit never goes right," Alex says.

"I can't believe what I'm hearing out of you." Lopez gives her a crooked smirk. "You're *defending* him. Seems like you butted heads with him every single day when you were younger. You and your friends."

She shrugs. "I grew up. Now it's just every third day."

For the next five minutes, she divides her attention between Ash and the sensor screen Lopez is watching. Nothing else is stomping out of the rainy fog to bear down on them, and the dog is quietly alert but no longer on edge. She doesn't want to go back out into the rain, and she really doesn't care to get back up on the hill where a Lanky walked past just a few minutes ago, but Alex knows that the dog's senses are more acute when he's out in the open instead of in an armored box. She checks the straps of the rain cloak she put on quickly right before the dog alerted and tightens the pull strings properly to make sure she doesn't get soaked right away. Ash watches her and gets to his feet the moment she reaches for his harness to make his gear neat and tight as well.

"Time to get back to it, I guess," she says to both the dog and Private Lopez.

"Turning off the camo," he says and taps the control for the mule's polychromatic cloak. She hears the soft whining of electric motors as the fold-out webbing contracts and pulls back into the storage receptacles all around the top of the vehicle's hull.

"All right, we're visible again. I'll keep the optics on you at all times. Something comes your way again, start running for the mule."

"Just be careful where you aim that thing," she says and reaches for the hatch control. She pushes the button for the tail ramp, and the air-quality light inside the cargo compartment goes from green to orange to red as the ramp lowers and the warm, moist outside air comes rushing in.

"You're short. I'll just shoot over your head."

"Watch who you're calling *short*," Alex says. She gets up from her seat and lightly snaps Ash's lead, but the dog is already in motion, eager to get out of the hold.

"Dog team up," she reports and walks down the ramp with Ash.

Outside, the rain has picked up, and she can barely see the top of the hill where the Lanky passed by a little while ago. She gives Ash a few seconds to stand still and take in his surroundings. He looks at her and wags his tail once. Alex turns around and gives Lopez a thumbs-up, which he returns.

Overhead, a long, rolling peal of thunder rumbles. To Alex, it sounds like giant boulders tumbling down a rocky slope. Rivulets of water are streaming down the slope of the access ramp, tiny flash floods of rainwater the rocky soil can't absorb quickly enough. She starts her walk back up the incline toward her original overwatch point. It's an unnatural act to be venturing out of safety and toward danger again, but Ash isn't alerting anymore, and she trusts the dog with her life at this point. Still, the anxiety knot in her stomach seems to triple in size and density as she reaches the top of the ramp to see what lies beyond the ridge. Up ahead, there's nothing except rain-swept rocks as far as she can see through the sheets of downpour. To her right, the passing Lanky is long out of sight, but she still feels as though she can sense the little tremors from its slow steps as it crosses the gravel field a few kilometers away.

She turns around and gives another thumbs-up in the direction of the mule a hundred meters downhill. Lopez responds with a quick flash of the sensor array's signal light. She knows that the private will watch over her with the gun mount and shoot anything that appears out of the mist, but she still feels exposed up on this hill even if it's only a fifteen-second dash to the safety of the vehicle. For a moment, and not for the first time since she went out on this mission, Alex finds herself thinking that she's an idiot for volunteering to be a dog handler, to stick her neck out to play trip wire with Ash on these salvage runs while all her friends are safe and dry in the Vault. But then she reminds herself that they're probably all busy with their regular chores right now, the mind-numbing and repetitive work that everyone needs to do in rotation to keep the colony running: picking vegetables, unclogging sewage lines, checking catwalks for rust and damage, feeding the reclaimers with waste to be reconstituted. It's not just that she feels like she's making more of a difference watching for Lankies out here than she would stacking meal trays in the galley back at the Vault. It's that she feels more alive on a mission, more in control despite the ever-present danger or maybe because of it, just like Ash seems to be happiest when he's working outside under a dark sky instead of repeating the same routines in the Vault all day.

We're probably both idiots, she concludes as she follows the dog on his patrol pattern, pacing in slow figure eights as lightning tears open the black-gray clouds overhead and another low, rumbling boom follows in its wake.

CHAPTER 5

The muffled metallic-sounding crash is loud enough to reach Alex all the way on the top ridge, even through the relentless wind and rain, and make her jump. She runs the last few steps to the crest of the access ramp to see what's going on, Ash in tow. It has been almost an hour since the Lanky passed through the neighborhood, and she has gotten more antsy with every passing minute out here in her exposed location because she knows that Lankies hardly ever show up alone.

Down at the main entrance, the colony's cargo crawler is slowly backing away from the building. One of the techs—she can't tell whether it's Andres or Cheryl—is directing the vehicle from the side with hand signals. As the crawler pulls out, Alex can see that it's dragging something through the rubble and away from the structure with its front-mounted towing cable. There are a few more grinding and crashing sounds, this time a bit less jarring than the first wrenching crack she heard, but she still flinches at the commotion. Noise avoidance is the second most important survival tactic in the colony after radio silence, but she knows that Blake and Sergeant Frye wouldn't make noise unless they had no other choice. The tech who was directing the crawler now walks over to the front of it and detaches the tow cable from whatever they yanked free from the interior of the smashed building. The crawler backs up and turns around almost on the spot, all eight wheels spinning at the same time, until the nose of the vehicle faces uphill toward Alex and she can see the driver through the thick windshield of the dimly lit cabin. When the crawler comes to a stop again, the driver hops out of the cabin and goes back to the trailer. The other techs and the soldiers have all gathered at the front of the main entrance, their helmet lights bobbing in the semidarkness as they roll up the tow cable and open the access hatches of the crawler's trailer. It's clear that they've gained access to something that's worth hauling back, and Alex is itching to go downhill again and see what it is. But her job is to stay out here with Ash and make sure they don't get surprised by another Lanky, so she turns around and walks back to the top of the ramp to continue her slow patrol.

The Lanky that walked across the ridge just an hour ago left a set of massive footprints in the rain-sodden gravel up here. Ash is pointedly avoiding the prints, leading her between them instead of across, but Alex feels the urge to stop and check them out. They're several meters long, clearly showing the shape of the Lanky feet that made them—a sharp heel and three massive toes, each wider than her entire body. She steps into one of the footprints and paces it from front to back. The depression in the ground is shallower than she expected it to be considering the size of the creature that made it, but it's still more than halfway to her knee when she measures the depth of it with her leg. At the bottom of the footprint, rainwater has pooled over the last hour, leaving deep puddles where the front of the Lanky's toes and its heel dug into the ground.

Alex paces slowly in the giant imprint—front to back, then the other way, then back again. It's so big that she would fit into it with all her friends, with room to spare, and use it as a pool if it were a little deeper. It's a little terrifying to be walking in the footprint of a creature that could squash her into goo without any effort, but there's also a primal sort of excitement to it, like pulling a dragon by the tail. She looks in the direction of the tracks and imagines the Lanky striding across the gravel flats in the rainstorm. They all move without haste or concern, as if they're aware that nothing on this planet can challenge their absolute supremacy. Without news from Earth, there's no way for Alex to know how far the Lankies have spread by now, how many human colonies are left in the settled galaxy. She was born on Earth, but she has no memories of the place. Her parents got selected for the colony when she was two years old, and she really only knows her home planet from pictures and network broadcasts. She can't imagine what it may look like overrun with Lankies because she can't really visualize what it's like there without Lankies, not after spending almost her entire life on this rough and mostly empty world.

Maybe we're the last humans alive in the universe, she thinks. It's not a difficult thing to imagine out here, walking underneath the dark skies in the stormy weather, and the only other humans within hundreds of kilometers barely visible in the driving rain as they toil away at the bottom of the hill. It's a glum thought but not one that she finds entirely depressing. It would be a far better reason for the silence from Earth than simply having been forgotten or written off by the rest of humanity.

Three hours after their arrival, the salvage team is still busy carrying things from the ruined building and loading them into the cargo crawler and the trailer they brought along. Alex keeps watching the activity from her vantage point every time Ash finishes his patrol loop along the top of the ramp. She knows that the team would never waste cargo space and weight on stuff that isn't undeniably valuable to the colony, and the fact that they're still at it tells her that the long overland trip was worth the time and effort. They haven't had a good, solid salvage in months, and she's eager to find out what the building yielded. But even with the excitement of the obvious find and the latent adrenaline in her system that comes from staying alert for signs of another Lanky approaching, Alex is tired and a little bored after a few solitary hours at her post. Her jumpsuit is supposed to be waterproof, but the downpour has been constant, and all the water getting in through the little gaps on her collar and sleeves has been enough to soak her thoroughly.

Finally, the light on the mule's turret flashes a signal in her direction, telling her to return to the vehicle. She clicks her own light on and off twice to acknowledge the message. When she gathers Ash and heads downhill, Alex feels her stomach growling. There's no opportunity for them to shower and get the grime off their bodies when they're out on a mission, but just the prospect of a hot combat ration pouch and some sleep inside a dry sleeping bag puts a bit of an extra spring into her step as she leads Ash down the access ramp and back toward the mule. As she makes her way downhill on the rain-soaked gravel, Private Lopez comes up the ramp to meet her halfway.

"This better be good," she says when they meet up. "It's going to take me a week to dry out."

"Oh, it's good," Lopez says. "It's more than good."

"You gonna tell me? Come on, Lopez."

He falls in line next to her and Ash for the walk back to the mule.

"We got down to the basement. Most of it is rubble. But there was one storage room in the back that looked like it was still in one piece. Door was wedged shut, so we had to yank it off with the winch. *Jackpot.* Bunch of spare comms gear. Fifty boxes of rations. And *sixty-four* power cells, still sealed."

"Holy shit," Alex says with a grin. Rations are great as supplemental or mission food, but the standard power packs that can run everything from vehicles to power tools are of immeasurable worth to the colony. It's a good day when a salvage mission comes back with six or seven used but intact cells. Bringing back more than five dozen new ones with only a handful of discharge cycles on them will make this weeklong slog well worth the effort.

"Trailer's crammed full of goodies. Crawler's just about full too. Be a cozy ride back for the civvies," Lopez says.

"As long as they don't rat fuck the rations and take out all the lemon bars," Alex replies.

"Don't worry. Nobody's opening those babies until we're back home. Blake will make sure of that."

"Wish I could have helped with the loading."

"Be glad you had something else to do," Lopez says. "Those large power packs are heavy as shit. I'm worn-out now."

Back at the vehicles, Administrator Blake is loading ration boxes into the back of the cargo crawler with Sergeant Frye and technician Andres. Ash trots past them and leaps into the back of the mule, his paws barely touching the tail ramp in the process. Through the open hatch, Alex sees that Corporal Bayliss is taking a turn at the gun mount.

"You two," Blake says to Alex and Lopez as they walk up. "You are aware that this is a salvage mission, not a matchmaking service, right?"

Alex feels the old temper flare up just a little, the reflexive defiance that got her into trouble with Blake so many times when she was younger and less in control of herself.

"That's not something you need to worry about," she tells him. "Why did you call me back down?"

"We're heading out. I want to get some distance between us and this place before we break for the night."

"We're not sheltering here?" Lopez asks.

Blake shakes his head. "I don't like the feel of it. We're at the bottom of a bag down here. There's only one good way in or out. We dodged a bullet already with that Lanky. No need to tempt fate."

"We also only have to defend in one direction," Lopez says.

"Sergeant Frye agrees with me, so we're moving in five. Get squared away for egress. We'll stop a few hours up the plateau for some rest."

He turns around and takes another ration container from Andres to pass it up to Sergeant Frye in the back of the crawler.

"Aww, and we just got here," Lopez says to her in a low voice as they walk over to the back of the mule to follow Ash inside.

"At least you got to see the inside," Alex says.

"Not much to see. The Lankies wrecked the shit out of it. We got lucky with that storage room in the basement. There's fuck all in the rest of the place except for rubble and scrap metal."

"Any bodies?"

Lopez shakes his head curtly. "Not in the places we could reach."

They take their seats and buckle in. Ash waits until Alex is settled in before he lies down next to her and pushes his snout against her hand. She pats him on the neck, then rubs his ear. He settles down with a little grunt and puts his snout between his paws, having received all the recognition he craved.

A few moments later, Sergeant Frye comes through the hatch and closes it behind him by slapping the button with his palm on the way into the compartment. He settles into one of the empty seats with a tired grunt. When the hatch locks into place, the relative silence that follows is quite loud to Alex's ears after listening to the driving rain for hours. She waits until the air-quality light has turned green once more and takes off Ash's mask, then her own. When she turns the mask upside down, a trickle of water runs out and spills on the floor in front of her boots. Alex rubs her face with her sleeve, but it's a futile gesture because her clothes are soaked.

Lopez grabs a towel off the storage rack under his seat and hands it to her.

"Thank you," she says. She dries her hands and face and then uses the towel to rub down Ash's head. "I'm going to have a mask rash for a week after this."

Without the mask, the smells in the compartment are assaulting her nose—wet dog, wet people, and the collective lack of hygiene that is an unavoidable side effect of multiday salvage missions—but she doesn't mind because even the smelly air in the hold is better than rebreathing her own exhalations inside of a wet mask for hours.

"Bayliss, you stay on the gun until our next stop," Sergeant Frye tells the corporal behind the controls for the weapons mount. "Take a breather, everyone. We got lucky today."

"Day's not over yet, Sergeant," Lopez cautions.

The mule lurches backward as the driver sets it into motion and reverses away from the rubble they used for partial concealment. Then they're on their way up the ramp. The crawler follows in their wake, its enormous tires shedding rainwater and bits of gravel as it climbs the slope with its heavy trailer in tow. When the mule reaches the top of the ramp where Alex has spent the last few hours making figure-eight patterns in the gravel with Ash, she looks over at the targeting screen of the weapons station, almost expecting to see another Lanky walking across the flats toward them. But when Corporal Bayliss rotates the gun mount to get a picture of their surroundings, there's nothing out there but silvery bands of driving rain pelting the barren landscape. Alex allows herself to relax a little in her seat and enjoy the cool, dry air from the overhead vents. She takes a drinking-water pouch out of the storage bin underneath her seat and opens the screw cap. One of the pouches on Ash's harness holds his bowl, and he perks up when she takes out the bowl and places it on the rubberized floor in front of him. When she pours water into the bowl, he glances at her with what she imagines is mild disappointment, but then he lowers his head and drinks.

"Water now, food later," she tells him. He wags his tail once at the mention of food—one of his favorite words—and continues drinking in loud, wet slurps. Alex drinks the rest of the water in the pouch. It's warm like everything else in the cargo hold, but it tastes clean and clear, unlike the plastic-flavored solution in her vest's hydration pack, and she sucks the bag dry until it collapses into a single layer. She replaces the cap and tosses the pouch into the reclaim container.

"When we get home, we'll open something better to celebrate," Sergeant Frye says.

"And now you're old enough to have some too," Lopez says with a knowing wink.

"Oh, boy," Alex replies. Lopez knows that she and her friends have been sneaking bottles of the colony's engineering moonshine back to their secret little hideout in the Vault since they were teenagers because he has joined them on occasion. She's pretty sure, however, that Sergeant Frye isn't aware of Misfit Cove, and she'd like to keep it that way. She shoots Lopez a stealthy warning glance, but he just smiles and shifts his attention to the weapons station. They're on the plateau now, driving back the way they had come just a few hours ago. Behind them, the ruins of the science outpost are already out of sight in the fog and rain. Her instincts tell her that it's safest to shelter in the cover of the buildings instead of underneath some rock overhang out on the plateau. But after eight years of playing cat and mouse with the Lankies, the remaining humans of 18 Scorpii b have learned that it's safer to stay out in the open and leave the encounters with the Lankies to chance than to loiter in the illusory safety of a fixed landmark.

Still, as they head out into the storm and leave the destroyed science station behind, Alex feels as though she's on a little boat that's leaving safe harbor and heading out onto a turbulent, monster-infested sea, and the thought sends a little trickle of a chill down her spine even though it's a sweat-inducing thirty degrees Celsius in the back of the mule.

CHAPTER 6

The jolt that wakes her up almost throws Alex off the makeshift bunk. Disoriented, she tries to sit up only to find that she can't, and the sudden panic she feels is like a steel vise closing around her chest. Then Ash's snout bumps into her side, and she blinks as she tries to get her bearings. She's still stretched out on the seats Lopez had turned into the sleep-shift bunk, but someone has strapped her in while she was sleeping, fastening two sets of lap belts around her.

"Easy," Lopez says from his seat across the aisle. "You're all right. Take a second."

The mule jolts again, this time a bit less vigorously. Alex unfastens the lap belts and swings her legs over the edge of the seat bunk, still trying to shake the fog of sleep from her brain.

"What's going on?" she asks.

"Bumpy ride," Lopez replies. "Weather's terrible. Lots of deep ruts from all the runoff."

Alex looks around to see that Sergeant Frye has taken over the gun mount. Corporal Bayliss is no longer in the back, which means she went up front to drive the mule with Private Harris. Frye glances at Alex and then returns his attention to his sensor screen. She sees that he has buckled himself in as well.

"How long was I out?"

"Three hours, give or take," Lopez says. "It's 0330."

"Should have kicked me awake."

"Nah, you needed the rest. You looked worn-out."

"Pretty sure we're all running on backup power by now," Alex says. She rubs her eyes and gives Ash's neck a squeeze.

Lopez doesn't disagree. He rubs his face, which is scruffy with several days' worth of beard stubble, and stifles a yawn. The excitement of the successful salvage has mostly worn off in the two days since they left the science outpost, and the mission has once again become soul-grinding monotony.

"Listen to that rain," Alex says. The rain coming down on the mule's hull is a constant low-frequency roar that is louder than the humming of the electric engines.

"I don't think the weather could get any worse, but here we are," Lopez says.

Alex switches sides in the hold and sits down next to Lopez so she can see the sensor screen at the weapon station. The view ahead is just headlights cutting through swirling fog and sheets of heavy rain. A readout in the corner of the display shows their current speed: fifteen kilometers per hour, a quarter of their usual overland speed. Behind them, the civilian cargo crawler is following closely to stay in sight, tailing the mule by just a few vehicle lengths, its headlights bobbing fiercely on the uneven terrain.

"Where are we?" Alex asks.

"We're off the plateau, finally," Sergeant Frye says. "We're on the southern ridge. Eighty klicks out from home."

She does the math in her head: almost six hours left to go at this pace, for a distance that would take them less than an hour and a half in better weather. The storms have been getting more frequent and severe since the Lankies arrived, but she has never been in a downpour like this. It feels like the planet is trying to wash them away, humans and Lankies alike. Her clothes are still damp even after three hours in her sleeping bag, but her discomfort is tempered a little by the prospect of a long, hot shower, a set of clean clothes, and a proper meal that doesn't come out of a pouch, all waiting for her just a few hours away.

"Want some chow?" Lopez asks.

"What do we have left?"

The private picks up the ration box that was on the seat in front of him and takes inventory.

"There's one chili left. And three of the spaghetti and meatballs in tomato sauce."

She considers the options and shakes her head.

"I've had my fill of all of those," she says. "I'll have a fruit bar if there are any left."

Lopez digs around for a moment. "Let's see. Looks like you're in luck. This is the last one in the box."

He takes out the requested item and tosses it to her. She catches the fruit bar and opens the plastic wrapper with her teeth. At the sound of the crinkling wrapper, Ash perks up and looks at her hopefully.

"Just a bite," she tells him. She breaks off a piece and holds it out. "Easy."

Ash takes the offered treat gently, swallows it in two bites, and returns his attention to the rest of the bar in Alex's hand.

"Only a little bit, buddy. Those are not good for you."

"They're not great for people either," Lopez says.

She takes a bite of the bar. It's a chewy blend of pressed fruit and soy binder and whatever additives give it a ten-year shelf life. Whenever they're out on missions, the military-grade stims they take to stay alert also suppress appetite as a side effect, and it took her a while to learn to listen to her growling stomach even when she doesn't feel like eating. Ash watches with envy as she finishes the bar. She shows him the empty wrapper.

"See? All gone."

She stands up to throw the plastic into the reclaim container, and the mule lurches to the side again. Lopez reaches up and grabs her by the arm to keep her from falling. Then the mule comes to a sudden stop, brakes sighing.

"What's going on?" Sergeant Frye calls into the intercom.

"Water obstacle," Corporal Bayliss replies. "Can't tell how deep it is. Someone's gotta get out and check it out."

"I'll go." Frye unbuckles his harness and reaches for his mask. "Lopez, get on the gun. Alex, get the dog ready. I'll call you out if it looks like it'll be more than a second."

They all put on their masks. When Alex has geared up Ash again and connected his air supply, Sergeant Frye opens the rear hatch of the mule. The sound of the downpour immediately doubles in volume. The rain is coming down so hard that Alex is getting splashed with some of the water that's bouncing off the open tail ramp. Behind them, the cargo crawler has stopped as well.

Sergeant Frye grabs a coiled-up safety rope from an overhead bin. He leaves the mule and walks down the tail ramp into the rain in a crouched stance. When he turns the rear corner of the vehicle and disappears from sight, Alex looks at the sensor screen and watches him walk to the front of the mule and check out the obstacle ahead, a fast-flowing stretch of water that's several meters across. He connects the safety rope to the front of the mule and clips the other end to his harness. Then he starts probing the water-filled rivulet ahead. Two steps in, the water is already up to his knees, and the current looks strong enough to make him plant his legs to avoid getting swept away.

"That doesn't look great," Lopez says.

"It's not that wide," Alex replies.

"Doesn't really matter. What matters is how deep it is and how strong the flow is. Remember, the contact spots on those wheels are only as big as your hand. Doesn't take all that much to get washed away. Even in this thirty-ton piece of shit."

They watch Sergeant Frye as he does his careful assessment of the obstacle. After a few minutes, he walks back to the rear hatch of the mule and signals the driver of the cargo crawler behind them. Then he walks up the ramp of the mule and sticks his head into the hatch.

"Dog team, you're up. We'll be here for a bit."

—

Outside, the rain is coming down relentlessly. Alex leads Ash away from the mule, but the visibility is so bad that she can barely see the mule and the crawler behind it from less than fifty meters away. They're in a precarious spot, an uphill slope that is hemmed in by a rock ledge to their left and a steep drop to their right. The obstacle blocking their path is a gully that's channeling the rainwater flowing downhill. Alex walks close to the edge to take a look at the drop-off. It starts at a shallow angle, but not far from the edge, the gradient steepens so much that the runoff from the gully shoots over the edge like a waterfall, spewing rainwater into the darkness with a dull roar. The hillside below Alex is full of jagged rock formations that stick up like giant shards. From her vantage point, she can't see the bottom of the canyon, which makes the sight all the more menacing, an endless chasm full of sharp, unyielding edges. Standing close to the edge makes her deeply uncomfortable, so she takes Ash back to the other side of the path, past the stopped vehicles. The civvie techs have gathered in front of the mule's open tail ramp with Sergeant Frye, who has to shout to make himself heard over the sounds of the downpour and the water rushing through the gully in front of the mule.

"It's at least a meter and a half. Fast-flowing water too. The mule can wade it, but the crawler's gonna have problems," he tells Administrator Blake, whose sour expression is obvious even behind his mask.

"Fucking fantastic," Blake replies. "Give me some options here, Sergeant."

Frye looks back at the crawler.

"We have just enough space up here to turn around. But we'd have to backtrack all the way to the flats, try to hook around to the western approach. That's a hundred-klick detour once all's said and done. Eight hours, give or take."

"We don't have the juice left for that," Blake says. "Power cell's down to twenty percent. Gotta make it across this ridge or we're walking home empty-handed. You sure about that crawler?"

"High center of gravity, especially loaded up like it is. And those oversized tires. I wouldn't feel good about trying it," Sergeant Frye says. "But you're the boss. Your call."

"Well, shit." Blake wipes his forehead and flicks off the rainwater. "You got any ideas, now's the time."

"We hook up the tow rig. Mule goes first. If it gets into trouble, the crawler can pull it back. Mule makes it through, crawler goes next. Crawler starts drifting, the mule can pull it out."

Blake considers the suggestion for a moment and nods.

"Let's do it," he says. "And let's be quick about it. Don't want to stay stationary for too long. Not in this shit."

—

Alex stands back with Ash while Sergeant Frye and the civilian techs reel off the thick steel cable that's mounted on the front of the crawler and connect it to the recovery hook on the back of the mule. When they're finished, the sergeant waves her back to the mule, and she gets into the back with Ash, both of them once again thoroughly drenched.

"Let's go, Bayliss," Sergeant Frye says into the intercom. "Nice and easy. Walking speed."

"Copy that," Bayliss replies.

The mule rolls forward and takes the slack out of the tow cable. A moment later, the crawler follows. When the front of the mule starts to dip down into the gully, Alex realizes that she didn't fasten her safety belt. When she reaches for it, Sergeant Frye shakes his head.

"Leave it undone," he tells her. "You don't want it to slow you down if this goes sideways."

She nods and puts her hands in her lap. The sounds of the water splashing against the bottom of the hull are getting louder as Corporal Bayliss carefully drives the mule through the flooded gully. The hull shudders and jolts with the force of the rushing current. Alex tries to think about the comforts waiting for them at the Vault instead of the rocky chasm that's only a few dozen steps to their right. She reaches down and pets Ash to give her hands something to do.

"It'll be fine," Lopez shouts over the roar of the water and the whining of the electric engines. *"This thing can ford much deeper water. It's amphibious."*

"All vehicles are amphibious, Lopez," Sergeant Frye shouts back. *"Some only briefly."*

Despite her anxiety, Alex has to crack a smile at the sergeant's offered wisdom. She knows the soldiers well enough by now that she can tell they're every bit as tense as she is, but she appreciates their efforts to look after her.

The mule pushes its way through the flooded gully and up the far side. Behind them, the crawler follows at the end of the tow cable. Alex watches through the half-open tail ramp as the nose of the bigger vehicle dips down and the front tires splash into the current. The tires on the crawler are much taller and wider than those on the military mule, and she can see that the water has much more surface to push against. Almost right away, the driver has to steer sideways a little to compensate for the sudden drift, which only increases as the second and then the third pair of wheels enter the rushing flow. For an alarming moment, it looks like the crawler is completely adrift, with all six wheels afloat and spinning without traction. Then the tow cable gets taut as Corporal Bayliss slowly drives the mule forward, and the front wheels of the crawler gain their footing again and begin to claw the vehicle up the side of the gully. Even with the tow assist, the crawler struggles against the incline and the force of the current. Just as the second pair of wheels bites into the ground again, the trailer enters the water and immediately floats sideways, pulling the rear of the crawler with it.

"Yank 'em out," Sergeant Frye calls into the intercom.

Corporal Bayliss throttles up the electric engines, and the tow cable creaks under the increasing strain. The front of the crawler is almost on dry ground, but the weight of the now free-floating trailer is yanking it back sideways. The driver tries to counter the sudden drift by steering into it. The crawler lurches up the little slope, then slides backward again with spinning tires. Finally, the efforts of the driver combined with the pulling power of the mule reach a stalemate against the force of the rushing water, but not before the unmoored trailer has pulled the stern of the crawler downstream and canted the vehicle sideways on the slope at a forty-five-degree angle.

"Gun it," Frye shouts.

"I'm trying," Bayliss replies from the driver's seat. "I can't pull them out like that. I'll tear that tow hook off if I try."

"*Goddammit.* Lock the brakes. Keep that crawler where it is. If they slide back, they'll float off and pull us with them," the sergeant says.

There's a sharp electric whining sound as the brakes clamp down on all six wheels. Sergeant Frye gets out of his seat and rushes over to the rear hatch. He slaps the button to open it all the way, then darts out as soon as the opening is tall enough to let him through. Alex gathers Ash's lead and gets up to follow the sergeant out.

Outside, the tires of the crawler are spitting gravel and mud as the driver is trying to drag the vehicle out of the ditch. The crawler is top-heavy, twice as tall as the mule, and the angle at which it sits on the little embankment looks dangerously steep to Alex. After a few moments of futile spinning of wheels, Sergeant Frye signals the driver to stop.

The crawler has a ramp in the rear just like the mule, but the tail end of the vehicle is still above the fast-flowing water, so Administrator Blake has to climb out of the forward personnel hatch next to the driver's station, which is now two meters off the ground. Alex watches with growing concern as Blake and the sergeant assess the situation together.

"We need to get some weight unloaded," Frye says when they have finished their unhappy survey.

"We can unload the ration boxes, but the crates with the power cells won't fit through the front hatch," Blake replies. "Not unless we open them up and empty them one by one."

"That'll take hours," Sergeant Frye says. "Tell your techs to dismount. Everyone needs to grab an entrenching tool and start shoveling. We need to get that middle port-side wheel something to grab. Hurry up before that tow cable decides to pop and we're all in deep shit."

—

After a few minutes, only the two drivers are left in the vehicles. Everyone else except for Alex, soldier and civilian tech alike, is taking turns digging away at the embankment, shoveling soil and gravel underneath the center wheel pair of the crawler. Alex is pacing what little open space they have with Ash, who is focused on his job as always. The ground here is stony and unyielding, and she flinches a little every time she hears the bright noise of a shovel blade hitting rocks. All the other sounds are drowned out by the steady rain and the rushing of the water in the gully.

The first attempt to get the crawler out of the ditch again is almost successful. With the fresh dirt and gravel under the center drive wheel on the left side, the tire finally grips, and the crawler lurches upward. It nearly clears the low ledge with the front wheels. Then the center wheel is on bare rain-slick rock, and it starts to spin in place again. The crawler stalls and slides backward until it's almost back in the spot where it started the attempt. Alex watches with increasing anxiety as her teammates climb down the side of the ditch and start shoveling again.

On the second try, the first row of wheels makes it over the ledge. The second row just barely mounts the ledge, but the crawler is still pulled sideways by the weight of the trailer in the fast-flowing water, and one tire settles on top of the little berm while the other one churns up the soil just below. Once again, even the mule's pulling power isn't enough to achieve more than a stalemate against the mass of the trailer and the canted crawler's awkward center of balance. The tow cable is taut and quivering with the powerful forces that are pulling it in opposite directions. Alex watches the tug-of-war between torque and gravity with clenched fists, willing the crawler over the obstacle even though she knows that the physics involved aren't going to be influenced by her desires.

The mule pulls again, altering its angle slightly to compensate for the cant of the crawler. The towing cable vibrates under the strain with a high-pitched metallic chirp. Centimeter by centimeter, the front of the crawler noses over the ledge.

"Come on," Alex pleads. "Almost there." Behind her, Ash barks.

The sound makes her flinch hard. It's not his usual low huff but an explosive noise that's only slightly muffled by the mask he's wearing. He barks again, even louder than before, and the bark morphs into a deep, sonorous growl that makes his chest vibrate with the resonance of it. Alex sees that the fur on his neck and spine is standing up. She has never seen him in the kind of posture he's assuming right now—hunched low, with stiff legs and flattened ears. She can't see his muzzle underneath the mask but she knows that his teeth are bared.

"*No, no, no,*" she says. "Not fucking now."

CHAPTER 7

This time, Alex senses the Lanky before she can see it. Somewhere down the slope, the swirling bands of fog and rain coalesce and disperse in response to something unseen, a presence so large and weighty that it bends the air currents around it with its passage. Ash barks again, even louder than the first time. She can feel the vibration of the growl that flows through the leash in her hand. Then he backs up a little, creeping backward slowly even as all his attention is still focused on whatever is alarming him. The sight of a scared Ash frightens her more than anything she's ever seen while out on a mission. Ash is always cautious, vigilant, confident, never afraid like this. The sudden flood of adrenaline rushing to her brain electrifies her senses better than any stim she's ever taken.

Down on the slope behind them, the Lanky materializes out of the haze like a nightmare gradually taking form—a massive cranial shield, twenty meters above the rocky path, then long and spindly limbs. The head slowly sways from side to side with the cadence of the creature's unhurried walk. Its gait is cautious and deliberate, as if the Lanky is making sure it has solid footing going uphill on the wet rock ledge. For a heartbeat, it looks like a mirage, something served up by a restless subconscious in the middle of a bad sleep. Then Ash barks again and yanks her out of her horrified paralysis.

Alex turns around and activates her signal light. Down by the vehicles, everyone is either shoveling gravel underneath the crawler's wheels again or helping to push it over the low ledge it can't quite mount. She takes a deep breath and undoes one side of her mask so it doesn't muffle her voice.

"Incoming," she shouts as loud as she can against the wind and the rain. *"We have incoming!"*

She pulls on Ash's leash and prepares to run for the safety of the mule, but the dog isn't moving. When she turns her head to shout at him, he's no longer fixed on the Lanky that's coming up the slope, now just a little more than a hundred meters away and closing in with long, slow steps. Instead, he's looking at a spot above the rock ledge that marks the left edge of their path, where the water is pouring out of a gap in the rock and rushing down the ravine that is holding them up. He barks again, but in a cadence she has never heard out of him, a high-pitched staccato that sounds like he's preparing to launch himself against someone and tear their throat out.

A second Lanky appears above the ledge right in front of her and Ash. For a second, Alex doesn't even fully realize what she's seeing. At this range, the thing is so massive that it looks like a part of the mountain has suddenly come alive. She looks up to see a massive head and then a leg coming down toward the spot where she is standing, transfixed by the sight. The Lanky's huge three-toed foot plows into the ground right next to her, and she throws herself forward and down reflexively to protect Ash even though she knows it won't make a difference. She lands on her belly in front of Ash and tries to pull him down to shield him, but the dog is standing firm, furiously barking at the Lanky that is now right above them. Alex rolls on her back, using Ash's harness for leverage. For a moment, the Lanky's foot is so close that she can almost reach out and touch it. Then the Lanky steps down from the ledge completely and strides toward the spot where the mule is still lashed to the crawler with the towing cable. Her teammates are scattering in front of the creature. One of the soldiers opens fire with his rifle. The thunderclap of the shot is followed by a second bang well above her head, the sound of the gas-filled rifle round exploding against the Lanky's head shield. The soldier fires again, and Alex rolls over and tries to take Ash down with her, but the dog doesn't budge, eighty pounds of unyielding, infuriated muscle. He launches himself at the Lanky as it takes another step away from them. She tries to pull him back by the leash, but he's so strong and determined that her effort doesn't even slow him down. He rips the leash out of her hand and darts after the creature, still barking those loud, shrill, enraged barks.

"No, Ash! No!"

Alex screams after him, but her voice is drowned out by the noise of the relentless wind and the gunfire. Everything has happened so quickly that she hasn't even had time to get scared, but the sight of Ash dashing after the Lanky terrifies her, and she scrambles to her feet and runs after him. The Lanky's long strides have carried it almost all the way to the vehicles in just a few steps. It's only when she gets dizzy that she realizes her mask is still dangling from one side of her head and that she is sucking in the atmospheric carbon dioxide with every breath. She reaches up and fastens the mask with clumsy fingers that don't quite seem to be under her control.

There's more gunfire now, a staccato of booms that cut through the storm noise and assault her ears like physical blows. The Lanky stumbles under the fusillade of rifle bullets and loses its footing. Then it screams. It's the loudest sound Alex has ever heard, a high-pitched, keening wail that feels like it's making every molecule in her body vibrate in response. She screams and covers her ears with her gloved hands.

The Lanky is almost on top of the vehicles when someone in the mule opens fire with the automatic cannon. The muzzle blast from the heavy weapon briefly lights up the darkness. Alex can feel the concussion from the muzzle blast even from fifty meters away. The cannon fires twice at what is now almost point-blank range.

Both cannon rounds slam into the Lanky's torso. The creature's scream changes pitch as it stumbles again and goes down, limbs flailing. It crashes into the water-filled gully, and the shock from the impact almost knocks Alex off her feet. There's another sound, the tortured groaning of metal and composites enduring forces well past their design tolerances. The Lanky's body crushes the cargo crawler's trailer and sends water splashing in all directions. The crawler, still connected to the destroyed trailer with its tow bar, gets yanked back from the edge of the gully and toward the prone Lanky that's flailing and screaming in the water. It tries to scramble back to its feet, but it looks like it can't get solid footing on the wet rock against the force of the runoff. It falls again, and the momentum of the movement makes it slide down the gully toward the nearby edge of the rock ledge.

The mule is no longer shooting. Instead, it's pulling against the strain of the weight of the crawler trying to yank the entire vehicle combination back toward the Lanky. The wheels of the mule spin in place as the tires claw for traction, and gravel sprays out from underneath the treads in long rooster tails. Alex finally reaches Ash, who is right up at the edge of the gully, barking his shotgun barks at the Lanky that is struggling to right itself just a few dozen meters away. She wraps her arms around his neck and tries to pull him back, but he stands his ground with a stubbornness she has never seen out of him. Alex has no doubt that if it wasn't for the mask he's wearing, he'd try to take a bite out of the Lanky.

To her right, the Lanky's keening wail is answered by another. In the few moments since the first one stepped off the ledge and almost flattened her, the second creature has already made it halfway up the slope from the spot where it had appeared out of the storm. Alex looks around frantically, but there's no cover out here on the rocky path, no hole or crevice where she can hide from the monsters.

Someone screams at her from the direction of the mule, but she can't make out the words over the din. Alex turns to see Sergeant Frye and Corporal Bayliss aiming their weapons at the second Lanky. From her angle, it looks like the gun muzzles are pointed straight at her, and she realizes that she's in their line of fire. She grabs Ash by his harness and yanks him back with all her strength, boosted by the adrenaline surging through her system. This time, he gives in and allows her to drag him with her even as he keeps up his furious staccato of barks.

The Lanky in the gully almost manages to get back on its legs, but it's clearly wounded or dying from the cannon shells that tore into its middle, and it has trouble finding traction in the water-filled rock trough. Alex pulls Ash away from the edge of the ravine and away from the huge flailing arms. Just as it's almost upright again, three more rifle rounds smash into its chest and explode with muffled cracks. The Lanky wails again and takes a step back. Then it loses its balance in the fast-flowing runoff and crashes back into the ravine. With one arm, it reaches out and tries to grab the edge of the gully, and its huge spindly fingers close around the crushed remnants of the crawler's trailer. When the Lanky tries to pull itself up, there's a sound like someone is crushing a freight container with a hydraulic press.

Alex drags Ash back to the rock ledge and hunkers down with him. The ledge on this side is five or six meters tall. It doesn't have any crevices she can use for cover, so she wraps her arms around the dog and tries to make herself as small as possible. It takes most of her strength to keep Ash from darting toward the stricken Lanky again. The other one is almost on top of them now as well. It looks even bigger than the first, and it's moving toward the gunfire and its fallen comrade with terrifying speed and purpose.

Sergeant Frye and Corporal Bayliss unload their rifles into the Lanky thrashing around in the gully. Alex looks over at the crawler, which is still trying to make it out of the ditch with spinning tires. She can see the face of the driver behind the cockpit's large side window, their fear evident by the wide-eyed stare that meets her own eyes. The

Lanky wails again, but the sound is weaker now, in a shakier timbre than before.

"Shoot it! Fucking shoot it!" One of the civilian techs is shouting through the open tail hatch at whoever is in the back of the mule. She recognizes Blake's voice. The administrator is standing between the mule and the soldiers, out of the line of their rifle fire. The mule's driver is alternating between throttle and brake, trying to pull the crawler free from the grasp of the Lanky that is pulling it back by the trailer's tow bar. The autocannon on top of the mule is still aimed at the creature, but there's a mechanical *clunk-clunk-clunk* noise coming from the mount that sounds like something isn't working the way it should. The other Lanky bellows as it makes its way toward the chaos. Ash barks a challenge in reply. Alex can feel his muscles tensing with each bark, taut as steel cables and vibrating with anger.

The Lanky in the ravine finally falls to the gunfire from Frye and Bayliss. It drops back into the water, still holding on to the smashed trailer as it falls. The crawler, still attached to the broken cargo pod, slides backward another meter or two. Only the tow cable and the efforts of the mule's driver keep the crawler from getting pulled all the way back into the ravine.

The stricken Lanky makes one last effort to get up, but its injuries and the force of the water rushing down the gully work against it. It falls backward, its legs buckling, and splashes back into the ravine. The crawler gets jolted violently as the Lanky's weight overcomes whatever pulling power the mule can muster. The towing cable chirps with the strain of the added load it suddenly has to bear. The mule's driver is going full throttle now, heedless of the smoke pouring from the rubber liners of the tires, the treads trying to get traction against the wet rock and the immense forces pulling the thirty-ton vehicle slowly backward.

The front tow hook on the crawler breaks with a sharp crack that's almost as loud as the gunshots. Alex watches in horror as the steel cable whips around in a wide arc with a high-pitched whistling sound. The end of the cable, with the tow hook still attached, hits Blake in the chest and knocks him off his feet before slamming into the back of the mule with the harsh ringing of steel on steel even as the armored transport leaps forward, cut loose from the weight that had held it in place. The mule takes off, its rear swinging from side to side for a moment with the shock of the sudden release and the uneven traction of the tires. When the vehicle straightens out, the driver doesn't stop. Instead, the mule races up the slope, away from the water-filled gully and the Lankies, leaving behind everyone who wasn't in the back when the towline broke. Alex shouts out a wordless curse in disbelief as she watches the armored transport accelerate and outrun the techs who were trying to catch up to it.

They fucking left us, she thinks. *They left us behind with these things.*

The stricken Lanky slides down the gully toward the edge of the rock ledge, driven by the momentum of its fall and the raging current rushing through the narrow ravine. Whether by intent or some alien nervous impulse, it's still gripping the crushed trailer it had tried to use for leverage, and Alex shouts again as the crawler gets hauled back into the water as the Lanky topples over the edge and disappears in the darkness. The crawler's driver tries to turn the wheels and get back onto solid ground, but it's mostly floating on its massive all-terrain tires now, and whatever propulsion the spinning wheels still provide is no match for the current and the weight of the Lanky. For a brief, heart-stopping moment, it seems like the driver of the crawler is looking directly at her, eyes wide with fear. Then the vehicle's front tips up as the rear goes over the ledge, and the crawler follows the Lanky down the side of the mountain. Alex gets one last glimpse at the underside of the transport, its wheels still spinning madly. Then it drops out of sight like a drowning person slipping beneath the surface of a dark lake.

The other Lanky is almost at the gully now, advancing with weighty steps that Alex can feel through the soles of her boots as they shake the rock ledge. It wails again, in a lower timbre than the earlier distress cry of its fatally wounded compatriot. It sounds sinister, like an angry challenge. The Lanky is only fifty meters from Alex now, and the noise is so loud that it feels like a physical push against her chest. Ash replies with a challenge of his own, barking in a near-hysterical pitch and frequency.

The remaining humans on the ledge scatter as the Lanky steps across the ravine. Sergeant Frye and Corporal Bayliss fire their rifles at the creature while they retreat backward. Blake is sprawled on the ground, unmoving. When the Lanky's massive foot comes down on the other side of the ditch, it misses the administrator's prone form by a mere meter or two. The Lanky pays him no mind. It's focused on Frye and Bayliss now, who are pelting it with explosive rounds. The soldiers empty their rifles as quickly as they can pull their triggers and bring the weapons back onto target after each shot, a steady drumbeat of muzzle blasts followed by the sharp cracks of explosive-tipped rounds detonating against the tough hide of the Lanky. It bellows again, and Alex screams and tries to cover her ears without letting go of Ash's leash. It's so loud that it's not even really a sound anymore, just a pressure spike that stabs her eardrums like a rusty nail covered in pure alcohol.

The Lanky leans forward into the rifle fire and drops to all fours to cover its body with its cranial shield. It's so tall that the move halves the distance between the creature and the two soldiers. Frye yells something at Bayliss and changes the magazine in his weapon. The Lanky is badly hurt by the gunfire, but it's still advancing undeterred, and it's clear that the two rifles aren't enough firepower to stop this charging monster.

Sergeant Frye finishes reloading his rifle and opens fire again, aiming low underneath the Lanky's head to hit the limbs. One of the exploding rounds tears into its front limb, and the impact makes the Lanky stumble. For a second, it looks like the thing hesitates. Then it wails again and lunges forward, faster than Alex thought an organism of this size could move. It lashes out with one spindly arm and smashes it into the spot where Sergeant Frye and Corporal Bayliss are holding their ground. It looks like someone sweeping a tabletop in a fit of anger.

When it withdraws the limb again, both soldiers are gone, hurled into the darkness beyond the rock ledge.

Alex hears a muffled shout and turns her head to see one of the civilian techs running uphill after the mule and away from the Lanky. The creature hauls itself upright again and follows the colonist.

"No! You son of a bitch!" Alex shouts after it. She picks up a fist-sized rock from the ground and hurls it after the Lanky. *"Over here!"*

The rock falls well short of the Lanky, and Alex is under no illusion that it would have noticed the impact even if it had struck. But she doesn't have a gun, nothing that can hurt this behemoth or give it pause. She watches helplessly as the Lanky catches up to the colonist in three long steps and walks right over them. Alex screams out in horror when she sees the human shape disappear underneath the dinosaur-like foot of the creature. The Lanky takes two more long steps and stops, then turns around as if it wants to survey the aftermath of its passage. Alex sees the massive head swing around, rainwater flying from the edges of its cranial shield, and even though Lankies don't have eyes, it feels like this one is staring directly at her.

Alex looks around on the ledge, but there's only Blake, lying on the ground eighty meters away, unconscious or dead. There is nobody left to help her. She is all alone with Ash now, and this nightmare is about to descend on them and squish them like bugs under a crawler tire.

I should have died with Mom and Dad eight years ago, she thinks. *To only get twenty-one years after all that. It's not right.*

The panic and horror that have been taking over her mind fall away when she recalls her parents, and the emotion that replaces them is a cold sort of anger. These things took away her world and her parents, and now they'll end her life as well as her birthday, denying her both a quick death with her parents and a full adult life. But if she has to go now, she won't be turning her back, won't be running away from the inevitable.

Ash is still barking and straining at the leash. She lets go of it, and he shoots off to charge his foe, ready and eager to take on a creature that's thousands of times his size and weight. She doesn't want to see Ash die in front of her, but if it must happen, she wants him to meet his fate head-on as well and go out on his own terms instead of being tethered to her.

The Lanky takes a step toward her and lowers its head a little. Alex reaches into her pocket and takes out her father's knife. She unfolds the blade and holds the knife out in front of her. The creature takes another step just as Ash gets close to it, and the dog swerves to avoid the foot as it comes down. With the mask covering his muzzle, he can't bite the Lanky, for whatever good it would do, but he's still darting in as though he intends to take the thing down all by himself.

"Fuck you," she tells the Lanky and raises the knife to point the tip of the blade at it.

The Lanky walks toward her, another slow step that makes the rock tremble under her feet. Alex feels the fear flaring up again when she sees the foot hitting the ground just a few dozen meters in front of her, and she tightens her grip on the knife and wills herself to stand firm despite the trembling in her legs. Ash darts toward the back of the Lanky's foot, barking madly, but the creature ignores him as it continues its advance toward Alex. She takes a deep and shaky breath to steel herself and tenses her leg muscles to run and charge the Lanky just like Ash did.

In the squall line up the slope behind the Lanky, two bright lights cut through the rain and mist, the distinctive cat-eye headlights of the mule. A few heartbeats later, the mule's cannon thunders, belching out a three-round burst that echoes across the ledge. The armor-piercing grenades slam into the Lanky's torso from behind and make it stumble in midstride. The mule is racing down the path toward the creature at high speed, firing on the move. The Lanky starts to turn around to face the threat, but the autocannon barks again, and three more rounds smash into the Lanky's body and explode. One of the grenades hits the lower part of the Lanky's right leg and blows it off in a spray of organic matter. The Lanky lets out a keening wail and topples backward. From Alex's vantage point, it looks like a building falling toward her. She turns around and runs, renewed panic flaring up and giving her a fresh jolt of adrenaline, certain that the thing is going to fall on her and turn her into a puddle of gristle on the rock just as her salvation is coming toward her with guns blazing.

When the Lanky crashes to the ground behind her, the shock of the impact makes her stumble, and the momentum carries her off her feet. She hurtles forward and smashes into the ground in a small-scale imitation of the Lanky's fall. The impact knocks the wind out of her, but instinct and fear make her scramble to her feet again even as her lungs are screaming for air.

Behind her, the Lanky is sprawled on the ground, limbs contorted at angles that look unnatural even for their strange physiology. It opens its maw, then starts to close it again slowly in a motion that looks reflexive. The Lanky's massive head is only ten or fifteen meters from where she is standing with shaking legs and trying to get her breath under control again. The huge creature shudders and stops moving. Its mouth is still halfway open, and Alex can see into its maw, which looks cavernous at this range. There are wisps of smoke rising from the ragged holes the autocannon shells have torn into its body.

As soon as Alex has enough air in her lungs for a shout, she pulls down her mask.

"Ash!" she yells. *"Ash! Come here!"*

For a few terrible moments, she's certain that the dog was too close to the Lanky when it fell, that he's now somewhere underneath this mountain of organic matter in front of her. Then Ash comes dashing through the gap between the Lanky's body and the rock ledge to her left, and Alex shouts his name again. The relief she feels at the sight of him almost lifts her off her feet. She puts her mask back into place and crouches down to receive Ash. When he reaches her, he crashes into her open arms and knocks her on her ass. She laughs and ruffles the fur on his neck.

"You maniac," she says. Ash wags his tail, but it's a furtive wag close to the ground, as if he's not entirely sure whether the levity is appropriate right now.

The mule comes to a stop on the other side of the Lanky with the sighing of pneumatic brakes. She can't see it directly because the enormous carcass is blocking her sight, but she can see the headlights spilling around the edges of the body and illuminating the rain that is still coming down relentlessly. Alex grabs Ash's leash and stands up. She doesn't want to get any closer to the Lanky body, but there's only the small gap between it and the rock ledge where Ash came through, so she gathers her resolve and rushes toward the opening with Ash leading the way.

On the other side of the felled behemoth, the mule is standing in the middle of the ledge, with its cannon still trained on the Lanky's body and slowly tracking from side to side. Alex turns on her light and waves at the vehicle to make her presence known.

"Over here," she shouts.

She hears the whining of the mule's rear hatch. A few moments later, Lopez comes around the back corner of the armored personnel carrier and runs toward her.

"Where the fuck *were* you?" Alex shouts at him when he is close enough to hear her over the wind and rain.

"I'm sorry," he shouts back. His voice sounds like he is close to tears. "I got two rounds off, and then the fucking dual feed jammed. I had to get clear to fix it."

He looks around with a harried expression.

"Where's the crawler? What the hell happened? Where's the sergeant?"

"They're all dead," Alex replies, her voice just short of a scream. "They're fucking gone. You took off and this thing killed them all. Why did you *do* that? How *could* you?"

"I had to clear the feed chute and cycle the cannon. That takes thirty seconds at least. Thirty fucking seconds, Alex. If Harris hadn't gunned it out of here, the mule would be gone too. We'd all be dead."

Alex rushes past Lopez and runs toward the drop-off on the other side of the ledge with Ash. Lopez follows her after a few seconds.

"The sergeant and Bayliss went over the edge," she shouts. "The crawler too. The Lanky pulled it along when it went over. Bring a light. Bring the mule over here and use the searchlight."

Lopez stops next to her at the edge of the rock ledge. The slope looks bottomless from here, a steep drop that seems to go on for half a kilometer before it disappears in the rain and fog. There's no trace of Sergeant Frye or Corporal Bayliss, nor the crawler and its trailer. To her right, the water from the gully arcs over the edge and gushes downslope with a noise that sounds like distant thunder.

Private Lopez turns toward the mule and signals Harris, who is in the driver's seat and watching them through the side window. The mule backs up and turns its nose toward them, then creeps forward cautiously. It stops a few meters short of the edge and locks its brakes again. Lopez runs back to the vehicle and dashes up the still-open tail ramp. A few moments later, the powerful searchlight mounted on the roof of the driver's station turns on and blinds Alex momentarily before Harris moves the light away from her and down the steep slope. Alex follows the beam with her eyes, but the bright pool of light only pans across jagged rocks and irregular fissures. Alex runs toward the back of the mule and up the ramp, Ash in tow. Inside, Lopez is back at the gunnery station, scanning the ravine with the weapon mount's sensor array.

"I don't see shit," he says. "Not even on infrared."

Alex goes up to the emergency supply locker and opens it. She takes out a trauma kit and checks the contents.

"Blake's on the other side of that thing. He's hurt bad."

"What happened?"

"The tow cable snapped. It came around and the end of it hit him," Alex says.

"The tow hook? Fuck." Lopez looks from Alex to the sensor screen, then back to her. "Fuck, fuck, *fuck*," he says again.

"We need to get the hell out of here," Private Harris urges from the driver's station in the front. "You know there's more of those things coming after all that gunfire."

Alex grabs another trauma kit and tosses it at Lopez. It bounces off his console, and he catches it before it can fall to the floor.

"Help me with Blake," she says. "I can't get him back to the mule by myself."

Lopez gets out of his seat with a curse. He joins Alex at the emergency locker and reaches up to get a collapsible stretcher out of the overhead rack.

"Harris, get back here and cover us. We have eleven rounds of AP left. Make 'em count."

"I can't drive and shoot at the same time," Harris replies.

"Get on the fucking gun," Lopez says. "We're not leaving. Not until we've found everyone."

CHAPTER 8

When she reaches Blake, Alex is almost certain that the administrator is dead. He's lying on his side, with blood coming out of the gap between his face and the mask he's wearing, and a dark puddle of it has formed under his head, mixing with the rainwater. But when she kneels next to him and carefully touches his head, he moans softly. Ash is keeping his distance from the prone and injured man, focusing his attention on the darkness beyond the rock ledge to their right again, where the first Lanky appeared seemingly out of nowhere a few minutes ago.

"You're all right," Alex tells Blake. "You'll be all right. Can you hear me? Blake. *Blake*."

She calls his name again and taps his collarbone gently to get his attention, but he doesn't respond. Behind her, Lopez arrives with the stretcher. The soldier gets on his knees next to her and puts the folded stretcher on the ground.

"Is he alive?"

"He's breathing," she says. "But I can't get him to wake up."

"Keep him on his side. That's a lot of blood. You want it to keep draining so he doesn't choke on it." Lopez lifts one side of Blake's mask a little with his gloved finger, and a fresh stream of blood pours across the administrator's cheek and drips onto the ground.

"Shit," Lopez says. "He needs that mask off or he'll suffocate. We have to get him back to the mule."

He unfolds the stretcher and lines it up next to Blake's prone form. Then he kneels on the other side of the administrator and gestures for Alex to take up position next to him.

"I have the neck and chest. You have the hips and knees," he says. "Smooth and easy. Ready? On three. One. Two. *Three.*"

They lift Blake and slide him over onto the stretcher. As they put him down carefully, he moans again. His chest shudders as he follows up the sound with a wet, rasping cough. Lopez reaches over and pulls one side of Blake's mask away from his face to let the blood drain from the inside. In the darkness, the globs that land on the spidersilk fabric of the stretcher look black like old oil.

"I'll get the front, you get the back," Lopez says. "Let me know if you need to put it down along the way. Try to keep things level. On three again. One. Two. *Three.*"

Alex's arms shake a little with the strain of lifting half of Blake's weight. They carry the stretcher past the Lanky's carcass and through the gap, which is barely wide enough for their inflexible combination of bodies and equipment. Ash follows them and dashes ahead to the mule, where he turns and waits for them to catch up.

"Shit," Private Harris says from the gunnery station when Alex and Lopez come up the tail ramp with their cargo. She starts to get out of her seat, but Lopez shakes his head.

"We got it. You stay on that gun. Don't take your eyes off the sensor screen."

They put the stretcher on the floor of the mule between the two rows of seats. Blake's breaths are slow and ragged, and there's an ominous gurgling sound coming from his chest when he draws in air from his oxygen supply.

"You know how to hook up an autodoc cuff, right?" Lopez asks Alex. She replies with a nod.

"Good. We only have the combat medic unit in this shit bucket. But it'll have to do. I'll go and look for the others. Once that ramp is closed, get that mask off him as soon as the AQ light turns green. Got it?"

Alex nods again. "You need the dog with you."

Lopez shakes his head. He picks up his rifle and checks the magazine.

"Keep him in the mule with you. I don't want him to run into the line of fire if another one of those things shows up."

He turns and heads for the tail ramp. When he's almost there, Alex calls his name.

"Lopez."

He turns around to look at her.

"That last one, the one you killed with the cannon. It got one of the techs. I saw it stomp on them," she says. "Thirty, forty meters up the slope and to the right. Halfway toward the drop."

There's a flare-up of emotions behind Lopez's eyes that's obvious to Alex even in the darkened troop compartment of the mule. He acknowledges her information with a curt nod. Then he turns and walks down the ramp without another word.

Alex reaches over and pushes the button for the tail ramp. When the rear hatch is sealed, she goes back to Blake to prepare the autodoc. When she opens the emergency gear locker to get out the equipment, she feels her heart thumping in her chest, and she takes a few seconds to focus on her breath and suppress the sense of panic that is threatening to bubble out of control and take over her brain. To steady her thoughts, she quietly reads off the step-by-step instructions that are stenciled on the inside of the locker hatch as she prepares the cuff and data link for use.

On the forward bulkhead, the AQ light switches from red to green, signaling that the air in the troop compartment has returned to safe levels of carbon dioxide. Alex pulls off her mask and wipes her sweat-soaked face. The front of Blake's jumpsuit is caked with dirt and blood.

There's an angular smudge across his chest where the hook of the tow cable hit him, and some of the fabric is torn. Alex uses the surgical scissors from the emergency kit to widen the holes and cut the heavy fire-retardant fabric away from his upper body. When she has freed his chest and right arm, she peels the protective film from the autodoc's contact patches and sticks them to his skin in the pattern she was taught in her medical training.

She breathes a sigh of relief when the autodoc comes to life and its control screen finishes its initial diagnostics, verifying that she connected everything correctly. The medical robot goes to work, scanning injuries and administering an initial round of medications through the cuff that's cradling Blake's right arm. Alex watches the screen for instructions, which start to appear after a minute of swift and near-silent robotic activities.

"How's he doing?" Harris asks from the gunnery station. She has taken her mask off as well, and her face is smudged with dirt and grease.

Alex looks at the diagnostic screen, which is scrolling medical updates in urgent shades of red and orange.

"Not great," she replies. "I'm not a medic. I don't know what half this shit means. But it says that we need to get him to a Level III or better trauma facility."

"No shit," Harris says. "Like we wouldn't do that if we had one nearby. The only 'Level III or better' on this rock went offline eight years ago." She shakes her head and returns her attention to the targeting screen. "Bayliss was the combat medic," she continues. "Without her, it's up to the robodoc. Let's hope it can keep him alive until we get back."

"You think we're going to make it back?"

Harris looks at Alex again, and the older woman's expression softens a little. "I am not an optimist. But I've seen the autodoc fix worse. And I know that I really don't want to die in this place."

With the autodoc working on Blake, there's nothing left for Alex to do right now, so she kneels on the floor in front of Ash to remove his mask. The dog holds still while she unfastens the straps. When she is finished, he turns and retreats to his little cave-like nook under the seats on the left side of the compartment. He settles down and looks at her with watchful eyes. Alex grabs a water bottle and fills his bowl. When she lifts the bottle to her mouth to take a drink, her hands are shaking, and she puts the bottle down in her lap. Now that the adrenaline is starting to ebb, she feels like her brain is finally processing just how close she came to getting killed a few minutes ago. She tries to focus on her breathing again, but the shaking gets worse, until she has to put the cap on the bottle to keep the contents from spilling. For a little while, all she can do is to sit with the water bottle in her lap and hold on to it with both hands until the tremors subside again.

When Lopez returns to the mule, the unexpected sound of the tail ramp's retracting locking bolts makes Alex jump in her seat. He comes up the ramp and punches the control button before the hatch has settled on the ground, and it reverses direction and locks into place behind him. Lopez unslings his rifle and puts it into the nearest holding rack. When he pulls off his mask, his defeated expression tells Alex all she needs to know even before he speaks.

"There's no way anyone survived that drop," he says. "It's a fifty-degree incline and it's at least half a klick to the bottom."

"That was our whole salvage," Harris replies. "What about Cheryl and Andres? Scott?"

Lopez shakes his head. "Andres was driving the crawler. No sign of Scott. And Cheryl . . ."

"What about Cheryl?"

"The thing fucking stepped on her. You don't want to see what's left. I wish I hadn't."

"The sarge? Bayliss?"

Lopez shakes his head again.

"They're gone, Harris. They're fucking gone."

"Fuck," Harris says. "Fuck, fuck, *fuck*." She raises her voice with every repetition of the word until the last one is almost a scream. She makes a fist and pounds it against the bulkhead to her right.

"What are we going to do now?" Alex asks. "We can't just leave them at the bottom."

"There's fuck all we can do," Lopez replies. "The tow cable isn't long enough to reach down there. And if those fuckers show up again, we're done too. We have eleven rounds left in the cannon."

"What the hell happened?" Harris demands. "They jumped us. How could they jump us? They're twenty fucking meters tall. Why didn't the dog alert? That was your job. That was your *only* job."

"Cool your jets, Harris," Lopez tells her. "It's not her fault. You know that shit happens sometimes."

"Ash did alert. He was focused on the first one. The second one came out of nowhere," Alex retorts.

"Weather's shit. We wouldn't have heard a fucking parade passing by on the other side of that ledge," Lopez says. "I'm surprised he picked up anything at all. Now lay off the kid and get your ass up front. We need to get as far away from here as we can before more of these things show up."

Harris glares at Lopez for a moment. Then she unbuckles her harness and gets out of the gunnery station. She ducks through the low opening to the cockpit of the mule and disappears behind the bulkhead. Alex hears the humming of the electric drivetrain powering up. Lopez ducks past her and takes over the seat Harris just vacated.

"I feel worse than useless right now," Alex says. "I can't drive this thing or fire that gun."

"You did fine," Lopez assures her. "Harris is just torn up. The stuff she said, don't take that to heart, you hear? You didn't screw up. Neither did the dog. It was just bad fucking luck."

Alex flashes a weak smile in response, but Lopez's eyes are already glued to the sensor screen again. She rubs her face with both hands and exhales slowly into her palms. She knows that Lopez is right, that she didn't do anything wrong. But as the mule lurches forward and accelerates up the ledge, she can't completely dismiss Harris's implication that it was her fault or Ash's. Five people are dead, all of them colony techs and soldiers she has known most of her life: Scott, Cheryl, Andres, Sergeant Frye, Corporal Bayliss.

I'm sorry, she thinks as they drive away from the carnage of the last few minutes. *I am so sorry.*

CHAPTER 9

Alex only realizes she had fallen asleep when the lack of noise in the troop compartment startles her into opening her eyes. For a moment, she feels a profound sense of disorientation, and her heart beats fast and hard in her chest. Then she remembers where she is and what she is doing, and the distress that had started to constrict her chest slowly dissipates. It takes her sleep-fogged brain a few moments longer to notice that the relentless drumbeat of the rain against the hull of the mule has ceased.

She sits up carefully and looks around. Blake is on his stretcher, tucked in snugly between the seat rows. His face looks ashen, and only the green light of the autodoc and the steady humming of the ventilator are evidence that he's still alive. Ash is snoozing in his little cubby underneath the seat next to hers. Lopez is still in the gunnery seat, staring at the sensor screen with eyes that look beyond tired.

"The storm passed," she says.

Lopez startles at the sound of her voice and looks over at her.

"Yeah," he says. "It stopped coming down maybe ten minutes ago. I thought it'd never quit. We haven't had a second without rain since we left the outpost until now."

Alex picks up the water bottle next to her makeshift cot, unscrews the top, and lets the cap dangle from the bottleneck while she drinks what's left in the container. The water is as warm as the air in the troop compartment, and she makes a face when she's finished even as she can feel the liquid soothing her dry mouth and throat. She gets out of her seat and kneels in front of Blake's stretcher to check the autodoc's status screen. The display has improved since the computer started its assessment of the administrator's condition, but the status messages are still mostly orange and red.

"I think it's just barely keeping him alive," she says to Lopez.

"It's not a combat surgeon. It's an automated field medic. It's supposed to stabilize someone enough for medevac. If this was a battlefield deployment, he would have been in the battalion aid station six hours ago."

Alex rubs her eyes and stifles a yawn. "Have you been in that chair since I fell asleep?"

Lopez nods with a little shrug. "Someone's gotta stay on the gun. Harris is driving. That leaves only me."

Alex thinks about Sergeant Frye and Corporal Bayliss, swept into a bottomless gorge full of sharp rocks by an alien monstrosity the size of a building, and she knows she can't keep the sudden anguish and despair she feels out of her expression because she can briefly see the same emotions on Lopez's face.

"You could teach me how to use that gun turret," she suggests.

Lopez replies with a tired laugh and a slow shake of his head.

"That would be so against the regs. You're not in the Corps."

"I'm riding in the back of this thing, aren't I?"

"Because you're the dog handler. The dog's a military asset."

"Come on. I'd feel more useful. And you could lie down and sleep for a bit. You really look like you need it."

Lopez rubs his eyes and blinks. He tries to stifle a yawn, but the attempt mostly fails. Alex smirks at him for proving her point. He looks back at the sensor screen and shrugs.

"Oh, what the hell. I'll show you how to run the damn gun. May come in handy at some point. Come over here."

Alex grins and crosses the hold to sit down in the seat next to the gunnery station. Lopez leans back a little so she can get a better view of the panel. He taps the control stick with his fingers.

"I'm sure you already get the idea. The reticle on the screen is where the rounds are going to hit. That's the easy part. Gun computer measures distance and crosswind and automatically adjusts the aiming point. Move the stick up and down, gun goes up and down." He demonstrates with slight movements of the stick. Alex watches the reticle shift on the screen as Lopez moves the gun.

"Move it right and left—you get the idea. The thumb switch here, that's your magnification. The hat switch here on top cycles through your sensor filters. Thermal, infrared, low light, multispectrum. The red button next to it? That's the lidar range finder and the target designator. You push that one, the gun will autotrack anything that's under the reticle. Got it so far?"

"Thumb switch magnifies," Alex recalls. "Hat switch for sensor filters. Red button marks the target."

"You got it," Lopez says. "Very good. You probably figured the whole thing out already just by watching us."

"I can neither confirm nor deny," Alex replies.

Lopez flashes a grin and checks the screen. He sends the gun mount on a 360-degree traverse to get a full view of the mule's surroundings. They're high up on the northern ridge, with the wide expanse of the gravel plain to their left and a deep valley to their right that's crisscrossed by rock formations and irregular ravines. Lopez repeats his survey sweep with the gun mount. Then he unbuckles his harness and slides out of his seat.

"Try it," he tells Alex. "See if you can get the hang of it. Nothing out there except rocks right now."

She climbs into the gunnery station and sits down on the seat Lopez just vacated. He's standing between the gunnery station and the forward bulkhead, so close to her that she brushes against him when she settles in behind the console.

"All right," Lopez says. "Before you grab the stick, make sure you don't flip that red cover away from the trigger. The one that says 'LIVE.'"

"Got it," she replies. She leans forward a little to get closer to the targeting screen and carefully wraps her hand around the control stick for the weapon mount.

"The sarge would shit a brick if he could see that I am letting you handle a loaded cannon," he says.

"I think Sergeant Frye would be fine with it right now," Alex says. "I mean, all things considered."

"You're probably right," Lopez concedes.

She moves the stick a little to test the resistance. In front of her, the image under the targeting reticle moves in synchrony with her input. Once she feels that she has gotten used to the sensitivity of the control stick, she sends the gun on a slow rotation, moving the barrel slightly up and down as she turns the mount. Above their heads, the electric motor powering the gun turret whines softly with the movement.

"Thumb switch back and forth for magnification, right?"

"That's right," Lopez says.

Alex moves the sliding button upward, and the picture changes as the optics zoom in on the area under the gun reticle until the screen shows nothing but cloudy sky. She decreases the magnification again and aims the reticle at a distant rock formation.

"Red button, target designator," she says to Lopez. He verifies her statement with a nod.

She presses the red button. Next to the reticle, a distance read-out blinks: 833m. Despite the movement from the rolling mule, the image on the targeting screen remains static, with the crosshairs on the rock formation and only the distance number slowly changing as they increase the range. Ever so slowly, the rock formation seems to turn to the left underneath the gun reticle.

"Look at you. You're a natural," he says. "Now you know as much about that gun as any trooper coming fresh out of Basic. It's really not that complex. The computer does most of the work for you. Just put the marker on whatever you want to shoot to shreds and let fly. Not right now, though," he adds.

Alex presses the red button on top of the stick again to cancel the target lock. She turns the turret to the right while zooming out to decrease the magnification at the same time. The gun mount obeys her input smoothly.

"Kind of fun," she says. "And they pay you for this?"

"Under normal circumstances," Lopez says with a crooked smile. "I haven't gotten paid in eight years. Not that there's anything to spend money on down here."

The lights in the troop compartment flicker and then go out completely. The screens in front of Alex turn off as well, and for a moment, the only light in the hold comes from the passage in the bulkhead that leads to the driver's station. Then the red battle lights turn on. The targeting and sensor screens at the gunnery station come back to life all at once. From Blake's makeshift cot, an alert chirps and flashes a warning on the autodoc's control screen.

"What did you touch?" Lopez asks.

Alex withdraws her hand from the stick. "Nothing. I was just turning the turret to face forward again. What happened?"

The steady hum of the mule's electric drivetrain falters and dies down gradually. Alex and Lopez exchange a look.

"What the fuck," Lopez says. He pushes the touch panel for the intercom.

"Harris, what's going on?"

"Hang on," Harris replies from her station in the cockpit. Without the background noise from the drive, Alex can hear the vehicle's tires crunching on the gravel-strewn ground as they coast to a stop. Lopez goes over to the cockpit passage and squats in front of it.

"Talk to me, Harris."

"Something's broken. I have power dropping on every subsystem," Harris says.

Alex climbs out of the gunnery station and checks the autodoc to make sure it's still busy keeping Blake alive. The administrator's chest is slowly rising and falling with the mechanical regularity of the machine that's breathing for him right now. Alex knows that the autodoc sedated him up to his eyebrows, and that he won't even be aware of it if the computer medic reaches the end of its supplies or programmed interventions and he dies.

The others should have been so lucky.

The thought brings back the fresh memory of the Lanky's foot coming down on the running Cheryl and snuffing her out like a roach caught in the middle of the kitchen floor. Alex tries to shake the image, but it feels as though it has seared itself deeply into her memory already.

She notices a movement out of the corner of her eye and turns her head to see that Ash has emerged from his sleeping cave for a long and thorough stretch.

"Make sure you limber up for that next nap," she tells him. "Wouldn't want to pull anything."

He rewards the advice with a yawn. Then he looks at her and wags his tail briefly in what she knows to be his "hopefully expectant" indicator. Alex smiles and reaches for his supply bag to get out one of his nutrition strips, glad to have a task to distract herself. She tosses him the treat in a gentle underhand throw and he snatches it out of the air. He turns and retreats to his nook to chew the snack in comfort.

Private Harris appears in the cockpit passage with a harried look on her face. She exchanges a glance with Alex and looks at the prone

Blake before turning her attention to Lopez, who is back at the gunnery station.

"We're in trouble," she announces.

"Well, that's a switch," Lopez replies. "Everything's gone so smooth until now. What's broken?"

"Power core number one is totally fried," Harris says. "All the cells are dead. Power core two just dropped from nineteen percent charge to *nine*. We're running in emergency deep-discharge mode."

"Fuck," Lopez says. "How the hell did we lose the whole primary core?"

"Something must have broken when we went full throttle to tow the crawler out of the ditch. We were at emergency power for a while."

"That shouldn't have knocked out the entire core."

"We've been using these cells for almost a decade without an overhaul. Everything's held together with polymer tape and prayers. Or maybe the towing cable hit something important when it snapped back. I heard it bounce against the underside."

"Great. Really fucking great." Lopez exhales loudly and runs his hands through his hair. "Do we have enough juice in the secondary core to make it home?"

Harris glances at Alex. Then she returns her gaze to Lopez and shakes her head slowly.

"We have sixty klicks to go. There's no way we can do that on nine percent. And that's assuming a regular discharge rate on those remaining cells. For all I know, the second core could shit the bed as soon as I put this thing back into drive."

"How far is that going to get us?"

Harris shrugs. She looks tired and defeated rather than distraught now. "We can probably get another twenty klicks. Maybe thirty if we're super lucky."

"What if we turn everything else off back here?" Alex offers. "Everything except the autodoc."

"That'll get us a few more klicks. Not enough," Harris replies. "The drivetrain is what really drains the power cells. Not the lights back here in the hold."

"Twenty, thirty klicks," Lopez repeats. "Fuck. Oh, that is *awesome*. Just wonderful."

"What are we going to do?" Alex looks from Lopez to Harris and back.

Lopez leans back in his chair and slowly rubs his eyes with both hands.

"Not much we can do," he replies. "We'll drive until this thing stops. Wherever that's going to be."

"And then we walk, or what?" Alex asks.

Harris shakes her head.

"You planning on legging it across this ridge for thirty or forty kilometers? Have you checked the elevation lines on the map? That would take us most of a week."

"I'm happy to give it a try," Lopez replies.

"What about Blake?" Alex nods toward the stretcher. "He can't make that walk. We'd have to carry him."

Private Harris huffs a humorless laugh. "We can't carry him and take along enough breathing air for the four of us, plus the dog, plus guns and ammo. Ever tried hiking in the mountains with a ninety-kilo pack?"

"We can't just leave him here," Alex says.

"No, we can't," Lopez agrees. "But we can't take him either. He won't make it without the autodoc. If we take the mask off and try to carry him with us on the stretcher, he'll be dead in half an hour. If he even makes it that long."

"Can't drive home, can't walk home. So what the fuck do we do now?" Harris looks around in the troop compartment as if she's looking for a hint at a solution among their inventory of weapons and gear.

"We'll drive toward home as far as this thing will go," Lopez says.

"And what then?"

"We'll figure it out when we get to that point. But sitting here won't get us closer. And we're using up power that can get us a few klicks farther down the road. Get us moving. I'll think of something on the way."

Harris puts her arm against the bulkhead and leans forward until her forehead rests on it. She lets out a distraught groan that's muffled by the fabric of her sleeve.

"What if we call for help?" Alex suggests. "Maybe they can send someone out in the other crawler."

Harris turns her head and looks at her.

"Call for help? On the radio? Are you nuts? We'll have every Lanky in the hemisphere heading our way."

"It's an idea," Lopez says.

"It's a terrible idea," Harris replies. She starts tapping the bulkhead with her fist in a slow cadence. Alex can see her jaw muscles flexing.

"At least it's an idea," Lopez says. "Maybe come up with a few of your own? And stop your *we're-so-fucked* commentary. Because you're not telling me anything I don't know already."

Harris shoots him a withering glare, but she doesn't retort. Instead, she raps her knuckles on the bulkhead one more time, harder than before, and turns around to disappear in the cockpit passage.

"They may not even notice," Alex says. "And what if they do? It's not like it can make things any worse."

"Suffocate or get squished. Not a great menu to pick from, is it?" Lopez is looking at his targeting screen again, and his right hand is on the control stick to rotate the gun mount for a look around the mule.

"It can make things worse all right," he continues. "Say we send a distress call and another team comes out to save our asses. And then the Lankies show up and wreck the last crawler as well."

"That would be worse," Alex concedes. She looks over at Blake, whose chest is still slowly rising and falling in sync with the soft beeps from the autodoc's control unit.

He's not going to make it, she thinks. *Neither are we. Everyone in here is going to be dead soon.*

The realization makes a wave of despair well up inside her. A few hours ago, she was seconds away from death when the Lanky advanced on her, but everything had happened so quickly that she didn't have time to let that reality sink in. Now, in the quiet troop compartment of the mule, surrounded by her fellow survivors and with the time to contemplate the notion, the weight and certainty of that knowledge settles on her chest and threatens to squeeze the air out of her lungs.

She gets out of her seat and crosses the aisle to get down on the floor next to Ash, who has long finished his treat. Alex wraps her arms around his neck and hugs him firmly. The smell of his fur and the feeling of his warm body pressed against hers usually comforts her, but the knowledge that the heart thumping in his chest is going to stop beating soon only amplifies the dread she feels. Ash doesn't usually like being grabbed around the neck, but she guesses that he's sensing her misery because he's holding still while she fights back tears.

"I told you it's not your fault," Lopez says behind her. "Or his. Our luck was bound to run out some day. Sorry it had to be on this run."

She wipes the tears from her eyes before she lets go of Ash and turns to look at Lopez.

"I knew what I signed up for," she says. "He has no idea. He'll go anywhere with us. Just because I tell him to."

"We all did what we had to. Including him. He's a good troop. We couldn't have done all those runs without him."

"I should go out with him and let him run. You know, when the time comes." She can't quite bring herself to say *when we run out of air* because it conjures the mental image of them all flopping around on the floor of the mule, gasping like dying fish on dry land.

"Hey," Lopez says. "Let's try our best to make sure that time doesn't come. All right?"

She knows he's probably just trying to make her feel better by keeping hope kindled, but she nods anyway because it's better than to give in to the dread she feels.

"If we call for help, they would come and try to get us, right?"

Lopez nods without hesitation.

"I would," he says. "They'll send out another fire team in the other crawler. Even if we were gone, they'd still try to salvage the mule. It's the biggest gun we have left. We lose that, we can't run salvage missions anymore. Not if we want to be able to fight off these things. The rifles just don't take them down fast enough at short range. And short range is all we get in this shit weather lately."

"We should at least tell them where to find it," Alex suggests. "Whether we're still here when they arrive or not."

Lopez thinks for a moment. Then he pushes the control for the intercom.

"Harris, stop pouting and come back here for a second. We need to make a decision."

Private Harris appears in the passageway a few seconds later. She sticks her head around the corner to look at Lopez.

"You acting sergeant now?"

"Acting corporal," he replies. "No need to get too ambitious. Are you monitoring the battery drain?"

Harris nods. "It's not bad on idle. The turret servos are pulling some amps, but we can last for a while if we don't engage the wheels."

"What if we find a spot to hunker down?" Lopez asks. "Somewhere sheltered. Where we don't sit out in the open like a sitting duck. We'll send a burst transmission back to base with our status and location. They can decide whether they want to risk a rescue."

"And if the Lankies home in on us?"

Lopez nods at Alex.

"The kid's right. We'd be screwed either way. But at least they'll know where to find the mule so they can tow it back home."

Harris bites her lower lip as she ponders the idea.

"Still not in love with the idea. But I like the whole *certain death* thing even less."

"Can't you send a message from the drone?" Alex asks. "Fly it out as high and far as it will go and then transmit from there."

Lopez shakes his head.

"Not a bad idea, but the drone isn't set up for long-range comms. We stripped the transmitters years ago for spare parts because we only ever used the drones in autonomous mode. If we want to reach the base, we'll need the mule's radios."

"Or the mobile command set," Harris says. "We still have one of the squad leader units stowed away."

"Shit, yeah." Lopez flashes a grin. "I could grab that and hike out a klick or two to make the call. May not be enough to throw off the Lankies if they come looking for the source."

"Sure as shit better than just popping up the antenna and shouting 'Lankies, come as you are.'"

Harris returns Lopez's grin, and Alex feels a little flare of hope. She has no idea whether the plan is feasible or the two soldiers are just grasping at straws with her, but having a plan for a shot at survival is infinitely better than sitting in this troop compartment and waiting for the power and air to run out.

"All right. Get on the stick and find us a nice quiet spot to hole up," Lopez tells Private Harris. "I'll get the comms kit ready in the meantime."

"Affirmative," Harris replies and ducks into the cockpit passageway again.

Ash looks up at Alex when the drivetrain comes back to life with a low hum and the mule starts to move forward again. She reaches down and scratches the spot on the top of his head between his perked-up ears.

"It'll be all right, buddy. We'll be fine," she says, as much to assure herself as to calm the dog.

"Don't you worry," Lopez says from his seat behind the gunnery console. "They'll come for us. If they get the transmission, they'll send out a team. Corporal Doran is in charge back at the barn. I know she won't leave us hanging. All we have to do is keep breathing until they get here."

"That's the trick, isn't it?" Alex replies, and he flashes a wry smile.

She sits back and tilts up her head to put her face into the feeble stream of cool air coming from the air-conditioning vent.

"If they can't make it before . . . ," she says, leaving the sentence unfinished because she doesn't even want to tempt the fates by giving voice to the possibility.

"If we run out of time, I'm going to check out with clean air in my lungs. Hypercapnia isn't a great way to go," Lopez says, and she can see his quick glance at the rifle that's stowed in the weapon rack across the aisle from his station.

Outside, the rain has started again, a steady white noise of water against titanium laminate that sounds a little like soy bacon frying in a pan somewhere in the distance. Alex closes her eyes to enjoy what she knows may be the last cool air she'll ever feel on her face as the mule continues its slow crawl along the ridge. She thinks of her parents and pictures them the way they were the last time she saw them alive. Even after eight years, she can still recall every detail on their faces, remember all their little quirks and expressions.

Maybe I'll see you soon, she thinks. *But don't mind if I hope it'll be a good while yet.*

CHAPTER 10

"This is the spot," Private Harris announces on the mule's intercom as the vehicle crunches to a halt. The parking brake whines and locks the wheels into place. Then the electric humming sound from the drivetrain fades away until the only background noise in the troop compartment is the soft beeping of the autodoc.

Alex unbuckles her seat harness and goes over to Blake to check on him. His vitals are unchanged from when she last looked at them a little while ago, but he appears worse than before, fragile and diminished. She gently places a hand on the administrator's chest to feel it rise and fall in sync with the soft hissing of the ventilator. From the way he looks, she knows that he'll probably be dead as soon as the autodoc runs out of power and stops pumping air into his lungs.

Behind her, Harris comes out of the cockpit and, with a deep sigh, drops into one of the fold-down seats along the side of the troop module.

"Secondary core dropped below five percent," she says. "If I wasn't so damn sure that I'm immortal, I'd start to worry right about now."

"If we had only stashed a few of those cells from the outpost back in the mule instead of cramming everything into the crawler," Lopez says.

"There's no telling whether they even had a charge after all those years in storage. And the civvie ones have a different interface anyway. I could have rigged something at home in a pinch, but not out here. Not with the toolkit in the mule. So let's not fret about it." She crosses the aisle and sits down next to Lopez, who is scanning the area outside. "Anything moving anywhere?"

"Nothing but the rain," Lopez says. "I can't see anything on the left side of the hull. Where exactly are we?"

"Southern Highlands, just off the plateau. I found us a cozy nook between a bunch of rocks. Inertial nav says it's thirty-three klicks back to the Vault."

"Thirty-three klicks," Lopez repeats. "We did thirty-klick marches between lunch and dinner back in infantry training."

"On Earth. Without having to carry around our breathing air. Not in this rocky hellhole. Vault's over a thousand meters higher than we are right now. You couldn't do that between breakfast and lunch even if you could breathe without a mask."

"I know, I know." Lopez sits back with a little groan and stretches. "All right, time to go for a walk. Thirty-three kilometers should be plenty close enough for the squad comms."

Alex pats her thigh to make Ash come out of his little cubbyhole under the seat. He obeys and sits down in front of her. She opens the pouch for his mask and checks the straps and fasteners.

"You should stay in here," Lopez says. "Lay low, get some rest. Maybe gather the spare air packs and set them up so we can use them as a last resort."

Alex looks back at him and shakes her head.

"I'll come. If you run into one of those things, nobody's going to find out where we are. You have better odds with Ash."

"Whatever you guys decide, do it quickly," Harris says. "We have just a few hours of juice left in the power cell. After that, we'll be sweating in the dark until the air tanks run out."

Alex puts the mask on Ash and tightens the straps.

"I'll come," she repeats. "Let us do our jobs, Ash and me. It's why I'm here to begin with."

To her mild surprise, Lopez acquiesces without further argument.

"Fine. One minute to dismount. Make sure you top off that tank all the way."

The tail ramp opens into the gloomy grayness of what has become a typical Scorpio day since the Lankies arrived, shimmering bands of rain underneath an unbroken canopy of low-hanging dark clouds. Alex walks down the ramp with Ash on a short lead. To their right, a cluster of rocks towers above the mule, a jagged formation of sharp ridges and spikes. When she steps off the bottom of the ramp, her boots splash into an ankle-deep puddle. Ash deftly avoids it by making a short leap across, and she lets out the leash a little more.

"You're going to get soaked anyway, you big baby," she tells him.

Behind her, Lopez comes down the ramp in his sealed battle armor. There's a mobile comms unit on his back, with a flexible antenna that's tied down into a U-shaped loop. He carries a rifle across his chest and another one in his left hand. When he's next to her, he holds out the spare rifle by its carrying handle.

"You still know how to use one of these, don't you?"

She takes the rifle from him. It's a heavy piece of gear, five kilos or more, but the weight in her hands is comforting. Every able-bodied adult in the Vault has received training on military small arms as a last-resort contingency for dire emergencies, and she can't disagree that their current situation qualifies.

"If we do come across a Lanky, you'll want something with a little more punch than that pocketknife," he says. "Two rifles are better than one."

She sticks her forearm through the loop of Ash's lead to free up her hand. Then she checks the magazine's loading status and the chamber of the weapon. She has never fired a live round, just simulated ones that shoot a marking laser instead of explosive rounds, but Sergeant Frye and Corporals Bayliss and Doran have made all the young adults in the Vault do refresher practice often enough that her hands can perform the weapon check automatically. Lopez gives her an approving nod when she finishes the motions and makes sure the weapon's safety is engaged. She transfers the leash to the other hand and sticks her head through the rifle's sling loop, then swings the weapon onto her back.

"Shoot when I shoot," Lopez says. "And shoot what I'm shooting at."

"I have a rough idea how this works," she assures him.

"All right. Let's go for a little walk and call for a tow."

Lopez turns to the open rear hatch of the mule.

"Stay on the gun, Harris. If we're not back in ninety minutes, you're on your own. Drive north as far as you can before the power core quits."

Harris shakes her head.

"Fuck that noise. Make the call and get your ass back here. I'm not going anywhere without you. Whichever way this spins. Now get your asses moving. That core charge is dropping more every minute."

Lopez doesn't argue. He taps two fingers against the brow of his helmet and flicks them toward her in a little salute. Harris nods curtly in reply and pushes the button for the hatch control. The ramp rises and latches into place. A few seconds later, the gun mount swivels a few degrees to the right, showing that Harris is back at the firing controls.

Harris has parked the mule in a little ground depression next to the ragged rock formation. With the vehicle as close to the rock as she could place it, the front and left side of the mule are shielded by the spiky geologic formation that rises at least ten meters above the height of the gun mount. Alex takes in the rest of their surroundings, a shallow slope littered with more rock clusters like the one that's partially sheltering the mule. To her left, Lopez is surveying the area as well.

"We need to get to higher ground," he says. "Some spot that's free of obstacles. Home base is to the north-northeast, thirty degrees." He points in the direction of the Vault. "Let's go up that way a klick or so and take a look around."

"You lead, I'll follow," Alex says. The unfamiliar bulk and weight of the rifle on her back are a little uncomfortable, and she shifts the weapon around on its sling to the front of her body until it hangs diagonally across her chest just like Lopez is carrying his own gun. The private is already trudging up the hill, the antenna loops on his radio pack bobbing slightly in time with his steps. Alex shifts the loop of the leash to her palm and gives Ash a slight tug to let him know that it's time to go to work.

When they're a hundred meters up the slope, she turns around to look at the mule. The low-slung wedge of the armored personnel carrier is now mostly hidden by the rocky outcrop, with only the autocannon mount peeking over the natural barrier.

The gradient of the slope is gentle, no more than two or three degrees, but the ascent is far more tiring than her usual patrol loops with Ash. Lopez doesn't head up the hill in a straight line. Instead, he takes a serpentine path, going from one rock formation to the next to stay in cover as much as possible. Whenever they have to cross the patches of open ground between the rock clusters, he rushes her along. After fifteen minutes of this leapfrogging, Alex is sweat-soaked and out of breath, and she resolves to put in a little more time on the cardio equipment back in the Vault's gym if they ever make it back. The rifle is now more hindrance than comfort, a heavy counterweight that pulls on her neck and shoulders, bounces around when she runs, and gets in the way when she crouches between the rocks. Lopez carries much more weight—his own rifle, the radio set, and the battle armor he wears—but he shows no obvious signs of fatigue as they make their way uphill and away from the mule, which is now well out of sight.

"Forget what I said about getting paid for this," she tells Lopez when they make another stop in the shelter of a rock cluster to catch their breath. "On second thought, I don't think this infantry stuff is for me."

He smiles at her and shakes his head.

"I don't know if you've noticed, but you've been part of the squad for a while now. You and the dog."

She looks down at Ash, who is on his belly next to her. He's not paying attention to them. Instead, he's focused on their surroundings, his ears moving slightly as he listens for the sound of approaching threats in the wind and rain.

"You'd both make fine grunts," Lopez says. "I guarantee there's maybe one or two out of a hundred raw recruits who wouldn't lose their minds if they had to go up against a Lanky out of the blue."

He taps a control on his wrist and consults his data display.

"Six hundred meters out. Let's give them a little more space down there before we start with the noise."

He stands up to peek over the rock they've been using for shelter. She gets up as well and looks in the same direction.

"See that little ridge over there?" Lopez raises his hand and holds up his fingers in front of his eyes. "Three fingers to the left of that tall rock that looks like a triangle."

She uses her own fingers to measure the distance.

"Yeah, I see it," she says.

"That looks like a good spot for comms. Elevated position, nothing nearby to block the signal. Three hundred eighty meters."

Alex wants to crouch here in the relative safety of their cover for another minute to catch her breath. But then she thinks of Harris and

Blake back at the mule, who don't have any time to spare as the energy cell depletes steadily—especially Blake, who can't just be connected to an air pack if the power goes out because he needs the autodoc to work his lungs for him. She stands up on shaky legs and adjusts the rifle dangling from its carry sling.

"Let's get it done," she says. "I want to go home and stand under a hot shower until my skin starts coming off."

"That's the spirit," Lopez says. "I'm getting a bit tired of this place myself."

Ash leaps to his feet without hesitation when Alex gives him the signal with the leash. She kneels next to him to check the air gauge on his pack. Then she gets up and follows Lopez, who's already twenty meters ahead of her.

All I have to do is keep breathing, she reminds herself as she catches up to the private.

When they finally reach the top of the ridge, it feels to Alex like they're the only two people left in the galaxy. Every time she has been out on missions before, there has been another group of humans and a vehicle or two in her line of sight, a reminder that she's part of a colony. Up here, with the wind blowing and the rain falling out of a sky the same color as the rock beneath her feet, it's easy to imagine that everyone else is dead and gone.

Lopez takes a knee and looks around to survey the area beyond the ridge. When he's satisfied that nothing is coming out of the rain toward them, he swings the comms unit off his back and puts it on the ground in front of him. Alex watches as he opens the unit and starts the setup process. Next to her, Ash is at the end of his leash, looking out over the broken landscape, his ears subtly moving to home in on distant sounds.

She wonders how much better at detection he would be if she could take the mask off and allow him to fully use his nose, his most acute sensory organ.

"All right. Powered up and ready to transmit. Hope we don't come to regret this," Lopez says. He opens the comms unit and folds down the keyboard that is protecting the data screen.

"I hope they get the message," Alex replies.

"They'll get it. The ops center keeps the antenna up when there's a team outside the doors. You know that."

"We've had some really bad luck with gear lately," she says.

"Ain't that the truth." Lopez brings the screen of the comms set to life and flexes his fingers over the keyboard. "Wow, it's been a minute. Haven't used one of these in the field in a long, long time."

He dashes off a series of command entries. When he is finished, he unfastens the holding bracket that keeps the antenna tied down and carefully guides it to its full extension with his gloved hand. Then he kneels down in front of the control unit again and checks the display.

"Message is cued up," he says. "Coordinates, status, emergency aid request."

He looks up at Alex.

"Once I hit the send button, it's going to repeat the transmission three times, every ten minutes. They're sure to catch at least one of those bursts back home."

"And after that?" she asks.

"We double-time it back to the mule as soon as I punch send. The repeat messages will go out automatically."

Lopez flexes his fingers again and lets his hand hover above the control unit. Then he extends his index finger and quickly pushes the transmit button, as if he doesn't want to give himself time to second-guess his decision. The control screen flashes a new status, and he leans in to check it.

"The beacon is lit," he says and gets to his feet. "We just set off a nice little EM flare for the Lankies to home in on."

"You're going to leave the comms set here?"

"If we need to use it again, I know where to find it. Now let's haul ass before one of those fuckers comes looking for the candy store."

CHAPTER 11

They manage the descent in less than half the time it took to climb to the top of the ridge, and their speed is only partially due to the return trip going downhill. Lopez backtracks their path, but this time they only stay in the cover of the rocks for a few moments to catch their breath. Every time they do, Alex looks over her shoulder, expecting to see a Lanky's cranial shield coming up above the ridge. But as much as she has convinced herself that every Lanky in the area is homing in on their radio signal right now, nothing bad happens beyond her slipping on the rain-slick slope a few times and scraping up her knees.

The mule is right where they left it, tucked into the shelter of the low ridge, its cannon slowly traversing from side to side. Lopez flashes his helmet light twice as they approach, and Harris quickly returns the signal with the gun turret's light.

"All done," he says to Harris when they're back in the troop compartment. "The antenna is a kilometer up the hill. Lotta rocks between here and there. We should be in the clear."

"I guess we'll find out before too long," Harris replies. "How long do you figure until the cavalry can be here?"

Lopez chews on his lower lip for a moment as he thinks about her question.

"Thirty-three klicks from the Vault to this spot. They'll need an hour to get the mission geared up and the other mule ready. Figure four hours. Three if we're lucky and they haul ass."

Alex looks up from her spot on the floor where she is securing Ash's gear on his vest.

"Three or four hours. Is the power going to last that long?"

"It's going to have to," Harris says.

"We'll shut everything off that doesn't need to run right now," Lopez says. "Lights, sensors, air-conditioning. Park the gun and power down the mount too. That turret draws a shit-ton of amps. We'll leave the autodoc and the battle lights on. Punch the fuses on everything else."

"If one of those things comes looking for us, it'll catch us with our pants down."

Lopez shrugs. "We have no line of sight to the top of the ridge. If one comes down from that direction, it'll be on top of us before we see it. We don't have the ammo left for a stand-up fight anyway."

"You can go out and spot. Take her and the dog. I'll keep an eye on Blake."

"It's not gonna make a difference. We're not going to stop shit with two rifles. I think we have better odds if we pretend to be part of the landscape."

Harris throws her hands up. "Fine. Let's shut it down, then. I'll take the cockpit. The back's all yours."

She gets out of the gunnery chair and disappears in the cockpit passage. Alex shoots Lopez a questioning look.

"We all deal with a shitty hand in our own way," he says in a low voice. "She'll be all right."

He swings himself into the gunnery seat and grabs the control handle to turn the gun turret into its rest position. Then he starts turning off screens and flicking switches. One by one, the displays surrounding the gunner's seat shut down, until the weapons station is dark and silent, illuminated only by the red battle light coming from the bulkhead.

Alex takes the rifle she had put on the seat on top of Ash's cubby and removes the magazine. She clears the action and hands the weapon to Lopez. The private waves her off.

"Put it in the clamp by your seat. Keep the mag in it. As long as you have that nearby, you have options."

She doesn't have to ask what he means. She puts the magazine back in the weapon and locks it into the receptacle next to her seat as Lopez suggested. It's an unwelcome avatar now, as if its presence next to Ash and her makes a violent end for them both more likely. But as dark as the possibility is, she agrees with Lopez that it's good to have options, even if all the choices are shitty.

Up front, Private Harris turns off the environmental controls that keep the crew compartment at a tolerable temperature. The soft whispering sound of the air-conditioning stops, and with it the welcome cool flow from the vent above Alex's seat.

When Lopez has finished shutting off all the nonessential gear, the only sound in the troop compartment is the regular soft beeping and hissing from the autodoc. Lopez gets out of the confines of the gunnery station and sits down at the head of the seat row on his side. He stretches out until his legs cross the aisle and his boots are on the seat on the opposite side.

"Now we wait," he says. "Try to hold your breath for an hour or two if you can."

Alex smiles weakly at Lopez's attempt at levity. Across the aisle from her own seat, the shadows of the dim, red illumination from the battle light make Blake look even more corpse-like than he looked before. The machine is keeping him alive, but there's no way to know if he's ever going to wake up again.

Maybe it would be a mercy if he doesn't, she finds herself thinking with something like envy. *Just slip away when the air runs out, while you're full of painkillers and sedatives. There are far worse ways to go.*

The faint background noise of raindrops drumming on the mule's armored top has stopped. Alex finds herself wishing they could lower the tail ramp because the complete lack of awareness of the outside world makes her feel uneasy. She's guessing that Lopez feels the same way because after a few minutes of them listening to the autodoc pumping air into Blake's lungs, he sits up and hauls himself out of his seat with a little grunt.

"I'm gonna go up front for a bit. Why don't you try to sleep? They won't be here for a few hours. I'll wake you up if something happens."

He ducks into the cockpit passage and disappears.

Alex is still wired from the trip to the top of the ridge and back, and she knows the slowly ebbing adrenaline will keep her eyes wide open for a while. But the cockpit of the mule only has space for two people, and she doesn't want to impose herself on Harris and Lopez anyway if they both want some time alone. She lies down on the bench and reaches down to pet Ash. The dog shifts his head slightly under her touch and huffs out a little sigh. Alex closes her eyes and listens to the autodoc softly hissing and beeping in the darkness, and she tries to time her breaths to the rhythm of the ventilator. The air-conditioning has only been off for a few minutes, but it feels to her as if the temperature in the troop compartment has gone up by five degrees already. From the front of the mule, she hears the murmur of a quiet conversation between Lopez and Harris, their voices too low and too muffled by the armor plating of the bulkhead for Alex to make out what they're discussing. After a while, she gives up trying to parse the sounds and focuses on her breathing again to ease the anxiety that has wrapped itself around her chest like a steel band. Whatever is going to happen will play out in the next few hours, and the only thing she can do right now to influence the outcome is to take slower breaths.

But lying on her back in near-total silence and darkness, the unwelcome thought pops into her head that the inside of the mule has never felt more like a coffin than it does right now.

CHAPTER 12

Alex only realizes she had fallen asleep after all when Ash wakes her up with a low bark and his cold nose nudging her hand.

She jerks her head up from the rolled thermal blanket she is using as a pillow and looks over at Ash with blurry vision. The dog returns her gaze, takes two steps backward, and lets out another soft bark. He follows it up with a low growl. The sudden surge of adrenaline clears the sleep from her brain almost instantly.

"Shit," she says and swings her legs over the edge of the bench to sit up. "What is it? What?"

Ash turns his head toward the forward bulkhead. His ears are perked up and twitching, homing in on some source of noise she can't make out yet. Outside, it sounds like there's another storm brewing, and she hopes that Ash merely got spooked by distant thunder. She gets up and walks over to the dog to kneel beside him and try to figure out what concerned Ash enough to wake her up.

For a minute or two, she listens to the noises that reach her ears from the outside, the wind whipping against the flanks of the mule and the faint hissing of the rain drizzling on the roof. Then there's a new sound, a faint rippling roar that comes and goes in short intervals.

"Lopez," she calls out. "Lopez, are you guys awake?"

She hears the rustling of movement in the cockpit. Lopez comes through the passage a few moments later, as bleary-eyed as she was just a few minutes ago when Ash woke her up.

"What's going on? Everything all right back here?"

"Ash woke me up," Alex says. "He heard something. *Listen.*"

They listen together, trying to make out the sound from the outside between the soft hisses and low beeps from the autodoc. A minute passes, then another. Then Lopez sighs and rubs the beard stubble on his chin with one hand.

"That's the storm you're hearing. It's coming in from the west. The clouds are getting rumbly. It's gonna be a full-on thunderstorm soon enough."

"It's not the storm," she insists. "It was something else. I heard it too, twice."

He gives the dog a skeptical glance but continues to listen. When the autodoc beeps again, he reaches over to the control screen and mutes the sound. Now the only background noise in the troop compartment is the sound from the ventilator pump.

"Wait." Alex holds up a hand. "There it is again. Hear it?"

Somewhere in the distance, that staccato roar sounds again, almost too faint to hear over the steady rain. It sounds like someone ripping a giant piece of canvas in half. Alex looks at Lopez to see dawning realization on his face.

"Oh, *shit,*" he says.

"What is it?"

Lopez stretches across the aisle for his mask by the gunnery station.

"Get your mask on," he says to Alex. "The dog too. I'm going to open the hatch. Hurry up."

He punches the intercom button.

"Harris, mask up. I'm going out."

Outside, the rain has filled in the tracks made by the mule's wheels on its way to the rock shelter. Alex keeps Ash's leash short and follows Lopez, who is walking to the front of the mule. When he's a few steps away from the vehicle's wedge-shaped nose, he stops and signals for her to do the same.

"What is it, Lopez?"

"Shhhh." He taps an index finger to the face shield of his helmet.

For a few moments, she only hears the wind and the distant rumbling of the approaching thunderstorm. Then the odd sound starts up again, somewhere to the north, two quick pulses of a humming sort of roar.

"Look, there." He points to the sky ahead, where some small and red-hot objects are rapidly rising until they disappear in the low cloud cover.

"Ricochets from tracers," Lopez says. "That's the tri-barrel on the other mule. They're firing short bursts."

She doesn't have to ask what the other mule is shooting at. A few seconds later, Lopez's assessment is confirmed by the unmistakable wail of a Lanky in the distance. Next to her, Ash stiffens and growls. The far-off gun raps out two more quick bursts that send another spray of ricochets into the dark sky like embers rising from a fire. Then everything is silent again except for the ever-present wind and rain.

"Three, three and a half klicks to the north," Lopez says.

"Can we do anything?" Alex asks.

He shakes his head. "We won't be much help. Not with a flat power cell and a dozen rounds of cannon ammo. And whatever went down already happened. Let's hope they handled the problem."

Behind them, the driver's hatch on the sloped front of the mule opens, and Harris's head appears above the rim of the hatch collar.

"Did you see it?" Lopez asks her.

"Yeah, I saw it. Looked like twenty mil. They must have really hosed something down."

"You think we can make it north about three klicks?"

Harris shakes her head slowly. "We're at two percent. That's in the margin of error for the charge gauge. Just turning everything back on will probably drain what's left."

"Well, shit." Lopez looks from Harris to Alex and back. "I'll head north, see what's going on."

"What if they didn't make it?" Harris asks, and the question hangs between them for a silent moment.

"At least we'll know," Lopez replies. "Instead of waiting here in the dark for a ride that'll never show."

"I'll come," Alex says.

"Stay at the mule. The relief team has the position. If they're coming our way, I'll link up with them. If I get lost, at least it'll just be me."

Alex doesn't try to argue. The way Lopez just said that last sentence tells her that he's not just going out to scout for the rescue team, that he wants to be alone if he finds out that there won't be any salvation.

"Harris, get me a thirty-mil flare round out of the small-arms rack," he says. "A red one."

Harris nods, and her head disappears back inside the driver station. A few moments later, she emerges again and tosses a pair of grenade launcher rounds to Lopez, one after the other.

"Take a spare in case the first one's a dud," she says. "We haven't test-fired any of those in a long time."

Lopez loads one of the rounds into his rifle's grenade launcher and tucks the other one into one of his magazine pouches.

"If I get there and things are all fucked to hell, I'll let you know with that," he says. "Keep an eye out to the north. You see a red flare going up, you know we're hosed. You'll be on your own after that."

Harris nods again.

"Good luck," she says. "Don't get squished."

"No need to get sentimental now," Lopez replies, and Harris flashes a smile.

He walks up to the mule and uses the foothold bars on the flank of the nose to climb the side of the vehicle. Alex watches as Harris and Lopez clasp each other's right hands briefly but firmly. Then he jumps down from the side of the mule with the metallic rattling of his rifle bouncing against his battle armor.

"Hey, you did all right," he says to Alex. "Sorry your birthday turned out to be so awful. We'll make up for it when we get home, okay? A proper party, with drinks."

Alex feels her throat tightening, so she just nods. When he offers her his hand as well, she hugs him instead, wrapping her arms around his bulky armor and squeezing it as hard as she can. He returns the hug, enveloping her in his arms and gently patting her back. When he withdraws from the embrace, he gets down on one knee in front of Ash and pats him on the head. The dog accepts the gesture calmly, as if he understands the gravity of the situation. Lopez stands up and knocks twice on the side of the mule with his fist.

"All right. I'll see you both in a few. Don't wait for me with dinner."

He turns and trots off in a steady jog without looking back. Alex watches him until his silhouette fades into the rainy darkness in the distance.

CHAPTER 13

Half an hour later, the power goes out again, and Alex thinks about the rifle by her seat for the first time since Lopez left.

The battle light flickers twice and comes back on, but it takes a few seconds, and the red glow seems a little weaker than before. Now the brightest thing in the troop compartment is the control screen for the autodoc, which is still keeping up the slow rhythm of its ventilator pump. There's a message flashing red in the center of the screen, and Alex gets up and goes over to Blake's stretcher to check it.

EXTERNAL POWER LOST, the screen informs her. BACKUP BATTERY 78% REMAINING (0H 34M).

"Harris," Alex calls out toward the cockpit.

"I know, I know." Private Harris comes through the cockpit passage with her mask in her hand. "The reserve cell is dry. Put your mask on. This ride is done making new oxygen. We're down to what's left in the air packs."

Alex straps on her mask. The inside of it smells like rubber and sweat. It feels moist and grimy against her skin after days of frequent use, and she knows she'll get a fierce case of zits soon for systematically mistreating her skin like that.

That's if we stay alive long enough for that to become a problem, she thinks as she puts on Ash's mask for what feels like the hundredth time this week. When she tightens the straps, she has some trouble with the buckles because her hands are shaking a little. Before, the idea of taking one last walk with Ash was still an abstraction. But now that the lights are out and the air is getting low, she feels the fearful anxiety returning, the rising panic of a condemned prisoner who's hearing the footsteps of the executioners coming to take her to the gallows. For all the talk with Lopez earlier, she doesn't feel ready to go, not even close.

Harris has finished putting on her own mask. She goes over to the weapons locker and takes out a rifle and a magazine. Alex watches as Harris puts the magazine into the weapon and slaps the bottom of it with her palm to make sure it's properly seated and locked in.

"I'm going to open the hatch," she says and squeezes past Alex and Ash to go to the back of the compartment. "I'm not going to die in this fucking box."

At the tail ramp, Harris opens the cover for the emergency hatch release and pulls the handle down sharply. The ramp opens with a loud blast of compressed air that makes Alex flinch. It hits the ground with a heavy thud and a splash of puddle water. Harris cycles the bolt on her rifle to load a round into the chamber. She turns to look at Alex.

"You coming or staying?"

Alex looks over at Blake's prone form.

"What about him?"

Harris shrugs.

"I can't override the autodoc to crank up the sedative and the morphine for him. And I sure as hell am not going to shoot him." She nods at the rifle in its storage bracket next to Alex. "Are you?"

Alex doesn't have to think long about her answer.

"No," she says. "I'm not."

"Then he'll go when the autodoc runs out of juice. At least he won't feel a thing."

Harris turns and walks down the ramp. When she's at the bottom, she turns to look at Alex again.

"I gotta keep watching for that flare. Are you coming, or are you staying in here?"

Alex doesn't really want to stay in the dark troop compartment with the unconscious and probably dying Blake. But the prospect of going out into the rain, only to have to watch whatever Harris is planning to do if her air runs out, is even less appealing to her. Lopez may prefer to go out alone, but Blake hasn't had the chance to make that choice.

"I'll stay with him until the machine shuts off," she says.

Harris nods.

"I'll see you," she says.

"See you," Alex replies. It seems like a terrible banality, but she can't think of anything else to say, nothing that can do justice to the possibility of saying goodbye to Private Harris for the last time.

Harris turns and walks around the back of the mule and out of Alex's sight. Then Alex is alone with Ash and Blake. A warm gust of wind drives a spray of rain through the open rear hatch and into the troop compartment. A flash of light ripples across the sky, and Alex's heart skips a beat before she realizes it's distant lightning and not a grenade launcher flare.

She switches seats, sliding along the bench row until she is in front of Blake's makeshift stretcher. On the control screen, the timer on the battery discharge status shows twenty-nine minutes until depletion. Alex touches Blake's hand, which feels clammy and cold. If not for the vitals updating continuously on the control screen, she would think he's already dead. She looks at his gaunt and sunken face and realizes she can't count all the times she got into it with him over rules back at the Vault when she was a teenager. It all seems unimportant and stupid now, playing cat and mouse with him over work assignments or schedules, hiding out in Misfit Cove with her friends and drinking pilfered alcohol instead of sifting soy or crawling around underneath the catwalks to check the supply lines for leaks.

"Well, here we are now," she says to him. "Sorry we were such a pain in the ass. We didn't know any better."

She squeezes his hand lightly. He doesn't give any indication that he heard what she said, but she feels better for having said it.

Ash is still lying on the floor of the mule under his regular seat. He isn't wearing his leash, but she knows that he would not go outside without her leading or telling him to. He has turned around a little so he's facing the open hatch, and she can see his ears moving a little as he listens to what's going on out there.

Alex slides out of her seat and lies down on the floor next to Ash. The center aisle of the mule's troop compartment is a tight fit for both of them side by side, but the snugness of the space and the proximity of his warm and soft body is a comfort. She settles in with her head on Ash's flank. He looks back at her, but he makes no move to reposition himself. Instead, he puts his head on his paws and lies still.

This isn't so bad, she thinks. *If we just fall asleep now and never wake up, it'll be all right.*

The wind is gusting into the back of the mule, and the breeze on her forehead is a little bit of relief even if it's just as warm as the air on the inside. With the steady background noise of the distant storm, it's almost peaceful out there. Alex closes her eyes and tries to focus on her breathing. She shifts her body a little until she can stick her hand into the pocket of her jumpsuit and wrap it around the familiar shape of her father's old pocketknife. Her father and grandfather both touched this knife a thousand times. She doesn't think there's magic in the object itself, and she doesn't believe in gods or spirits. But if this is her time to go, it feels right to recall the people she loves who came and went before her, and not to think of rifles and monsters and empty oxygen tanks. There's no fear or anguish in remembering the faces of her family, no anxiety in recalling their voices.

She doesn't know how long she has been lying on the floor with Ash when she feels him tense up a little. He raises his head and starts a low growl deep in his chest. The fear that had been receding in Alex's mind while she was drifting off comes back, an unwelcome emotion that tastes sour and metallic in her mouth. She sits up and looks at Ash to see that he's focused on the space beyond the open rear hatch.

"What is it?" she asks him, her voice barely above a whisper.

Ash doesn't look at her. He just keeps staring at the open hatch. His growl is soft but steady, like an ancient combustion engine running on idle. Then the noise that stirred him up is loud enough for her to hear it as well. The wind carries a faint whining sound that's accompanied by a low rumble.

There's an indistinct shout from the outside. It's Harris's voice, coming from somewhere in front of the mule, but Alex can't tell whether it's alarm, surprise, or something else. She scrambles to her feet and pulls the rifle from the weapon bracket next to her seat. Ash leaps up from his snoozing spot, instantly ready to charge out with her.

They run down the ramp together. She cycles the bolt of the rifle and chambers a round as she turns the rear corner of the vehicle. Fifty meters in front of the mule, Harris is standing on a small rock cluster, with her hand in the air and her rifle dangling from her side on its carry sling. She's holding the detachable helmet light and waving it in a slow back-and-forth motion at something in the distance. Alex runs over to her, with Ash by her side matching her pace in an effortless stride. When Harris hears her coming, she turns around and laughs.

"Looks like we may not kick the bucket today after all," she calls out to Alex. "Come up and look at this."

Alex joins the private at the top of the little elevation point. She doesn't have to ask what Harris has spotted. Less than a hundred meters ahead, a pair of thin horizontal strips of light is cutting through the darkness and coming toward them, the distinctive shape of a military mule's headlights. A moment later, the broad wedge shape of the vehicle materializes out of the rain. Harris waves her signal light again with barely restrained enthusiasm.

Alex's relief at the sight of their approaching salvation makes her feel like she could jump the fifty meters back to their damaged mule in a single leap.

"That's the most beautiful thing I've ever seen," Harris says.

Alex laughs and goes down to one knee to hug Ash, who is watching the new arrival with his usual vigilance. She gets up and leads him off the slope and back to the stricken mule that is sitting dark and silent in its shelter. Inside, she rushes to the autodoc and checks the screen. The charge-status timer is blinking red now: BACKUP BATTERY 19% REMAINING (0H 9M). She grabs Ash's leash and dashes back outside to meet their rescuers.

The headlights of the second mule are sweeping over the rainy rocks as the other vehicle pulls up next to its stablemate and stops with the soft hiss of pneumatic brakes, followed by the whine of the tail-ramp hydraulics. The first trooper coming down the ramp is Lopez, and the relief and joy she feels at the sight of him rushes her brain so intensely that it makes her dizzy for a moment.

"Found these guys on the road and hitched a ride," he says to her when she runs up to him. Instead of replying, she wraps her arms around him again, as much to steady her suddenly weak knees as to express her emotions.

"Easy," he says. "It's all right now. We're going home."

"The autodoc is about to quit," she says as she lets go of him again. "The mule's out of power. He only has a few minutes left."

Behind Lopez, three more troopers in battle armor come down the tail ramp of the second mule, weapons at the ready. Private Harris has come down from her elevated spot as well and trots up to the group.

"We gotta get Blake over into the other mule right now," Lopez tells them.

"Loftus, Stokes," one of the armored figures orders. Two of the troopers go up into the back of the broken mule.

"Are you all right?" the other trooper asks Alex. In the darkness, she has to check the name stencil on the armor to recognize her as Corporal Doran, the garrison squad's second-in-command.

"I'm okay," she replies. "I'll be fine. But Blake's in bad shape."

"We'll take care of him, don't worry," Doran says. "Lopez, get them out of the weather. We need to get the hell out of here."

Lopez leads Alex to the other mule and helps her into the back with Ash. He takes the rifle from her and unloads it on the tail ramp as she moves up to the bulkhead and takes the seat that's furthest from the rear hatch. Ash lies down underneath her seat and puts his head on his front paws. She fumbles for the air connector by the seat to hook it up to Ash's pack. When she tries to clip the end of it into the valve on the pack's tank, her hands are shaking so much that she needs three tries to make the connection. The high from the joy of spotting the rescue mission has worn off, and now she only feels drained and exhausted from the emotional whiplash of the last few minutes.

The troopers bring in Blake on his stretcher a few moments later. One of them quickly flips down the backrests of the seats across from Alex's side to make a flat surface. When Blake is strapped down, they connect the autodoc with swift and practiced hands. One of the soldiers leaves the compartment again once the device is in place. The remaining trooper glances at her and flashes a quick smile before returning his attention to the autodoc screen.

For the next few minutes, the mule is the center of hurried activity taking place outside. The tail ramp closes, and the driver moves the vehicle in front of the damaged mule. Alex hears metallic thumping from the rear of the hull. When the rear hatch opens again, she sees that the soldiers have linked up the two armored personnel carriers with two thick steel cables.

As soon as the tail ramp hits the ground, the soldiers from the rescue team climb back into the rear of the mule one by one and swiftly fill up the remaining seats on both sides of the compartment's center aisle. The last one up the ramp is Lopez. He moves up through the group and takes the seat right across from Alex and Ash. Next to the hatch, Corporal Doran hits the ramp switch and toggles the intercom.

"Squad and cargo secure. Get us the hell out of here, Clark."

"Copy that. Throttling up," comes the reply from the driver station.

The mule sets itself in motion with some hesitation. Alex can hear the driveshaft whining under strain as the electric engines work to overcome the inertia of both the vehicle and the twenty-odd tons of dead weight tethered to it. Then they are rolling along, bumping and swaying over the uneven rocky ground.

When the air-quality light jumps from red to green, there's a ripple of movement going across the troop compartment as troopers remove their helmets. Alex bends down to unfasten Ash's mask and tuck it back into its storage pouch. Unprompted, Lopez reaches for a water pouch and hands it to Alex.

"Thanks," she says. She takes Ash's collapsible rubber bowl out of his little backpack and unfolds it. When she pours the water, Ash nudges her hand aside with his nose and starts drinking before she has filled his bowl halfway. She puts the pouch between her knees, takes off her own mask, and drinks the rest of the water in one long and greedy gulp. It's warm and it has the stale foil-and-plastic taste of water that has been in storage for a long time, but she doesn't mind because she suddenly feels parched just like Ash. Lopez wordlessly hands her another pouch while she is still squeezing the last few drops out of the first one. She takes it and drops the empty pouch on her lap, then opens the new one and tops off Ash's bowl before chugging the rest.

"Go easy," Lopez says. "Don't make yourself throw it all up again."

With every seat in the back of the mule taken, the interior of this troop compartment feels much more cramped than the other one despite their identical dimensions.

"I hear you guys got two," Private Loftus, one of the newly arrived troopers, says to Lopez.

"We did," Lopez confirms. His voice sounds as tired as Alex has ever heard it. "One with rifles and the cannon. The other with the cannon alone. Blew through most of our ammo."

"We got three," Loftus says. "Stitched 'em up with the tri-barrel. That's five. Gotta be some sort of Corps record for a single squad. Never killed that many in one day before."

"Neither have they," Corporal Doran says from the back of the compartment. "Now cut the rah-rah bullshit. The sarge and Bayliss are gone. And Cheryl. Andres. Scott. We've got a broken mule in tow, and we've lost a crawler."

The litany of losses out of Doran's mouth makes Loftus shut his mouth and shrink into his seat a little.

"Those spindly bastards did all right for themselves. Five for five was a shit trade for us," Corporal Doran says. "Nothing to brag about."

Alex feels her cheeks flush a little. She wasn't the target of Doran's rebuke but she can't help feeling chastised as well. It was her job to stand guard, to make sure they didn't get surprised and demolished at short range by those things. As much as Lopez insisted that it was just bad luck and shitty circumstances, she can't shake the conviction that those five people are dead now because she failed at her task.

A tense and uncomfortable silence settles in the troop compartment, broken only occasionally by the sounds of the autodoc working on Blake. In her corner by the bulkhead, Alex makes herself small and avoids looking around at the other troopers so she won't have to make eye contact with anyone except Lopez for a while. She's glad the private is sitting directly across from her. Without him here, she'd feel more alone in this compartment right now than she did when she was by herself with Ash in the back of the dark and silent damaged mule.

CHAPTER 14

When Alex hears the familiar *thump* of the Vault's outer airlock door closing behind the mule, it's the sweetest sound she has ever heard. It means that they're home, safely sheltered underneath a hundred meters of solid granite, back in the tiny bubble that contains everyone and everything she cares about in the universe.

The mule comes to a stop in the airlock. Every time a salvage team comes in from a mission, they have to wait in the lock for two minutes until the air is safe to breathe again, and every time, those two minutes feel like an hour to Alex. When the airlock control finally sounds the all clear, she quickly unfastens her seat harness, ready to not see the inside of a mule again for a good while.

When she gets out of the mule, there are many more people in the airlock than usual for a salvage-team return. It looks like the entire medical team has turned out, along with the rest of the garrison squad and Conley, the colony administrator. The biggest flurry of activity is the spot by the tail ramp where Dr. Bailey and her helpers are transferring Blake from his makeshift stretcher to the mobile medical cradle. Alex hops off the side of the ramp with Ash to avoid getting in their way. There's usually levity when a team returns, but there's no laughing or joking around now. Death isn't a new thing in the colony—they've lost people to sickness or accidents before—but those deaths came one at a time. Losing five of their friends on the same day is a trauma nobody here has had to suffer since the day the Lankies arrived. The weight of everyone's anxiety and somberness brings back memories for Alex that she doesn't want to have refreshed. She leads Ash away from the mule and toward the ramp to the military section and the dog kennel.

"Alex," Conley calls after her. Then again, louder, when she doesn't respond. *"Alex!"*

If she could have claimed ignorance of his first hail due to the noise from all the personnel in the airlock cross-talking, the second call is loud enough to make that excuse implausible. She stops Ash, who is already eager for his post-mission treatment, and turns on her heel.

"Sir," she says.

Conley strides toward her through the crowd.

"Where are you going? You need to have Dr. Bailey or one of the medics check you out," he says. "You know the drill by now."

"I have to take care of Ash before I square myself away," she replies. "*'First the horse, then the saddle, then the man,'* right?"

Conley flashes the hint of a smile.

"So some of Blake's wisdoms did stick after all," he says. He looks over at the spot where Dr. Bailey and her team are swarming the assistant administrator's medical cradle. "What the hell happened out there?"

"Everything that could go wrong did," she says around the lump that is forming in her throat. "The crawler got stuck. They tried to tow it out. They almost had it, and then—"

She has to stop midsentence to clear her throat, which takes her several attempts. Conley shakes his head.

"You know what, never mind that right now. I'll hear the details when you all get debriefed. In the meantime, you will get yourself checked out by the medical team before you do anything else. Understand?"

"I'm all right," she says. "I'm fine."

"Like hell you are. Not after what happened. Just because you're not bleeding doesn't mean you're fine."

She looks at Ash, who is standing by her right side but glancing at the ramp to the kennel and then looking at her as if to remind her where she needs to be taking him.

"He's been cooped up in a little box for almost a week," she says. "He needs a bath and some real food and his bed. I think he's earned all of that without having to wait for me to get cleared. He charged a *Lanky* to protect me."

"Did he now?" Conley smiles and crouches down in front of Ash to pet him. "Good boy. Fearless like your sire."

"Let me get him clean and fed, Mr. Conley," Alex says. "Then I'll go straight to medbay to get checked out. I promise."

She looks over at the medical team, who have started to move Blake's cradle onto the main ramp to the upper cave.

"They're busy right now anyway. I can do something useful while I wait."

Conley follows her gaze and watches the medics silently for a moment. Then he sighs.

"All right. Go take care of the dog. But then you report in with Dr. Bailey. No detours, no stops between here and medbay."

"Got it," Alex says. "Thank you, sir."

She turns and continues her walk to the military section. When she has taken a few steps, Administrator Conley calls after her again.

"Hey, Alex."

She stops and looks back at him.

"I'm really glad you're safe," he says.

Alex feels her throat tightening again at the genuine concern on the administrator's face. She doesn't think it's right for her to be safe when so many others are hurt or dead. But she doesn't know how to wrap that feeling into words just yet, so she merely replies with a nod before she walks off, glad to be able to turn her back on Conley so he can't see the tears that are starting to well up in her eyes.

There's so much grime in Ash's fur that it takes three rounds of soaping and rinsing before the water coming off him starts to run clear. When Alex has finished rubbing him dry, he remains still on the drying mat and looks at her expectantly.

"You're done, buddy," she says to him. "Towel rub's over. You already got the top-tier spa package today. Unless you want me to throw in a nail trimming."

She reaches into the plastic container with all the dog care items and pulls out the nail clippers. At the sight of the familiar device in her hand, he walks off the mat and out of her reach.

"Didn't think so."

She puts the clippers back and gets up from the kneeling position she's been in for the last thirty minutes. The front of her jumpsuit is wet and smells of soap, and her hands and forearms are now by far the cleanest part of her body.

"Let's get you fed. And then I get a turn too," she says. Ash's ears perk up, and he eagerly follows her as she walks from the kennel's washroom into the galley, but he keeps out of arm's reach, she knows, because he suspects bait-and-switch treachery with the nail clippers.

In the galley, she fills his bowl with wet food while he supervises from a safe distance. When she puts it into his feeding rack, he waits until she steps away before he goes for his bowl and starts eating.

"You try to take on a Lanky, but you're scared of a little pair of nail clippers."

When he has finished eating, Alex leads him to the kennel's run, where his brother Blitz is waiting. She lets Ash into the run and watches as the two dogs greet each other with tail wags and much sniffing. When they've completed their little ritual, Ash trots over to one of the dog beds in the corner and plops himself down on it. Blitz comes over to Alex to get his share of attention as well, and she rubs the spot between his ears while he sniffs her pocket for treats. Over in the corner, Ash is rolling around on the dog bed and making little grunting sounds as he does his usual post-bath calisthenics. She smiles as she watches him rub his back on the fabric, his tongue lolling out of the side of his mouth.

If only we were all so easy to make whole again, she thinks as she latches the door of the dog run.

CHAPTER 15

"We're a little busy right now," a voice says from the back of the room when Alex walks into the medbay. "Hope it's not urgent."

Alex takes a few steps into the room to see who addressed her. One of the medical techs is emptying an autoclave behind a partition, her back turned toward the door.

"It's not urgent," she says.

At the sound of her voice, the technician turns her head and drops the scalpel handle in her hand onto a medical tray, where it lands among other instruments with a clatter.

"Hey, Lauren," Alex says.

Lauren pulls off her medical gloves and walks quickly across the room toward her. She's one of the old techs from before the Lanky arrival, part of the original staff of the facility before it became the last refuge for the colony survivors. She wears her hair undercut and shaved close to her skull on one side, and she does the fastest and cleanest manual blood draws of any of the medical personnel.

"*Alex.* Holy shit. How are you doing?"

"I'm fine," Alex says. "Conley told me to have Dr. Bailey check me out before I go Downtown. I promised him I would."

"The doc is in the surgery pod with Blake. She's got everyone in there with her. They called all hands on deck for the medics."

"Is he going to make it?"

"God, I hope so," Lauren says. "He's a mess. But if anyone can fix him, it's Bailey. We'll just have to wait and see."

"I can come back later. Just tell Conley that I was here if he checks."

"Nonsense." Lauren nods at one of the medical cradles in the room. "I can do the scan. If something pops up, I'll punt it to the doctor. Come on, sit down."

Alex walks over to the nearest cradle and sits down as directed. She unzips her jumpsuit, slips her arms out of the sleeves, and pulls the top down to her waist. Her undershirt is ringed with salt stains from her sweat, and the odor of stale perspiration wafts up from her T-shirt. It's much more difficult to ignore in this clean and air-conditioned pod than in the field. "God, I really need a shower," she says as a preemptive apology because there's no way Lauren isn't noticing the smell. "Does that thing have an express cycle?"

Lauren smiles and turns on the control screen to activate the device. It lowers itself into a semi-reclined position, and the cradle conforms to her body shape in a snug embrace.

"Five minutes and you're out of here," Lauren says and taps the control screen. "Here we go. I'll be right back."

She moves the screen out of the way and walks off. Alex closes her eyes and enjoys the cool, dry air coming out of the medbay's overhead vents while the cradle goes through its diagnostic protocol. It's the first time in nearly a week she hasn't had to keep the possibility of a sudden Lanky attack in the back of her head, and she can feel the tension starting to ebb as she focuses on her breathing.

"You look like hammered shit," a familiar voice says next to her cradle.

Alex opens her eyes to see a pair of light-blue eyes looking at her from above.

"Thanks, Velasco," she replies. "I'm glad to see you too."

"I *am* glad to see you," Val says. "Just pointing out the obvious, that's all." She leans in for a hug and recoils when Alex waves her off and airs out her undershirt by the collar.

"May want to wait with that until I've had a shower and a change of clothes," Alex says.

"You've smelled worse."

"I have no doubt," Alex replies, and they grin at each other. Val was her podmate for more than two years when they were teenagers and had to share a living pod. She knows Alex better than anyone else in the Vault, even if they both have their own pods now that they're adults.

"I heard what happened," Val says. "I mean, I heard that *something* happened. Rumor mill's been going wild since the second team went out. But nobody in Uptown is sharing any details. I couldn't even get anything out of my mom."

Alex takes a long, shaky breath.

"We lost five people, Val," she says. "And the Bravo crawler. The Lankies got them."

Val's expression turns serious instantly. "Holy shit. Holy *shit*."

"Yeah," Alex agrees.

"Who?"

Alex needs to gather herself for a moment before she answers.

"Sergeant Frye, Bayliss, Cheryl. Andres. Scott. And Blake's in bad shape. They have him in surgery right now."

"Holy shit," Val says again. "*Sergeant Frye* is dead?"

Alex just nods.

"What the hell happened?"

Alex tries to find the words, but when she recalls the memory of those few minutes on the rock ledge, the last moments of the people who died, she feels that she can't find a way to begin without choking up. She just shakes her head and clears her throat.

"Later," she says, and the word comes out with a little croak. "I'll tell you. Just not right now, all right?"

Val nods somberly.

"All right. Later. Is Ash okay?"

"He's fine. He went after one of those things, if you can believe it," Alex says. "Charged right at it."

Val chuckles. "That dog is all balls."

The scanning arc of the medical cradle starts its slow head-to-toe examination of Alex, and Val takes a step back to get out of the way of the device.

"Hey, listen. If you're not going to die soon, come out to Misfit Cove after you're done here. I'm going to round up the others. Dallas and Athena are off today. Luther's check duty but nobody's going to notice if he ducks out early. Not today, anyway."

"I need to get a shower first," Alex replies. "What's the time right now?"

Val checks her watch. "It's 1300 hours."

"Make it 1400 for the Cove. No, wait, 1500. I really need to clean up first."

Val takes half a step toward her and does a theatrical little sniff. "Yeah, you do—1500 it is. It'll take me that long to find all these slackers. See you then."

"See you," Alex says. She smiles as she watches Val walk out of the medbay.

When Lauren returns to the medical cradle a few minutes later, the medical tech has a harried expression on her face.

"Any word on Blake?" Alex asks as Lauren swings the control screen of the cradle back into place and checks the readouts.

"I think it's touch and go," Lauren says. "I know they're burning through a ton of meds and supplies. All right, let's see what the word is on you."

She flicks through the data on her screen and swivels it around so Alex can see it as well.

"You're looking good. No injuries other than a few bumps and scrapes. Blood pressure, oxygenation, organ function all normal. The only thing that's out of range is your cortisol level. Have you had a lot of workplace stress recently, maybe?"

Alex laughs at the joke and its dry delivery.

"I guess you could say that," she says.

"I am clearing you on your post-mission check," Lauren says. "I'll have Dr. Bailey look at the results. I'm sure she'll call you back in if she sees something to worry about."

"Thanks, Lauren." Alex sits up and swings her legs over the edge of the cradle. She pulls her jumpsuit top up and slips her arms into the sleeves again. "And now I am going to see if I can scrub my skin right off my body if I try hard enough."

CHAPTER 16

The upper and lower cave have been called Uptown and Downtown by the colonists as long as Alex can recall, even before the Lankies arrived and the Vault turned from the colony's administration center into the last refuge of the survivors.

The upper cave contains most of the colony services—medbay, kitchen and dining, school, gym and community room, the office of the colonial constable, and the administration pod where the colony leaders do their work. Alex walks from the medbay toward the ramp that leads down into the much larger lower cave, where all the residential pods are set up. After a week away, the thick layer of anechoic nonslip coating that's on the cave floor and walls up here always feels weird under her feet, too cushy and springy, with much more friction than the rock and gravel surfaces outside. Every time she comes in from a multiday mission, it feels like her legs need half an hour to relearn how to walk in the Vault again.

At the end of the ramp, Alex takes a right turn into the pod village. Her pod is on the third tier, and she takes the stairs of the central staircase two and three at a time, eager to get to her little private den. It's the middle of the day, and most colonists are busy with their assigned jobs. She encounters nobody on the stairs or the third-tier catwalks, which suits her fine because she doesn't have to stop for hellos or small talk.

As much as she wants to catch up with her friends, right now she craves her little bathroom and its shower more than anything else.

The living pods are all identical modular units, six meters wide and three meters tall and deep. The ones on the bottom tier of the pod village are combined into double and triple units for the families that live together. Alex's pod is a single unit because she is by herself, and it's more than enough for her. Some of the older colonists sometimes grouse about the lack of space and only half-jokingly compare the single pods to prison cells, but Alex finds hers cozy instead of confining. She spent more than two years sharing a pod with Val, and when she turned eighteen and got her own pod, the space seemed almost excessive for one person after all this time with a podmate. But the biggest luxury her own unit affords her is not the extra shelf space or elbow room, but the ability to shut out the world and have privacy.

Alex kicks off her boots and starts peeling off her jumpsuit the moment the pod door closes behind her. She strips out of her sweaty underwear, starts the hot water flow in the shower, and uses the toilet while the water heats up to the maximum fifty-five degrees Celsius she has dialed in. By the time she has finished relieving herself, the tiny bathroom is filled with steam.

Standing under the hot water stream and scrubbing the dirt and sweat off her body after nearly a week of stewing in her own perspiration comes as close to a spiritual experience as she can imagine. Much like Ash, she needs three rounds of thorough scrubbing before every bit of grime is gone. Even after she feels clean again, she stands under the fine jets from the showerhead until long after her fingertips have turned wrinkly.

When Alex has dried herself off and wrapped her hair in a clean towel, she walks into the living space on legs that feel shaky with the relieved tension from the hot water. She collects her dirty clothes from the floor and stuffs them into her laundry bin. She turned the sleeves of her jumpsuit inside out when she took it off, and as she pulls them back right side out, she feels something firm and a little weighty in the sleeve pocket. She unzips the pocket to find the lemon bar Lopez gave her as a birthday gift, two days and what feels like an eternity ago.

Alex takes the lemon bar out of the sleeve pocket, and the slight shaking of her fingers has nothing to do with the hot shower water. When Lopez handed her that bar with a light stick to stand in for a candle, Frye and Bayliss and all the others were still alive, and Blake was still unhurt. She walks over to her desk and puts the lemon bar into one of the drawers, wishing she had eaten it quickly in the back of the mule instead of letting it become a memory-laden souvenir from the disastrous mission.

Now that she is clean and dry, the sleeping nook beckons, and Alex almost gives in to the temptation to slip under the blanket and enjoy the comfort of her bed for just a little while. But she knows that she would fall asleep almost right away, and that she wouldn't wake up for the next eight hours. She gets a fresh set of underwear and a clean jumpsuit out of her closet instead and gets dressed with some reluctance.

—

Misfit Cove is at the far end of the Vault's underground lake, a freshwater pool that's two hundred meters long and almost a hundred wide. To get to the Cove, Alex has to make the trek halfway around the circumference of the lake. It takes a while because the access path that rings the reservoir alternates between catwalks, gravel strips, and sections of nonslip coating covering bare rock. Most of the older techs and administrators don't like to make the walk out to the Cove unless they have a compelling reason, and chewing out Alex and her friends ceased to count as one of those reasons some time ago.

The Cove itself is a small, narrow cave that splits off from the lake cavern. It's only accessible through a gap in the rock wall that forces the taller members of their group to shuffle through sideways and with their heads lowered. In the beginning, the administrators declared the cave off-limits once they discovered where the colony's teenagers were gathering clandestinely, but they gave up on enforcing the rule once it became clear that keeping the kids out of their clubhouse would require either a full-time guard or a dozen cubic meters of concrete to close the entrance. Alex suspects that someone upstairs recognized that the Cove served as a social pressure valve of sorts, a place for stressed teens to blow off steam in private, and it became a semi-sanctioned hangout. The only concessions they had to make to keep their nook was the installation of a wired comms set for emergencies and a soundproof coating of the Cove's walls and floor, two tasks which—according to Blake—they finished much faster than any similarly laborious task they had ever been assigned.

"Knock, knock," Alex says into the cave entrance.

"Green light," someone replies from the inside, and she ducks through the opening. She pushes the canvas aside that serves as a privacy blind on the inside of the entrance.

"Hey, Spaceborne Commando," Val greets her when she's past the canvas. Her friends are sitting on the varied collection of folding chairs and cots they've carried back here over the years to make themselves comfortable. Val gets up and walks over to Alex to pull her into a firm hug.

"You smell much better. How are you feeling?"

"All right," Alex says. "Better now after the shower."

Four pairs of eyes are following her as she walks over to one of the empty folding chairs and sits down with a slow exhalation. Val sits back down next to Dallas, who is sipping something bright orange from a squeeze bottle. Athena and Luther are sitting on one of the stretchers, her head resting on his shoulder. The mood in the Cove seems far more subdued than usual.

Alex looks at the bottle in Dallas's hand. "Got any more of that?"

Dallas holds out the bottle to her. "Don't you want to know what's in there?"

"Don't care," she replies as she takes it from his hand. "I've been drinking nothing but bagged water all week."

"Bug juice from the galley, carbonated and upgraded with a shot of the chief's finest."

She takes a sip and makes a face.

"More than one shot, I think."

Dallas flashes his white and even teeth. He has started to grow a beard since she went out with the salvage team, and the red scruff on his cheeks and chin makes his complexion look even more pale than usual.

"Maybe a few. I was in a hurry when I mixed it," he says.

Alex takes another sip and hands the bottle back to him. "I may need some more of that before the day is done."

She looks around at the faces of her friends, all watching her with expressions that tell her Val has given them the broad strokes of the news already.

"I thought I'd never see any of you again," she says, and she feels close to tears as soon as the words come out.

"Hey," Val says. She gets out of her chair and squats in front of Alex to squeeze her hands. "Don't talk about it if you don't feel up to it."

"I don't think I'll ever feel up to it," Alex replies. She lets go of Val and wipes her eyes with the back of her hand. "So I guess now's as good a time as any."

She tells her friends the details as she remembers them, from the time they pulled up to the research station to the moment the rescue force arrived with the second mule. Recalling everything is easier than she had anticipated, and something about being able to describe the events out loud helps her to look at them with a little bit of distance. When she has finished her story, there's a long silence in the Cove. Alex leans forward to take the bottle out of Dallas's grasp again and swigs another long gulp of the spiked bug juice.

"That is the scariest shit I've ever heard," Luther says finally. He runs his hand through the dreadlocks that fall all the way to his shoulders. Athena and Dallas nod their agreement. Val holds out her hand for the bottle, and Alex gives it to her. The bug juice makes the round until, now mostly empty, it arrives back in Dallas's hand.

"They won't be able to run salvage missions anymore," Dallas says. "Not with one mule and one crawler left. Nobody's going to want to go out without backup."

"There's hardly anyone left to go out," Athena says. "With Sergeant Frye and Corporal Bayliss gone, I mean. And Andres and Scott."

"It killed Cheryl," Alex says. "It walked right over her. Like she was a bug. Then Lopez came back with the mule and blew it away. Ten seconds sooner, and she would have been all right."

"That wasn't in your hands. Sometimes shit goes sideways," Val says.

"That's what Lopez told me. It's not really a comfort, though."

"Val's right, and so's Lopez," Luther says. "You start going down that path in your mind, there's never an end to it. *If* the crawler hadn't gotten stuck. *If* the gun on the mule hadn't jammed. *If, if, if.*"

He shakes his head and looks down at his folded hands.

"If the Lankies hadn't come," he adds. "Lotta things wouldn't have happened if they had left us alone. But they didn't. Everything was their fault. Not yours. Not Lopez's. *Theirs*. You got that?"

He looks at Alex with nothing but sincerity on his dark and handsome face, and she nods. Her friends and Lopez are right, of course, and she knows it on an intellectual level. But that knowledge isn't erasing the doubt she still feels, or the memory of Cheryl dying an awful death right in front of her.

"Fuck," Dallas says. He shakes the bottle in his hand, where the tiniest bit of orange liquid sloshes around at the bottom. "We're going to need some more of this, I think."

On the cave wall by the entrance, the red light of the comms set starts flashing. Val gets to her feet with a curse and walks over to the unit.

"Not fucking now," she says. "The soy picking can wait for a few hours."

She picks up the handset. "Go ahead."

Alex watches as Val listens to the person on the other end of the line and the irritation disappears from her friend's expression. Val takes a long, shaky breath.

"All right. Thank you. And I'm sorry."

Val slowly returns the handset to its cradle and turns to look at her friends.

"That was Kari. Blake didn't make it."

CHAPTER 17

The four SI troopers in dress uniform slowly march onto the platform in perfect precision, each step of their polished boots falling precisely in time. Between them, they are carrying a black metal tray covered by a small North American Commonwealth flag. Underneath the flag, Alex can see the bumps made by the half dozen burial capsules lined up evenly on the tray.

This is only the second time she has seen the soldiers wear their formal dress uniforms. There have been burials in the colony before, but none of them involved military ritual except for the symbolic ceremony they held for the casualties of the invasion eight years ago. This funeral is largely symbolic as well because Alex knows that five of the six capsules underneath the NAC flag are empty. Only Administrator Blake's capsule contains ashes, the cremated remains of the only body they managed to bring home.

Over a hundred colonists are lined up in front of the Uptown overhang, all watching the procession in total silence. Not even the soldiers' boots make a sound as they slow-walk their cargo to the rack in the center of the platform. They line up on either side of the rack and lower the flag-covered tray onto it with a calm precision that makes it look like they've practiced the formal funeral drill every day for the last eight years. When the tray is in place, the troopers step back as one and stand at attention on either side, still as statues.

When Administrator Conley steps forward to give the eulogy for the fallen, he looks a decade older than he did yesterday. He delivers his speech in a halting voice, and he has to stop frequently to gather himself. Nobody here needs to be told who the dead were, of course. With only a hundred and fifty-odd people in the Vault, everyone here has shared meals and jokes with them, worked alongside them, gotten to know their likes and quirks and individual histories. Alex looks at the bumps under the flag for the entirety of the eulogy, recalling the faces and voices of the dead and trying to etch them into her memory. Eight years ago, she had been so numb with grief, so shell-shocked by the suddenness and violence of the Lanky invasion, that it felt like she was sleepwalking through a terrible dream. She knew that her parents were dead, but she never saw them die, or her friends Micah and Aurora. For a long while after the invasion, she had held out hope that her mom and dad were still alive, holed up somewhere like she was, and she had only let go of that hope gradually as the months and years went on. But she has seen these people get killed, soldiers and techs who have been a close part of her life for half a decade. This loss feels more raw, as if the much smaller scale of it makes the pain cut deeper.

When Administrator Conley has finished his eulogy, he steps back from the flag-covered tray and joins the row of colonists in front of the platform. The soldiers turn toward the corners of the tray. One of them gives a quiet command, and two of the troopers pick up the flag at the corners with the same precision as their earlier march. They lift the flag from the tray and fold it in half, then again and again. Finally, one of the soldiers holds one end of the flag while the other folds it from the other end until it has the shape of a triangle. The soldier holding the flag turns on his heel and walks forward in slow and measured steps until he stands in front of Administrator Conley. He presents the flag to Conley, steps back to stand at attention, and renders a slow and precise salute.

—

There's no graveyard in the Vault. When the soldiers carry off the tray with the six burial capsules, she knows they will place them in storage down in the military section by the main airlock. Back before the Lankies, the capsules would get repatriated, carried back to Earth by the next supply ship to make orbit. Without the supply flights from Earth, Alex guesses that the capsules of their dead will be in storage for a long time, to be discovered by someone else long after everyone in the Vault is gone.

Then the soldiers and their somber cargo are gone, the colonists have started to disperse, and the funeral is over. Alex watches someone take down the rack for the funeral tray and carry it off.

I almost ended up on that thing myself, she thinks. *Or rather, just a capsule with my name on it. They'd be carrying it off to storage right now with the others.*

"You all right?" someone says behind her. She turns to see Private Lopez in his dress uniform, his white cap under his arm.

"No," she replies. "Not yet. It'll be a while, I think."

"I know what you mean."

"We worked so hard to keep him alive," Alex says. "And then he died anyway."

"He died here. Among friends. Not alone in the back of a mule somewhere out on the ridge. I don't have any regrets."

She's not entirely sure that she feels the same way, but it's an unpleasant thought, so she changes the subject.

"How's the mule? Are they going to be able to fix it?"

Lopez shakes his head. "The power core is trashed. We don't have a spare one around. Could have maybe rigged something with those cells we got from the outpost. But that's not an option anymore."

"So they towed it back for nothing," Alex says.

"It's going to be a spare-parts bin. And we can swap the cannon mount to the other mule, transfer the tri-barrel to the crawler."

"I don't think I am ready to go out there again, Lopez."

The private shakes his head lightly.

"Neither am I," he says. "Not yet. But we'll do it again. And when we do, we'll want to have you along. You and the dog."

She knows he's probably saying that just to lift her spirits, but she gives him a little smile in response, and he smiles back.

"Take a time-out. It'll be a while before we go out again. Just don't keep telling yourself this was all for nothing. Sometimes you get a shit hand. Doesn't mean you let them have the table. You reshuffle the deck and go again. All right?"

"All right," she says, even though she doesn't share any of that sentiment right now. But whether he really feels it or he's just trying to lift her spirits, she finds that his pep talk does give her a little bit of solace.

He takes the cap out from underneath his arm and puts it on his head.

"All right. I gotta get out of my dress blues and go back to work. I hope I won't have to wear these again for a long time."

"See you," Alex says.

"Not too soon," he replies. "And I mean it. Take some time. Take care of yourself. Tell Conley you're off for a few days. You've more than earned it."

"I'll ask him," she says.

"Don't ask him," he replies over his shoulder as he walks off. "*Tell* him. You stood your ground against a *Lanky*. Conley shouldn't be a problem for you."

"You can quit the pep talk now," Alex calls after him, but she finds that his obvious flattery makes her smile anyway.

CHAPTER 18

When Alex wakes up, the dream that had stirred her out of a restless sleep has already faded from her memory, leaving behind only a vague sense of menace and danger.

She picks up the wrist computer from the shelf above her head and looks at it. It's 0415 in the morning, the dead time of night when most of the Vault is asleep and only the firewatch shift is keeping an eye on things.

Alex lies back and tries to drift off to sleep again, but the unnerving feeling from her dream won't go away no matter how much she concentrates on her breathing. She gives up on the exercise and listens closely to her surroundings. There are no indications of danger, no fast footsteps, no alarms buzzing. The Vault is silent as always at this time of night. But she can't shake the sense that something is wrong, so she gets out of bed and slips into her jumpsuit.

Outside in the cavern, the overhead lights are dimmed to their nighttime level. Alex walks down the main staircase of the pod cluster with quiet and cautious steps. The only sound out here is the ever-present low humming of the electrical systems and the faint whispering of the environmental controls.

You're getting paranoid, she chides herself when she reaches the bottom of the staircase. *It's just the stress from the mission fucking with your head. Get your ass back to bed, or you'll be dragging it tomorrow.*

For a moment, she is about to turn around and climb the stairs back to her pod to do just that. Then she decides to listen to whatever nagging little voice woke her up and made her uneasy, and she walks over to the bottom of the ramp that leads to Uptown. If she has learned one thing from her time out in the field with Ash, it's that ignoring those primal instincts can be a grave mistake.

—

The upper cave is as quiet as the lower one. Alex walks through Uptown, past the empty dining hall and medbay, and she tries to filter anything unusual out of the regular nighttime background hum. There's nothing out of the ordinary up here either, but she can't shake the feeling of wrongness, or the low-level dread that makes her want to hide or run away like a frightened animal.

On the far end of Uptown, she stops at the railing that overlooks the ramp to the main airlock. The military section is off to the side at the bottom of another small incline. The dog kennels are just out of sight from her vantage point, around the corner from the end of the ramp. Alex checks her wrist computer. It's only 0433, much too early for breakfast for the dogs, but she decides to go down there anyway to check on Ash and Blitz, and she knows they'll at least be happy to see her.

Two smaller caves branch off from the airlock vestibule, the military section to her right and the motor pool to the left. When she walks through the vestibule, she looks into the motor pool cave, where the two mules and the remaining crawler are parked. The damaged mule is missing its gun mount, which is suspended from a nearby gantry, ready to be swapped onto the intact mule, which will in turn donate its less powerful tri-barrel gun to the crawler and transform it into a fighting vehicle. The crawler is a civilian utility transport that was never meant to accept military weaponry, but Alex has no doubt that the soldiers will make it work. If the colonists in the Vault have gotten very good at anything, it's the fixing of broken things with seemingly incompatible parts salvaged from other broken things.

Alex walks down the ramp to the military section. There's a light on inside the pod for the firewatch on duty, and she sticks her head into the open door. Inside, Private Loftus is sitting behind the desk with his feet on the tabletop, reading something on a tablet. He looks up when he hears her.

"I don't know how you're not fast asleep," he says to her. "Every time I come back from a salvage, I feel like I could sleep for three days straight."

"I wish I could," Alex replies. "My brain doesn't seem to be on board with that right now."

"What are you doing down here? Restlessly wandering the halls until the chow hall opens?"

"I was going to go to the kennel and check on Ash," she says.

"I think he's fine," Loftus says. "Last time I saw him, he was sleeping on his back. All four paws in the air. But go ahead. Just keep it down. It's another hour and a half until reveille." He returns his attention to the tablet in his hands.

"No bark parties, got it." She leaves Loftus to his reading and walks past the row of barracks pods to the back of the cave where the kennel is tucked away in a natural niche in the rock wall.

When she rounds the corner of the detention pod and turns toward the kennel, Alex can see instantly that something is off. Blitz is panting and slowly pacing in the run with his head down. Ash is on his bed in the corner of the run, lying down on all fours. His ears are perked up, and he is focused on a spot on the cave wall somewhere behind Alex.

When he sees her, he doesn't give her his customary tail-swish greeting. He just glances at her and shifts his gaze back to the cave wall.

Maybe I am not paranoid after all, Alex thinks.

She opens the kennel door and goes inside. Blitz looks up when she walks in and wags his tail furtively.

"What's wrong, boy? Dinner not sitting well with you?"

She checks the floor of the kennel for puke or blood, but the run is clean, without so much as a rogue puddle of pee. Their water fountain is working, and the temperature back here is normal. Ash and Blitz are both very smart, and sometimes they manage to steal treats out of unattended combat packs or from desks in the barracks pods, which has caused the occasional upset stomach and attendant vomit cleanup. But there's no evidence of any pilfered snacks anywhere, no torn-up cake-bar wrappers or ration pouches. She kneels next to Blitz and runs her hand through the fur of his neck. He stands still for a moment to let her pet him, but then he continues his restless pacing, still panting as if he is in mild distress.

Over in his corner, Ash starts to growl. It's a quiet growl, just a soft rumble in his throat, but it sets Alex on edge instantly. She looks at him, but he isn't paying attention to her or Blitz.

"What is it, buddy?" she asks him. "Are you seeing ghosts?"

Ash stands up and takes a few steps toward the center of the run in a slow, stiff-legged gait. Then he freezes, body tense, tail unmoving, and growls again. Alex looks in the direction Ash is pointing, but there's nothing but a granite wall there.

Then he barks. It's his danger bark, the one that's usually muffled by a breathing mask. Without the mask and in the confines of the cave, it sounds like a shotgun blast. Alex recoils involuntarily and falls on her ass from her crouched position. She gets to her feet quickly and walks over to Ash. When she puts her hand on his collar, she feels his body vibrating with the silent growl he's holding in his throat. She knows what his body language is telling her, of course. He's not growling at the wall. He's growling at something on the other side of that wall.

If only he were seeing ghosts, she thinks.

"Buddy, do I ever hope you're wrong this time," she tells him.

"You need to wake up the rest of the squad," Alex says as she rushes into the firewatch pod.

"It's 0440," Private Loftus says. He puts his tablet down on the table and pushes his chair back. "You want me to shake everybody out of their bunks? What for?"

"Something's not right," she says. "The dogs are really spun up."

"You spun them up by going into their kennel at four thirty in the morning," Loftus replies. "Now they're itching for breakfast."

"I know the difference. Something's out there. Close enough for the dogs to pick it up."

"We're under a hundred meters of bedrock. What could they possibly pick up from down here?"

"Just listen to me, please," Alex pleads.

"If I sound the alarm and raise the whole garrison and you're wrong, everybody's going to be extra pissed."

"And if you don't sound the alarm and I'm right?"

Loftus chews on his lower lip for a moment.

"Fuck it. This is so above my pay grade. Let's go up to ops. They can take a look."

The colony's operations center is the brain of the Vault's hardwired networks, and someone is on duty here every day of the week and every hour of the day. When Alex walks in with Private Loftus, she sees that

Administrator Velasco has the firewatch tonight. Val's mom is sitting at one of the consoles, sipping coffee from a steel mug and slowly spinning a stylus in the other hand.

"Morning, Mrs. Velasco," Alex offers.

"Alex," Gina Velasco says. "I saw you walking past earlier. I was wondering what you were doing up so early. What *are* you doing up so early?"

"Alex thinks the dogs are sensing trouble," Loftus says.

"Trouble," Mrs. Velasco repeats with a raised eyebrow. "I haven't noticed any trouble. It's been quiet all night. Too quiet. I've had to mainline coffee since 0200."

"How long has it been since you checked the feed from outside?" Alex asks.

Administrator Velasco nods at the control screen on the wall next to her, which is subdivided into two dozen different camera feeds, from the airlock vestibule to the hydroponic farm.

"The outside of the airlock is on the live feed. The topside one I check every hour or so."

"Can you check it right now?"

Administrator Velasco raises her eyebrow again.

"Sure. It'll take a minute to extend the sensor mast, though. You want some coffee? I just made a fresh pot."

"No, thank you," Alex says. "That stuff makes me jumpy."

"You seem plenty jumpy without it right now. Here, have a seat. I'll pull up the sensor controls."

The administrator pulls the chair away from the console next to her and nods at it. Alex walks over and sits down.

"Have you caught up with Val since you got back?"

"Yeah. She came to see me when I got my checkup in medbay," Alex says.

"She's mad with envy whenever you go out, you know. You're the only one of her friends who gets to go on salvage."

Alex chuckles at the thought of Val riding along in a mule and living off combat rations for a week. Val often tries to trade her soy farm shifts because she hates the slimy feeling of the pods on her hands. Going for days without hot water and air-conditioning would drive her into frothing insanity.

"All right. Mast is going up," the administrator says.

Alex looks at the control screen and focuses on the camera feed from the outside of the airlock. It's another gray and gloomy day out there. Dark clouds are rushing across the sky, and fog is rising from countless puddles. The camera has a limited field of vision because the airlock is at the end of a short tunnel, but the slice of the surface she can see from this angle doesn't show anything that could have spooked the dogs, just the barren and weatherworn rocky landscape beyond the mouth of the access tunnel. Behind her, Private Loftus leans against the wall by the door, his arms folded across his chest.

"Here we go," Velasco says. "The mast is extended. Let's take a look around topside."

She taps the controls, and the status screen on the wall changes as the tiles of the surveillance camera feeds are replaced with a single high-resolution feed from the sensor mast on the mountain slope a hundred meters above them. The camera is so high up that it looks like it's almost scraping the bottom of the low cloud ceiling. Below, the empty landscape stretches for kilometers before it disappears behind a distant curtain of precipitation.

"See?" Loftus says behind Alex. "Nothing out there. Just the rain and the rocks."

Administrator Velasco rotates the mast, and the image from the feed pans slowly to the right. A kilometer from the entrance to the Vault, the ruin of the old terraforming station comes into view, reduced to a few mangled sections of its outer walls.

"Weather's not too bad today," Velasco says. "I bet you can actually see all the way into town."

She pans the camera further to the right to follow the path of the old access road into the nearby settlement, the place that was home for most of the Vault colonists before the invasion. The town is right on the edge of visibility in this weather, the long rows of destroyed residential domes partially shrouded by rain and mist.

"I can't even remember where our old house—"Alex begins, and then the sentence dies in her throat, and the thought behind it disintegrates in her mind.

Even from this distance, the Lankies striding across the old airfield next to the settlement look immense, their size put into scale by the remains of the buildings behind them. It's the largest group she has ever seen in one place, at least a dozen of them, and more are coming into view as the camera keeps turning to the right. They pass over and through the ruins of the town like an enormous gray wave.

"Dear God," Administrator Velasco says. She gets out of her chair and takes a step away from the screen. Without her hand on the control panel, the camera stops its rotation.

So many, Alex thinks. *So many of them.* The sight on the screen paralyzes her for a moment as her brain is trying to rein in the instincts that are screaming at her to run away and hide in a deep hole somewhere.

"Oh, *shit,*" Private Loftus says. He enunciates the words slowly and with deliberation. Then he turns to rush out of the ops center without another word.

"They're coming this way," Velasco says. "Oh my God. They found us. They know where we are."

She looks at Alex in shocked bewilderment. "How can they know where we are?"

Alex can only shake her head in reply. The adrenaline flooding her brain makes her feel like she just touched a live wire with her bare hands. The panic that is rushing to replace the numbness from the initial shock is so strong that it almost makes her retch.

"Oh my *God*," Velasco says again. She snaps out of her stunned bewilderment and rushes over to the other side of the admin center pod, where a large red push button is mounted in a box on the wall. Velasco flips the safety cover up and presses the button with shaky fingers. Outside, the soft trill of the emergency alert sounds. Alex knows from countless drills that the lights in every pod and on every ceiling in the Vault just switched to a red blinking pattern that flashes in synchrony with the chirp of the alarm. The administrator picks up the wired handset on the console in front of her and toggles the transmit button.

"All hands on deck, all hands on deck," she says. "Administrative staff, report to the ops center immediately. This is not a drill. I repeat, this is not a drill."

She puts the handset back and rests her hand on it for a moment. Then she looks up at Alex as if she had forgotten that someone else is in the pod with her.

"What's your assigned emergency station?" she asks.

"Dog kennel," Alex replies automatically.

Administrator Velasco nods at the door. "Then get down to the dog kennel and tend to your duties, please. And good luck."

"To you as well," Alex says, despite her sudden certainty that their collective luck has finally run out this morning.

CHAPTER 19

Ash's mission vest is still on the drying rack where Alex left it yesterday after scrubbing it clean. When she picks it up, she can feel that there are still some damp spots on the ballistic material.

Didn't even have time to fully dry, she thinks. *We're not ready to do this again.*

She attaches the gear pouches and air pack to the vest and checks the gaskets of Ash's mask for cracks. When she's satisfied that everything is ready and working, she picks up the vest and carries it out of the equipment room.

In the run, Private Clark is already busy putting Blitz's gear on him. Alex exchanges a somber nod with the other dog handler and walks over to Ash, who greets her with a brief wag of his tail.

"Here we go again," she says to him while she lays out the vest. "At least we won't have to spend four days in the mule this time."

On the other side of the run, Private Clark chuckles.

"That's certainly one way to look at it," she says.

When Alex has finished dressing Ash in his battle gear, she realizes that the panic she had felt in the ops center at the sight of the Lankies is almost completely gone. She still feels the tightness in her chest that comes with the anticipation of a violent death, but she's no longer scared the way she was when she faced it by herself in the back of the mule. She reaches into the leg pocket of her jumpsuit to touch her pocketknife and feel the familiar smoothness of the worn scales on her fingertips. Everybody is here with her, and whatever happens next, she won't be alone.

"Ready to kick some ass?" Private Clark asks Blitz. He sits down in front of her and licks his chops.

"That's the spirit. You ready too?" she asks in Alex's direction.

"Ready," Alex confirms.

"Then let's go to war."

—

The military section is noisy with the din of hurried battle preparations. All the soldiers are in their armor and carrying heavy weaponry. Up on the central vestibule, the working mule rolls up from the motor pool and turns to face the airlock. When Alex leads Ash past the armory pod, Lopez comes out with a rocket launcher tube under each arm. He nods a greeting and huffs past her with his heavy load.

"Gather 'round, people," Corporal Doran calls out from the top of the ramp. "Listen up for a second. We don't have much time."

The troopers form a semicircle in front of the corporal. Lopez stacks his rocket launchers next to a row of ordnance lined up along the wall and joins the group at a trot. Alex stays a few steps behind everyone and makes Ash sit next to her.

"Loftus, you're working the tri-barrel from the back of the mule. Harris and Walton, get all the armor-piercing twenty mil we have left and lay it out next to the mule. Take the side cover off the gun pod and feed the belts directly. No time to roll 'em up into the pod. We're not driving anywhere anyway."

"Copy that," Private Loftus says. "I'll give a heads-up for reload when I'm down to fifty rounds."

"Lopez, you're in charge of the second fire team. Take Cooley, Carbone, Walton, and O'Toole. Get up on the Uptown ramp with the MARS stash. You'll be backstop when the tri-barrel reloads. Just don't shoot the mule in the ass by accident."

"How many of them are there?" Private Walton asks.

"Lots," Loftus supplies. "Twenty at least."

There's some unhappy tittering in the squad at that.

"You think we can hold off twenty Lankies with one tri-barrel and small arms?" Cooley asks.

"I don't think it'll come to that," Corporal Doran replies. "That airlock is fifty centimeters of titanium laminate. The locking lugs are two meters deep in solid granite. And the outer access tunnel is barely big enough for a mule. I doubt they'll be able to squeeze in that far."

"And if they do?"

"Then we'll shoot 'em," Doran says. "If they knock down the airlock somehow, they still have to get through one at a time. We'll plug the hole with the first one."

She takes a deep breath and lets it out slowly.

"We've got a hundred and forty people up there to protect. Whatever happens, we will hold the line. There's nowhere else to go. And if this is gonna be our day, make sure you've used up all your ammo before you show up down in hell. Got it?"

There's a low chorus of muttered "oo-rah" from the squad.

"All right." Corporal Doran nods with satisfaction. "Let's get to work. Last one with a confirmed kill scrubs the shitter."

The troopers disperse and take up their tasks. Alex walks up to Corporal Doran and clears her throat.

"Where do you want us?" she asks.

Doran points one thumb over her shoulder toward the Uptown ramp.

"I want you up there. We're going to lower the secondary airlock in front of the ramp. You should be on the other side."

"I'm on the team too," Alex protests.

"You're the dog handler. There's nothing for the dog to do right now. I don't want you down here if we need to start shooting. This place is all granite. Too easy for you or him to catch a ricochet. And you're not wearing armor."

"What about Clark and Blitz?"

"I already sent them up there," Doran says. "Now stop arguing. I don't have the time right now. If you're really on the team, you need to know when it's time to zip it and follow orders."

Alex knows that Doran's argument makes perfect sense—that she would only be in the way down here with Ash. She can't contribute to the fight without a weapon anyway, and she's sure that Doran wouldn't give her one if she asked. But as she leads Ash up the ramp, it still feels like she's being dismissed from the team right at the crucial moment when everything is on the line, only to wait with the other colonists for her fate to play out instead of being able to shape it a little.

When the secondary airlock door comes down behind her to seal off the rest of the Vault from the central vestibule, Alex has never felt more useless. Uptown is full of people now, everyone at their assigned emergency stations, but she is shut off from hers. She walks Ash across the upper cave, past the medbay and the galley, until she reaches the admin pod. Inside, administrators Conley and Velasco are standing in front of different consoles, each holding their own conversations with someone through the wired comms sets. Constable Morrissey is in the pod as well, geared up in his police armor. He has a small automatic weapon hanging from a sling across his chest. When Alex walks into the pod, he looks up at her from the screen he was monitoring.

"Shouldn't you be at your station?" he asks.

"Corporal Doran sent us up here. She says we'll just be in the way if there's any shooting."

"There's no good place to be in here if there's gunfire. That'll mean they breached the main airlock."

"Doran thinks it'll hold."

"I hope to God she's right," the constable replies.

Alex looks past him at the wall-mounted screen and feels her mouth going dry. The screen is now showing only four feeds. One of them is the image from the observation mast's optics. It shows a wide-angle view of the surface in front of the Vault's semi-hidden entrance. The square kilometer covered by the camera is dotted with Lankies. They have spread out on the plateau between the Vault and the abandoned settlement, and they're milling around, their head shields bobbing with the cadence of their slow steps.

"They're looking for us," she says. "It's a search."

Constable Morrissey turns around to see what she's looking at.

"Yeah. They're combing the area. They know we're here, but not exactly where. I'd love to know what tipped them off after all this time. Maybe you guys killed a few too many the other day."

Alex thinks about her hike to the top of the ridge with Lopez to call for help with the comms set, and she feels a sharp pang of guilt. Lopez said the transmission would only take a fraction of a second. She doesn't know how the Lankies can sense radio transmissions—nobody has figured it out for certain yet—but she is suddenly convinced that their emergency message is to blame, that it's her fault and Lopez's that there are more Lankies gathering outside the Vault right now than she has ever seen together.

"We showed them where to look," she says. "When we used the radio."

"We only received," Administrator Conley says. He has finished his low conversation, and he's holding the comms handset against his chest.

"We never sent a reply. And you sent that from sixty kilometers away. They probably spotted the mules and followed you home somehow."

Alex nods without much conviction.

"Doesn't matter now anyway, so don't dwell on it. You did what you had to do," Conley says.

On the other side of the pod, Velasco puts back her handset and looks around the room.

"Head count complete. Everyone's at their stations. We're as ready as we're going to get. For what it's worth." She exhales shakily. "God, I've been dreading this moment. I had almost convinced myself it would never come."

"We've played a running game of hide-and-seek with these things for eight years. It was bound to happen at some point," Conley says.

"Corporal Doran says they won't get through the airlock," Alex says into the silence that follows the administrator's words. They all turn their heads to look at her. She waits for someone to agree with that opinion or contradict it, but nobody does.

They know it's the end of the road, she thinks.

"Why don't you go and see if you can find a quiet spot for him?" Velasco says and nods at Ash. "Maybe that hideout of yours in the back of the cistern. It's bound to get noisy soon."

She locks eyes with Alex and nods her encouragement. "Go. Leave us to it. I'll see you later. If you run into Val, tell her the same."

Alex nods. She can't think of anything fitting to say as a goodbye to her best friend's mom, and her throat feels so tight right now that she's not sure she could squeeze out the words anyway. She pulls Ash's lead taut, and he jumps to his feet from his sitting position. She turns and walks out of the admin pod on legs that feel like her weight has suddenly tripled in the last few seconds.

CHAPTER 20

She's almost at the bottom of the ramp into Downtown when a deep, sonorous booming sound rings through the Vault. It feels like the cave floor under her feet is vibrating minutely at the same time. Alex stops in her tracks and reflexively looks up at the ceiling. Overhead, the fiber-optic lines for the environmental lighting are swaying slightly in the wake of the concussion that just traveled through the bedrock.

Her first thought is that the troopers have opened fire with one of the rocket launchers, and she turns to run back up the ramp to Uptown. A few moments later, the booming crash repeats. It sounds like someone dropped a giant metal serving tray onto the top of the mountain. When Alex is back on the overlook platform with Ash, there's a third concussion. The noise has a dull, metallic quality to it, and it takes her a moment to figure out that she's not hearing exploding rocket warheads.

They're at the airlock, she realizes. *They're trying to break it down.*

At the other end of the central Uptown corridor, the secondary airlock is still lowered, blocking her line of sight into the entrance vestibule where the soldiers have taken up their defensive positions. Up here, the booming crashes are much louder, and the shocks from the impacts are making the closed rolling door of the nearby constable pod rattle softly in its frame. Whatever is pounding against the outer airlock has settled into a rhythm now, a slow and relentless drumbeat of heavy thuds that feel like they're shaking the mountain itself: *boom, boom, boom.*

To her left, the door of the school pod stands open, and she can hear the titter of frightened young voices from within. She takes a few steps back to look through the door. Inside, the colony's teacher is half sitting on the edge of her desk, reading something off her tablet to the kids in the pod. Miss Buckler looks over at the door when she notices Alex. For a moment, the two women look at each other, and Alex is sure that the barely restrained fear on Steph Buckler's face is mirrored on her own. Then Miss Buckler looks down at her tablet again and continues to read out loud. Behind Alex, the thunderous booming sounds continue in the same slow cadence.

On an impulse, Alex pulls Ash close and walks up the few steps to the door of the school pod. When she stands in the door, the titter of young voices ceases, and every pair of eyes in the room is suddenly on her. There are only half a dozen school-aged kids left in the colony since her cohort of friends aged out, and they're all in the room, staring at her with wide and fearful eyes.

"Hey, everyone," she says and pulls Ash into the room with her. "I brought someone who wants to say hello. You remember Ash?"

At the sight of the dog, even the apocalyptic noises from the airlock lose their hold on the classroom's collective attention. As a military working dog, Ash stays in the kennel most of the time instead of roaming around the colony, and the young kids rarely get to interact with him. Having him in the classroom is a novelty that manages to get some smiles of delight even now. She walks into the middle of the room and sits down on the floor.

"You can come and say hi," Alex tells the kids. "Just be easy with him. He doesn't like it when you pull on his fur. And don't grab him around the neck."

The children get out of their chairs and gather around her and the dog. Before too long, Ash has six pairs of small hands stroking his fur.

She knows all these children, of course: Willis, Elissa, Malik, Pedro, Irene, and Lilia. The youngest, Pedro, is eight years old, born just two months before the Lankies upended their world. The oldest is Irene at twelve. Every young adult in the colony goes through monthlong apprenticeships for almost every job, to let them determine their aptitudes and make sure that everyone can do everyone else's tasks in a pinch. Alex spent a month in this classroom under Miss Buckler's tutelage, learning how to impart knowledge and deal with the daily challenges of keeping children busy and interested. Of all the apprentice months she had to do, the month in the school was the most exhausting one to her, far more demanding than harvesting soybeans or cleaning out clogged water pipes. All these young kids were born on this planet, and Alex feels an almost overwhelming sense of sadness at the thought that they will die here as well, long before they've had a chance to choose their own life paths, as limited as the options are for them in the Vault. But right now, they get to pet a dog, and if their world ends with that experience, it will at least end with a little bit of joy.

Miss Buckler walks over from her desk and kneels next to Ash and the kids to join in. When Alex looks over at her, she mouths a silent "thank you."

Outside, the thundering impacts continue. Alex knows the Lankies haven't managed to break down the airlock yet because she hasn't heard any gunfire, but she wonders how long it can stand up to so much relentless force.

"Why is he wearing a vest?" Lilia asks.

"Those are his clothes for work," Alex replies. "Remember how the dogs go out with us when we look for supplies? He's got all his stuff in the vest. His mask, so he can breathe outside. And his water bowl."

"He has a water bowl in there?"

Alex opens the pouch for the collapsible bowl and pulls it out. She flicks her wrist to open it, and it extends into its drinking shape with a little pop. Lilia chirps with delight, showing off the gap left by her missing front tooth.

"Can I give him some water?"

Alex hands her the bowl. "Sure."

Lilia jumps to her feet and dashes over to the classroom sink. She fills the bowl and brings it back, then places it on the floor in front of Ash. He sniffs it and politely laps up a few licks of water. Miss Buckler gets to her feet as well and walks back to her desk. She taps the embedded control panel, and classical music starts playing in the classroom. She opens a desk drawer and takes out a box to carry back to the group. When she puts it on the floor in front of her, Alex sees that it's full of dessert cookie bars from field rations.

"Everyone may pick one," she says.

The kids descend on the box in a flurry of movement, with some quiet bickering when a popular flavor quickly gets claimed first.

"Want one too?" Miss Buckler says and holds the box out to Alex when all the kids have grabbed a bar.

"Sure," Alex says. There's no lemon bar—there never is—but the kids left three blueberry ones, which are usually her second choice. Ash looks at her with interest while she unwraps it.

"Ah, what can it hurt at this point?" she says to him and breaks off a piece. He sniffs it and takes it gingerly from her open palm.

She makes the rest of the bar stretch, nibbling on it and savoring the taste of the sugar and the artificial flavoring. The hammer blows against the airlock ring through the Vault with a slow monotony that is starting to grate on her nerves.

The damn thing just needs to break it down so the squad can shoot it, she thinks. *Let's get it the fuck over with already.*

Miss Buckler seems to share the sentiment because she gets up and walks to the door to close it. When she passes her desk on her way back to the group, she increases the volume of the music.

"What are you learning about today?" Alex asks the kids, as much to distract herself as them.

"Earth," Willis says. He's the son of Constable Morrissey, and one of three kids in this group who has a living biological parent in the Vault. "The cradle of our civilization," he adds, intoning it like the first line in an educational video. "You know about Earth, right?"

"Yeah, I'm familiar with it," Alex says with a smile. "I was born there."

"Really? What's it like?" Elissa asks.

"I don't remember much. I was really young when my parents came here with me. Younger than you are now. I know we lived in a place with very tall buildings. And there was always a lot of noise."

"Did you know Earth has seasons?" Willis says.

"Yes, I did. Do you know *why* it has seasons?"

"Because of the axial tilt?" he hazards, and Miss Buckler nods her head with an approving smile.

"That's right," Alex says. "Who knows what the four seasons on Earth are called?"

Several hands shoot up reflexively, and Irene supplies the answer without waiting to be called on.

"Spring, summer, autumn, winter," she recites.

"It stopped," Pedro says in mid-chew.

Alex has been distracting herself with the conversation and her memories of Earth so well that it takes her a moment to realize that Pedro doesn't mean the planet or its seasons. The hammer blows against the airlock have just missed a beat or two in their steady cadence.

Alex exchanges a look with Miss Buckler. She holds her breath as they wait for the crashing booms to resume. She knows that the soldiers in the airlock will open fire with every weapon at their disposal as soon as the Lankies breach the lock. But there's no gunfire, no yelling, no sound of air-quality alarms blaring. Ten seconds tick by, then twenty, and the sudden silence outside is almost more unnerving than the battering-ram sounds. She wants to tamp out the little flame of hope that has kindled in her chest when a full minute goes by without another strike because she doesn't want the Lankies to extinguish it when they resume their assault.

They're trying to find a different way in, she thinks. *They gave up on the airlock, and now they're all over this mountain, checking for weak spots.*

Miss Buckler cocks her head very slightly. *What's happening?*

Alex shakes hers in the same almost imperceptible manner. *I have no idea.*

There's a little piece of her cookie bar left. She pulls it out of the package and holds it out to Ash, who plucks it from her fingertips. Alex stands up, mindful to make the motion slow and casual.

"Will you watch him for me for a minute?" she asks the kids, who each nod or voice their consent around a mouthful of cookie.

"Stay," she tells Ash and gives him the hand signal that goes with the command. She walks over to the door of the classroom pod and opens it to stick her head out.

There's an eerie silence out in the Vault. It feels like the whole colony is collectively holding its breath. The only thing she really hears over the background hum of the environmental system is the muffled din of voices in the nearby admin pod. She keeps listening for a few moments, but the banging from the airlock doesn't resume.

"I'll be right back," she says to Miss Buckler.

—

Over in the admin pod across from the classroom, the door is still open. Alex walks in and sees the three people in the pod standing in front of the big monitoring screen on the back wall, covering the view of the screen with their bodies.

"What's going on?" Alex asks, and all three heads turn toward her.

"I thought I said for you to find a quiet spot for the dog," Gina Velasco says.

"I did. He's over with the kids in the school pod. What's happening?"

"Looks like Corporal Doran was right," Administrator Conley says. "They didn't manage to break the airlock."

Alex walks into the middle of the room to get a better look at the screen. The screen is still split into four different views. One view shows the inside of the entrance vestibule, where the soldiers are still in position, their weapons pointed at the airlock. Another view is the stream from the camera above the airlock on the outside. Whatever was pounding on the door is no longer there. Instead, Alex sees the familiar view of the entrance tunnel and the landscape beyond the tunnel mouth.

"Where did they go?"

Administrator Conley enlarges the view of one of the quarters until it fills out the entire screen. The answer to her question is made obvious by the sight of two dozen Lankies from the high angle of the observation mast's optics. They're moving away from the cave mouth and dispersing in different directions. One small group is moving to the left of the camera's field of view, in the direction of the plateau where the mule broke down and Lopez sent their emergency call. Another group, bigger than the first one, is striding out of the right edge of the view, back toward the abandoned settlement. A few individual Lankies are walking off in what looks like random directions, as if they're unsure which group to follow.

"What are they doing? Did they just . . . give up?" Alex asks, fully aware of the ludicrousness of the notion that one slab of titanium alloy has stopped so many Lankies cold after they finally came across the hideout of the last humans on this planet.

"Damned if I know," Constable Morrissey says. "But I don't really care, as long as they're going away."

"They'll be back," Conley replies. "Now that they know where to find us."

There's a new sound reaching Alex's ears, a low and steady rumbling. It's so faint at first that Alex thinks she may be imagining it, but as she tries to home in on the source, she can tell from the way Morrissey and Velasco cock their heads that they've noticed it as well. Gradually, it increases in volume until it's louder than the background noises of the Vault. It feels like the entire mountain over their heads is trembling the tiniest bit. Then the sound fades into inaudibility again, as gradually as it had come.

"What the hell was that?" Morrissey asks.

"Earthquake," Velasco replies.

"There's no *earthquakes* on this rock," Conley says. "You know it's geologically inert."

"It *was*. God knows what these things have done to it in the last eight years."

Conley lowers the magnification of the lens on the observation mast until the field of view contains all the Lankies again as they walk away from the Vault's entrance. From this height, the off-white bodies and cranial shields look tiny, like a bunch of insects scurrying around on the red-and-brown surface. Conley slowly pans the optics to the right, back in the direction of the settlement, where the bigger group of Lankies is headed.

For a few moments, Alex's brain refuses to parse what she is seeing on the screen when the camera's field of view pans over the ruined town. There are clusters of lights coming out of the sky, descending onto the settlement like emergency flares dropped from high altitude. They emerge from the clouds and spiral down in slow, wide arcs. When they're just above the crushed and broken domes of the town's buildings, they continue parallel to the ground and swarm toward the airfield beside the settlement in regular intervals. One by one, they start to descend the last few dozen meters to the surface and begin setting down on the ground.

"Oh my *God*," Administrator Velasco says, but the tone of her voice is rising with jubilation instead of dread or despair.

Ships, Alex realizes when she sees the orderly lines of light forming on the far-off airfield runway. *Those are spaceships.*

Constable Morrissey laughs at the screen with a hand in front of his mouth. Conley looks back at Alex, and she can see that the administrator's eyes are filling with tears. Velasco lets out a high-pitched squeal Alex has never heard out of Val's mom. Then she hugs Administrator Conley and tries to lift him off the floor, which is most definitely something Alex has never seen her do.

Something white and very fast streaks into the camera's field of view from the direction of the light show on the airfield. A moment later, bright red-and-orange fireballs start blossoming in front of the approaching Lankies, who are still a kilometer away from the settlement. There's a second lightning-fast object that transits the screen too quickly for her to make out in any detail. Astonished, Alex watches as the fireballs start multiplying until the plateau between the Vault and the town is crisscrossed with long patches of hundreds of expanding fireballs rising into the sky. The sound of the explosions reaches the sensor head's microphones a few seconds later, a stream of rapid-fire booms and cracks that seem to go on for half a minute. When the noise finally abates, there's nothing but a glowing carpet of orange and red between the airfield and the middle of the plateau. To her amazement, Alex can make out a few individual Lankies coming out of the inferno at the edges of the fire, ablaze and trailing white smoke. She watches as they collapse one by one, still burning brightly, and twitch violently a few times before lying still.

The constable lets out a jubilant shout that sounds like a war cry.

"Get some, you bastards," he hollers, with a wild joy she has never heard in the voices of any of the adults in the Vault.

Administrator Conley turns up the magnification and zooms in on the airfield. The spaceships already lined up on the runway are joined by more every few seconds, a seemingly unending procession of bright lights coming out of the clouds and descending swiftly and with precise spacing between them. There are people pouring out of the backs of the newly arrived ships, and hundreds of them are already on the ground behind the rows of ships.

"What are they?" Alex asks.

"Military drop ships," Constable Morrissey replies. "I've never seen the type, though. Could be the Russians or the Chinese."

"I don't give a shit if it's the NAC, the SRA, or the goddamn Icelandic Coast Guard," Conley says. "They're *our people*. They're humans from Earth."

"Those are short-range attack craft. There's got to be a carrier task force in orbit right now."

Alex can't tear her eyes from the screen. There are so many people out there on the airfield already, many more than in the Vault. At this distance, they're a little indistinct, small silhouettes moving around behind the bigger shapes of the landing ships, but they're unmistakably human in the way they move. She hasn't seen a spaceship in the air in so many years that the sight of them is a little surreal, as if she just slipped into a different reality.

"Get the comms antenna up," Conley says to Velasco. "This is a large-scale landing. There has got to be radio chatter all over the place."

Administrator Velasco activates the communications array with a flurry of taps on her control screen. A graphic pops up on the side of her screen, a visual aid showing the extension status of the antenna, and Alex wishes she could hurry it along by sheer will as the antenna crawls up the shaft to the top of the mountain.

When the comms panel finally shows a green light, Administrator Conley takes over the console.

"Haven't had to do this in ages. Let's take a listen. Frequency scan is active."

He puts the audio feed on the admin pod's speakers. At first, Alex only hears white noise, the low static hiss of a dead frequency. Then the radio tunes in on one with active transmissions. They're not words, just short bursts of electronic chatter that sound like two machines talking to each other.

"What the hell is that?" Velasco asks.

"Encrypted military comms," Morrissey replies. He has walked up to the comms console, and now he's looking intently over Conley's shoulder. "That's a new algorithm. We don't have the encryption keys for that."

"So we can't talk to them?"

"We can," Conley says. "We can talk in the open. It doesn't matter at this point. It's not like the Lankies don't already know where we are."

He taps the controls for a few moments.

"Here we go. Standard colonial emergency band, unencrypted."

Conley picks up the wired comms handset. He looks at the other people in the room and smiles curtly.

"I never thought I'd ever use this thing again, to be honest."

Conley clears his throat and squeezes the transmit button.

"Mayday, mayday, mayday. This is Scorpio Alpha. Is anyone receiving me?"

He repeats the transmission, then lets go of the send button on his handset with a long exhalation.

The seconds tick by in the nearly silent admin center as they're waiting for a response. Just as Conley lifts the handset again to repeat the broadcast, the reply sounds from the speakers. It speaks in a crisp and terse military cadence, with a North American accent.

"Unknown station broadcasting on an open channel, please identify yourself. I repeat, party broadcasting in the clear, identify your station."

"This is Scorpio Alpha One, Colonial Admin center, Chief Administrator Charles Conley. Who is this?"

The next reply takes even longer than the first one, twenty seconds of silence that makes Alex's anxiety spike again.

If they're here for us, why are they asking who we are? Shouldn't they already know?

"Alpha One, this is the NAC Defense Corps, Task Force Normandy. What is your status and location, over?"

Conley exchanges a look with Morrissey before replying.

"Task Force Normandy, we are in the old colonial operations center, two point two kilometers to the southeast of the Scorpio City settlement. What's left of it, I mean. We see a whole lot of activity on the airfield. The Lankies just paid us a visit but you torched half of them and ran off the other half. What do you want us to do, over?"

The next reply comes much faster.

"Alpha One, please advise your personnel head count. We will relay to the assault team and send assistance. Do you require medical attention?"

"Negative on the medical, Normandy. We're all fine here. Head count is one hundred fifty. That's one five zero personnel, over."

"Alpha One, copy one five zero personnel, no medical emergencies. Stand by on this frequency. The mission commander on the ground will contact you shortly to coordinate your evacuation. Wait for their arrival and let us take care of the rest."

"We'll have more of these things coming our way very soon, Normandy," Conley replies. "This is the first time we've made an active transmission in eight years. They'll home in on it, have no doubt."

"Alpha One, copy that. If they do, they'll do our flyboys a favor, and save us some fuel and time. There are four carriers in orbit, with twenty warships in support. You have a heavy regiment of SI on the ground two klicks away and two more coming down right now. Let the Lankies be our worry. You're safe now, over."

When Conley ends the communication and returns the handset to its cradle, he still looks like he's in disbelief. While Morrissey and Velasco laugh and cheer, he puts his palms on the console in front of him and lowers his head. Then he exhales, and Alex can practically see the tension starting to leave his body. He stands in that hunched-over position for a few moments before he straightens up again and picks up the handset. When he presses the transmit button, the soft chime of a general announcement rings out overhead.

"Everybody, this is Conley. You may stand down from emergency stations." He pauses and takes a shaky breath before continuing. "The Lankies are gone from the neighborhood. There's an NAC task force in orbit. They are landing their ships on the airfield at Scorpio City right now. We're safe now. At long last."

His voice breaks on the last sentence, and he hangs up the handset without the customary sign-off. When he looks up, Alex sees that he has tears rolling down his cheeks.

"Two years in," he says. "That's when I stopped hoping that this day would come."

Velasco is now crying as well. She quickly walks up to him and embraces him in a tight hug.

Alex feels relief, but no elation like the other people in the admin pod. The ups and downs of the last hour have left her exhausted. She turns and walks out of the admin pod to leave the others to their celebration.

Outside, there's no chorus of cheers in the Vault, no shouts of elation. The need for silence is too ingrained in everyone after all these years of avoiding all unnecessary noises. But there are people coming out of pods now, looking dumbstruck with joy and relief, talking to each other in low and excited voices as they emerge. As Alex walks back to the school pod, Dr. Bailey comes out of the medbay next door, followed by Lauren and Alex's friend Kari. Kari rushes over when she sees Alex and gives her a hug that almost squeezes the air out of her.

"Easy there, Monaghan. I don't want to asphyxiate *now*," Alex tells her.

"I never got to see you after you came back in," Kari says. "We were so busy with Blake. I thought I'd never see you again."

Now there are suddenly so many people out of their pods at the same time that their many low-volume conversations have added up to an impressive background din that keeps getting just a little louder every moment. The spot where Alex and Kari are standing is right in front of the admin pod, and people are walking up to gather in front of the door for more news. Alex nudges Kari over to one side until they stand next to the door of the school pod to make space for all the curious and elated colonists who are coming up the ramp from Downtown.

"Listen, I need to get Ash and bring him downstairs to his kennel. It'll get busy in here very soon," Alex says.

"All right, all right," Kari replies and gives her another hug, this one a quick one-armed squeeze. "Hey, I'm ever-so-fucking glad we won't die after all."

"We won't die *today*," Alex cautions. "Probably. But we'll almost certainly die at some point."

Kari laughs and turns to walk with the crowd that's heading for the inner airlock.

Alex walks up the steps to the school pod's door and opens it. Inside, Ash is still where she told him to stay, lying down on all fours in the middle of the classroom. The kids are still huddled around him, surrounded by empty cookie wrappers. Miss Buckler walks around her desk and hugs Alex as well.

"We're all right," Alex says to her in a low voice. "They're all right."

She turns toward the children, who are watching with great interest.

"Big news," Alex says. "It's a good thing you all brushed up on Earth knowledge today. Because there are people from Earth here right now. They're going to take us with them."

"Today?" Irene asks.

Alex nods. "I think so. They're on their way right now."

Most of the kids look excited at the prospect of this adventure, but Irene looks upset by the news. When Alex steps into their middle to collect Ash, she kneels next to the dark-haired girl with the big eyes and the serious expression.

"You're not happy about going away?" she asks.

"I'm not sure," Irene says. "I don't really want to go. All my friends are here. And my stuff."

Alex smiles at the girl's earnest face.

"You'll get to take your stuff with you. And all your friends are coming as well. All right?"

Irene nods, but it's a slow and unsure nod. Alex strokes the hair on top of Irene's head.

"It'll be okay. I'm a little scared too. But we can't stay here right now. It's not safe for us anymore. And we're all going together. We'll be back before you know it."

The girl nods again, this time a little more assertively, and rewards Alex's pep talk with a tiny smile.

Ash hops to his feet as soon as he sees Alex reaching for the leash. She kneels in front of him and gives him a hug as well. He tolerates the violation of his dignity stoically, possibly in hope of some more treats as compensation.

"And you're coming too, stinker," she tells him, suddenly buoyant with the elation that's permeating the Vault outside now. "There are so many new smells out there, you're going to lose your mind."

CHAPTER 21

When the massive main airlock starts to open, Alex is almost convinced that the Lankies have bent it out of shape with their blows, that it will seize in its frame any second as the interlocking halves separate. But the big white slab of titanium and nanocarbon opens as slowly and steadily as ever, locking into its wall recesses with a muffled thump.

A full squad of soldiers is lined up behind the airlock with their weapons held at low ready. They slowly walk into the central vestibule in patrol formation. Their armor looks different from that of the garrison squad's troops, sleeker and more angular, and painted with a new camouflage pattern. The faces behind the helmet visors are the first new ones Alex has seen in almost a decade. They're all big and strong and bulky and armed to the teeth. Behind them, Alex can see more soldiers on the plateau beyond the access tunnel and the flashing position lights of several drop ships.

Doran steps forward to greet the trooper in the lead, who strides ahead to meet her. She stops and renders a sharp salute.

"Welcome to the Vault, sir. Corporal Doran, NCO in charge of the garrison squad. You have no idea how glad we are to see you."

The trooper returns her salute. "Captain Grant. First Battalion, Tenth SI Regiment." He looks at the other troopers behind Doran. "Is that the entire garrison?"

"Yes, sir. What's left of us."

The garrison troopers come forward and meet up with their newly arrived counterparts. The contrast between the older, battle-worn uniforms and armor of the Vault troopers and the advanced new gear the newcomers are wearing is jarring, as if the two groups belong to entirely different militaries. Alex stays behind Doran. For the first time since she started going out on missions with the squad, she feels like an outsider.

Behind the newcomers, the orange warning light on the ceiling starts rotating, and the airlock closes again. When the air-warning light jumps from orange to green, the garrison troopers take off their helmets, and the new arrivals follow suit one by one.

"You have no idea how glad we are to see you," Doran repeats.

"I can imagine," Captain Grant replies. "I'm sure you all have one hell of a story to tell."

Alex looks at all the new faces, and she is glad that she had a chance to bring Ash back to the kennel right before they arrived, because she has no idea how he is going to react to seeing unfamiliar people.

For a few moments, there's lots of handshaking and shoulder patting going on between the two groups. She sees curious glances from the new soldiers in her direction, as she is the only person in the group wearing a civilian jumpsuit instead of a uniform and battle armor.

The inner airlock in front of the Uptown ramp rattles open and retracts into the ceiling. At the top of the ramp, both administrators and the colonial constable are stepping over the threshold. Behind them, Alex can see dozens of people standing on the overhang in front of the airlock. When the colonists see the new soldiers, someone cheers. The dam broken, the crowd starts clapping and cheering loudly. None of the administrators attempt to curb this breach of Vault noise protocol. They stride down the ramp and walk over to the spot where Doran and Captain Grant are standing.

"Conley," the chief administrator says and shakes hands with the captain. His hand almost disappears in the palm of the soldier's armored glove. "I'm the colony lead. This is Gina Velasco, my second in charge. And Constable Morrissey."

Captain Grant shakes hands with all three colony leaders. Alex is painfully aware of Blake's absence from the tight-knit little group. Blake worked as hard as any of them to keep the Vault running, and he died less than a day before the rescue, when the soldiers that just walked in were probably already gearing up for their mission.

The captain looks up at the cheering and clapping crowd at the top of the ramp.

"How many people do you have down here?"

"A hundred and fifty total," Velasco replies.

"And you held out for all this time. Unbelievable."

"We did what we needed to do," Conley says. "There was no alternative."

"No, I suppose there wasn't. *Sergeant Armstrong*," he shouts over his shoulder.

One of the troopers from the new group jogs up from behind.

"Sir."

"Get on the link with TacOps. Let them know we're going to need enough birds down here for a hundred and fifty pax plus kit. It's still a hot LZ, so tell them not to dawdle. I want these people out of here and in the air within the hour."

"Aye, sir." Sergeant Armstrong trots back to the group and puts his helmet back on.

"Where's your senior NCO, Corporal?" Captain Grant asks Doran.

"He's KIA, sir. Sergeant Frye. Also Corporal Bayliss, the other section leader. They died three days ago on a mission."

"I'm sorry, Corporal. I really am. I know it's no consolation, but they'll get all the honors when we lay them to rest at home. And the rest of you—dear God. You're going to be the most famous faces in the Corps very soon. Holding out in this place for as long as you did."

"Yes, sir," Corporal Doran says stiffly. "We held our own."

"And with these antiques," the captain says with a glance at the nearby mule with its scuffed and battered exterior. "Unbelievable," he says again.

He turns to the administrators.

"I need everyone ready for evacuation in forty-five minutes. Personal effects only, one bag per person. Do you have enough breathing units for everyone to make it to the drop ships once they are on the ground?"

"Yes, we do," Administrator Conley replies. "But we can't secure the data storage modules and put the reactor into safe mode in forty-five minutes. We'll need a few hours for that."

"You'll keep everything up and running. The Corps engineers will sort it out when they get here. But this is now a combat zone. The enemy is going to come at us with everything they have, now that we've made our presence known. When things get hot down here, I can't spare any personnel to keep all these civilians safe."

This place has been a combat zone for eight years, Alex thinks. *And we all managed okay. You just said so yourself.*

She looks at Doran's face, and she can tell from her pinched expression that the corporal is chafing at the way this officer assumed command.

"What about the garrison, sir? We have arms and munitions to account for down here. I can't hand everything over without a proper inventory and command transfer," Doran tells the captain.

"Today you can," he replies. "I relieve you of the responsibility, and I am taking charge of the garrison as of right now. Get your people ready for evac and be ready to get on the drop ship in forty-five, Corporal."

"I stand relieved," Doran replies. She flicks her arm up in a quick and sharp salute.

"You heard the captain," she shouts at the Vault troopers, who are now intermingled with the new arrivals. "This will be quick and dirty.

Get your gear and get ready for dustoff. Final roll call in front of the firewatch pod in thirty. Snap to it, folks."

Back at her pod, there's not much to pack because nobody in the Vault really owns anything beyond their clothes, and most of those are the standard colonial jumpsuits the facility had in storage with the emergency supplies. She was wearing civilian clothing when the Lankies came and they had to make a run for the admin center, but she was twelve at the time, and she long since handed those clothes to one of the younger kids once she grew out of them.

Alex fills a bag with a few spare sets of jumpsuits and underwear. She has a second pair of boots that are in slightly better shape than the ones she is wearing right now, and she sits down on the bed to swap them.

There's not much personal stuff in her pod. Her most precious possession is her father's knife, which never leaves her pocket. The minimal amount of items in her desk drawer worth taking are the book reader she kept from school—one of the few things the colony had in surplus—and a scattering of small items crafted for her by her friends on various occasions: little figurines made from painted rocks or reshaped scrap material that escaped the reclaim bin on the way to the recycler, a stainless steel cup engraved with her name by Dallas with an electric pen. She wraps the handful of keepsakes in a clean undershirt and tucks them into a corner of her bag, then places the book reader on top of the small stack of clean jumpsuits. When she's finished, the little kit bag with her name on it is still pitifully empty. Alex goes to the bathroom to collect her few toiletries.

The last items she takes are the photographs of her parents on the wall above her bed, printed out years ago from their personnel files. Alex carefully pries the little laminated sheets from the wall and slides them between two layers of clothes in her bag.

Then she's packed and ready to go. She sits down on the bed again and looks around the pod that has been her home for the last three years. Like almost everyone else, she personalized the walls a little with various items—pictures of pretty or interesting things, etched into polymer sheets with a color laser by the school printer. The walls around the door are adorned with a wreath of Earth wildflowers, hand-painted by Val using pictures from the Earth botany section of the teaching database. It's a small pod, and it's the same size and shape as every other living pod in the Vault, but it was hers for a long time, and Alex feels a sudden, aching sense of loss at the thought of leaving it behind forever.

She stands up and walks out of the door before that feeling can grow and take hold. With all that has happened in the last week, there are many things to be sad about right now. Having to leave her tiny living capsule behind for good shouldn't even make the list.

CHAPTER 22

"We will leave in groups of thirty," Administrator Conley says. He raises his voice to just short of a shout to cut through the conversations of all the people lined up on the main walkway in the Uptown cave. "Quiet down and listen up, please. Have your masks ready. Constable Morrissey will check you off the list before you enter the airlock with your group. Don't worry about staying with a particular group. We're all going to the same place at the same time."

Up ahead, she can see movement ripple through the line as people try to count off to figure out if they'll be in a group with their preferred companions despite Conley's directive. She's standing near the back of the line with Val and Dallas. Athena and Luther are farther ahead, together as usual, and Alex already pities the trooper who tries to separate those two if one turns out to be thirtieth in line. This far back, it makes no sense to even try to count the heads ahead of her, so Alex doesn't bother.

"This is it," Val says. "No more soy harvest. No more shit scooping in the treatment plant." She has always been the bubbliest member of their group, relentlessly positive and cheerful, but right now she's absolutely giddy with excitement.

"I just hope we're not heading somewhere worse," Dallas says.

"Can't be worse than this," Val scoffs. "Wherever they put us, at least we'll get to go outside again. We've been locked in for eight years. Well, except for the Space Commando here." She nods at Alex.

"Outside isn't all that great," Alex says. "Not anymore."

The line starts moving in predictable intervals as the inner airlock admits thirty of their number every few minutes. When Alex and her friends get to the front of the line, Constable Morrissey is waiting with his data pad. He checks their masks and marks them on his list.

"Two minutes and you're out of here," he says. "Take one last look around."

"I need to get Ash out of the kennel," Alex tells him. "I'll have to go with the last group. I need five minutes to get him ready and packed."

He looks at her in mild surprise.

"He's already gone. Private Clark took Ash and Blitz with her. They went on the first drop ship."

The constable's words feel like a physical punch in the stomach, and she looks at him in wide-eyed disbelief.

"That was *my* task," she says.

"He's a military dog, Alex. He went with the soldiers."

"He'll be scared on that drop ship," she says. "He's never flown before. I should be next to him."

"I can't help that. You'll see him up on the ship. Now put on your mask and give me a thumbs-up for function. You're holding up the line here."

She puts on her mask with trembling hands and slides open the valve to the air reservoir. When she smells the stale air from the emergency tank, she gives the constable a thumbs-up, and he nods and ushers her through the inner airlock into the central vestibule. To her right, the military section is busy with activity, but all the troopers she sees are new arrivals in their intimidating angular battle armor. She suppresses the urge to run down the ramp and make sure Ash is really no longer in his kennel. Not being able to check on him feels wrong, and the disappointment makes her eyes fill with tears. Behind her, the vestibule fills up with the next batch of thirty evacuees. Val and Dallas join her, aware of the reason for her dismay, and Val squeezes her shoulder lightly.

"Morrissey's right, you know. You'll see him again in thirty minutes," Val says, her voice muffled by her mask. Next to her, Dallas tugs on one of the straps of his own mask and shifts it around a little on his face.

"You got it twisted," Alex says. She reaches out and fixes his rubber mask strap.

"Thanks," he says. "I have no idea how you can stand hours and hours in these things for days on end. I only wear mine when there's a drill."

"Be glad. They give you zits like you wouldn't believe," she replies.

Over by the main airlock, the alarm sounds and the orange warning light starts flashing.

"Shit," Val says and grabs Alex's hand. "Gonna be completely frank here. I am kind of scared."

Alex gives her friend's hand a reassuring squeeze. "It's fine. I've been outside a hundred times."

"I can deal with that part. *Probably*. I'm just not so sure about the whole 'going into space' thing."

"We've done it before, Val. We got here on a spaceship."

"Yeah. When we were in diapers," Val replies. "Not the same at all."

The main airlock doors pull apart as the lock starts its opening cycle. Two SI troopers are standing just outside in the access tunnel. When the doors have retracted fully into their recesses, the troopers wave them on.

"This way, people. Single file. Let's go, let's go."

They follow the directive and walk through the airlock into the access tunnel and then into the open space beyond. When they come out of the mouth of the tunnel, Val gasps in shocked astonishment, and Alex can't help echoing her. She has seen the landscape outside of the airlock many times, but it has never looked like this. The horizon in the distance is crimson red, as if the planet below their line of sight is glowing red-hot. On the plateau in front of the Vault, three military drop ships are lined up wingtip to wingtip with their tail ramps open, position lights blinking and landing lights pouring out wide pools of illumination between the ships and the tunnel entrance. A few hundred meters to the right, the ground is still ablaze with countless little fires spread over half a kilometer. There's smoke rising from dead Lankies on the ground everywhere, their bodies still enormous in scale despite the distance. Beyond this field of death and devastation, the airfield in the distance is a hive of activity, more landing lights on the ground and descending out of the dark sky than Alex can hope to count.

"Keep it moving," one of the soldiers shouts behind them. *"They're dead, they can't hurt you."*

Another soldier is standing in front of the drop ship on the right, directing them around the immense war machine with a fluorescent green wand. Once the ships' landing lights are no longer blinding her view of their hulls, Alex sees that all three are painted in a bright white, with orange markings on their wings and long light strips along their hulls.

"Still scared as shit, but this is the coolest thing I've ever seen," Val yells at her over the roar of the drop-ship engines.

On the tail ramp of the drop ship, two troopers wave them along into the hold, where two rows of fold-down seats are lining the padded walls of the compartment.

"Go all the way to the back. Fill the rows from back to front. Back to front," one of the soldiers instructs. Alex picks the left row and claims the first seat right next to the bulkhead. Val drops into the seat next to

hers, clutching her bag like a lifesaver. When Alex straps in, she finds that the safety harness is the same design as the ones in the mule, and she tightens all her straps with practiced fingers before leaning over to help Val and Dallas, who are fumbling with theirs. The rest of their group quickly fills up the other seats in both rows. Even before the last colonists are in their seats, the two soldiers come in from the tail ramp and go down the rows to check and adjust safety straps.

"Put your bags on the floor between the rows. All bags on the floor. No loose bags on your laps."

Alex does as she's told and places the little kit bag with her stuff on the nonslip lining of the deck in front of her feet. The soldier who's checking the harnesses picks it up and moves it to the middle of the floor between the rows. The soldiers repeat the process on both sides of the drop ship until all the bags form a neat row on the centerline. When they're finished, they detach a cargo net from the overhead liner of the compartment and drape it over the luggage row, then hook the sides of the net into receptacles set into the floor and tighten the webbing until the row of bags is tightly wrapped and held down. One of the soldiers folds down a seat on the bulkhead in front of Alex and straps himself in as well. The other pushes the button for the tail ramp and sits down in the last free seat at the end of the row. Alex snatches a last glimpse of the planet's surface through the slowly narrowing gap as the ramp closes. The horizon is still red, and even the bottom of the cloud cover in the distance looks like it's on fire.

It looks like the end of the world, she thinks.

The drop ship's hold has no windows, and even though the ride into orbit is the most bone-jarring experience of her life, Alex wishes she could see her world from above one more time. From the flights with the puddle jumpers she took with her parents to go out to the spaceport once or twice a year, she remembers wide fields of red and brown under a ragged cloud cover. But she consoles herself with the knowledge that the old world of occasional sunshine and breathable air no longer exists, and that she would just be looking at the other side of the perpetual dark cloud blanket that has covered the entire planet for years now.

Next to her, Val has given up on squeezing Alex's hand every time the drop ship hits a particularly rough spot in the atmosphere because the bumps are so frequent now that she'd have to squeeze almost continuously. Instead, Val has just made herself small in her chair, and every time the ship gets jolted, she closes her eyes and clenches her teeth.

"We are going to die," she says to Alex with a tone that conveys absolute certainty. "This thing will come apart, and we'll fall out of the sky. I hope a heart attack gets me before I hit the ground."

"No, ma'am," the trooper sitting next to Alex says over the roaring of the engines and the creaking of the ship's hull. "We've got the best pilots in the Fleet. They've flown in much worse. And this is a brand-new ship."

"Where are we going?" Alex asks the soldier.

"We're going up to the carrier. After that, I'm heading back down. I don't know what they'll do with you. But I'm sure they'll put you somewhere safe."

They had to scramble to call the ships down for the evacuation, Alex realizes. *And they don't know yet where to put us. They had no idea we were still alive.*

"You didn't expect to find us down there, did you?" she asks.

The trooper shakes his head.

"We came to take the planet back. This is a miracle. It made the whole thing a success already, right from the start. Everyone's talking about you. The whole task force heard your radio call."

He shifts and turns toward Alex and Val as far as his harness will allow.

"Can I ask how you managed to survive for so long down there? I mean, we lost that colony seven years ago."

"Eight," Alex corrects him. "Eight years and three months ago."

"We went underground," Val answers for her. "We closed the door. And we didn't answer it whenever they came knocking."

The soldier laughs. "That simple, huh?"

"We got lucky," Alex says. "That's the truth of it. We were just close enough to the Vault when they showed up. Everyone else died."

The smile quickly drops from the soldier's face. "I'm sure that must have been rough."

"You have no idea," Alex replies.

"They'll go crazy back home when they hear about you. Everyone's going to want to hear your story. This has never happened before."

"Nobody has ever been rescued from the Lankies?"

"They rescued a few hundred from Mars. Some science station, I think. But they had a fully stocked nuclear shelter. And they got picked up within a year. They didn't hold out seven—eight years," he corrects himself.

The thought that Earth wrote them off years ago, that this rescue was just a lucky coincidence, makes her angry and dismayed at the same time, and she sits in silence for a little while to let the two emotions fight it out. But then she looks around in the hold while Val talks with the soldier, and despite the scary turbulence shaking the craft every few seconds, she sees upbeat faces and smiles. Even Val has forgotten her fear of flying momentarily as she chats up the trooper, and her friend is clearly happy to have a new face to talk to after so many years of seeing the same ones every day.

It doesn't matter, Alex tells herself after the initial swirl of negative emotions has settled. Whether their rescue was a lucky coincidence or not, everyone in the Vault would be dead or dying now if it hadn't happened. Letting herself feel anything other than gratitude for that unfathomable luck would be tempting fate in the worst way, she decides.

CHAPTER 23

The drop ship's tail ramp opens onto a new world.

Everyone in the hold is craning their necks to see what's waiting for them outside. The space beyond is brightly lit and so expansive that it looks to Alex as if they're on the surface of a sunny planet and not inside a spaceship.

When they've all unbuckled and gathered their things and the first colonists are walking down the tail ramp, led by one of the soldiers, there's a noise starting up outside that sounds like a rainstorm is passing overhead. As Alex steps off the end of the ramp and onto the deck of the carrier, she realizes that it's applause. All over the immense expanse of the flight deck, hundreds of soldiers and deck personnel are cheering and clapping at the new arrivals. The wave of sound washes over her like a storm gust, and combined with the sights in front of her, it's enough sensory overload to make her feel disoriented for a few moments.

There are dozens of smaller military spacecraft of all sizes lined up on the flight deck, which stretches for hundreds of meters. The ceiling of this deck is easily twice as high as the one in the Downtown cave, which was tall enough to accommodate living pods stacked four levels high. It looks like it could fit the entire Vault in it with room to spare, even with the underground lake. The noise in here is incredible to her ears after all this time in the Vault. There's the thrumming of engines, the whining of hydraulic machinery, the buzzing from the electric motors of utility vehicles carrying ordnance or equipment, and the din from hundreds of voices. Nobody here makes any effort to moderate their volume. On the contrary, it sounds like they're having a contest to see who can cheer and whistle the loudest.

Next to Alex, Val and Dallas appear as thunderstruck by the sights and sounds as she is. Even Val, who is the least shy among her friends, seems to wilt a little under the weight of all this focused attention.

The soldiers lead them across the flight deck, and the applause and cheering follow them like a wave whenever they pass by groups of personnel. Alex wants to take in all the sights and sounds, but there's so much here that trying to process it all is more than she can ask of her brain right now. It's too loud, too bright, and too full of new faces, and when the soldiers lead the line of colonists through a bulkhead door and into a passageway, she's thankful for the relative silence inside the ship.

The soldiers shepherd them through the narrow confines of the ship's interior for what seems like half a kilometer. Every time they encounter crew members in the passageways, Alex sees smiles and hears words of encouragement. Finally, their long procession through the carrier ends in a large room that looks like a mess hall. Alex sees that the other colonists who went up in the earlier drop ships are already here, sitting around tables in small groups and talking in low Vault voices. There's a long counter on one side of the room that has trays of food and a lot of drink dispensers on it, along with stacks of plastic plates and cups. Two officers in unfamiliar blue-and-teal uniforms are standing near the door, obviously keeping an eye on things.

"Please help yourself to food and drink and find a place to sit down," one of the officers says to the newcomers as they file in. "Someone will be along shortly to take your personal information and get you processed."

Alex looks around in the room for Private Clark and Ash, but she can't spot them in the crowd even after a quick round of the mess hall.

The garrison soldiers should be obvious in the crowd, but the only people in the room wearing a uniform are the two officers by the door.

"They're not here," she says to Val when she rejoins her friends in the line for the food counter. "None of our soldiers are here."

"Neither's Conley. The constable isn't here either. Wonder what they're doing," Val says.

"Someone's gotta tell the new troops where everything is," Dallas chimes in. "Conley and Morrissey are the only ones who know all the access codes. They're probably still shutting everything down in the Vault."

"I can't even imagine the place empty," Val says. She spots someone in the back of the mess hall and waves at them. Alex follows her gaze and sees Athena and Luther, sitting around a desk with Lauren and Dr. Bailey.

"Well, at least the Misfits are all accounted for," she says.

"I was having visions of Dallas or Luther sleeping off a little buzz in the Cove and missing the evacuation call," Val says, and Alex chuckles at the mental image of a bleary-eyed Dallas walking into a silent and empty Downtown cave and wondering where the hell everyone went.

The galley counter has trays full of sandwiches on it, assembled with bread slices that are perfectly uniform in thickness and shape, and layered with a variety of ingredients that Alex hasn't seen on a lunch plate in a very long time: sliced meat and cheese and leaves of fresh green lettuce. She picks a sandwich at random and fills a cup with vitamin drink, marveling at the bright and vivid orange color of the liquid in its clear dispenser. Next to her, Val loads up her plate with two sandwiches.

"Hungry, are we?" Alex asks.

"Who knows when they'll feed us again? If I can't finish this now, I'll stick it in my bag for later."

"It doesn't really look like they have any shortages around here. There's nobody watching how much we take."

"Better safe than sorry, I say. Don't come crying to me when you get hungry tonight and they closed the mess hall," Val says.

They sit down at an empty table, and Val wastes no time taking a big bite of her sandwich. She starts chewing and lets out a muffled groan.

"Oh my *God*. This is the best thing I have ever eaten in my life," she says with a full mouth.

Alex cautiously bites off a corner of her sandwich to check the veracity of Val's claim. There was never a shortage of calories in the Vault, but everything was a variation of the few things they could grow in the hydroponic farm: lots of soy, beans, spinach, and potatoes. She was never hungry, but she also never had a desire for seconds. The piece of sandwich she is chewing right now feels like it's waking up taste-bud regions on her tongue that have been dormant for years.

"It's like I am eating in color," Val says around another mouthful of sandwich, and Alex laughs at the strange accuracy of the statement. She picks up her glass and takes a sip of the orange beverage only to do a double take at the intensity of the flavor.

"Holy crap, that's sweet," she says.

"Piece of advice, ladies," Dr. Bailey says from behind them. "Your digestive tracts aren't used to processed food. Don't eat too much or you'll regret it later today when you have to camp out on the toilet."

"Thanks for the image," Val replies. She takes a bite from her sandwich. "If I do, it'll be worth it. That's not even soy. That's real meat."

"Sort of," Dr. Bailey says. "The worst parts of the animals. The little chunks of meat that stick to the bones. All pressed through a mechanical separator, ground up finely, and laced with salt and preservatives. Enjoy your lunch, girls."

She pats Val on the shoulder and moves on to the next table, and Alex grins.

"Boy, she really knows how to sell somebody on Earth food," Val says dryly.

In the middle of their meal, a dozen Fleet officers with data pads in their hands walk into the mess hall and spread out in the room to go to different tables. One of them comes to the spot where Alex and Val are sitting.

"Good afternoon," he says. "I'm Lieutenant Kinsey. Can I sit down and get your personal information?"

"Sure," Alex says and nods at one of the empty seats across the table from her.

"Thanks." He sits down and puts the data pad on the table in front of him. "Can I start with you?"

"I guess."

"I don't suppose you still have your NAC passcard?"

"No, I don't," Alex replies. "It was a little busy on the day when the Lankies came. We didn't get a chance to grab anything."

"I can understand that. Not a problem. Let's start with your full name and date of birth."

"Archer, Alexandra," she says. "Seventeen November 2103."

He takes the information down on his pad.

"Any family in here? Are you related to anyone in this group at all?"

She shakes her head slowly.

"My parents both died when the Lankies came. Anna and Gregor Archer." She tells him their birthdates as well.

"I still remember my colonial ID number," she adds. "I memorized it a long time ago, when I was bored in school."

He looks up from his data pad with a smile. "Sure. Let's hear it."

She rattles it off, then repeats it to show him she's not just making up a string of numbers. He finishes taking down the ID number and smiles at her again.

"Very impressive. That will make my job very easy," he says. "I can pull everything I need right out of the colonial database."

"Can I ask you something, Lieutenant?"

"Certainly," he replies.

"Where are the soldiers that were with us? Corporal Doran, Private Lopez, and the rest? I don't see them anywhere."

"They're down in what we call Grunt Country," Lieutenant Kinsey says. "The part of the ship where the SI regiment is housed."

"And the dogs? There were two dogs with them. Ash and Blitz."

"If they came up with your SI troopers, they went to Grunt Country too. Everything that came with them on that drop ship."

"Can I go and see them? I really want to check on my dog."

He shakes his head with an approximation of regret on his face.

"No civilians allowed down there, I'm afraid."

She bristles with sudden indignation.

"I've been around them every day for years. I've gone on patrol with them. I'm one of the handlers for the dogs. An hour ago, we were getting ready together to fight Lankies. And now I can't see them? Just because we're up here instead of down there?"

"Those are the regulations. Sorry."

He moves on to Val's side of the table and starts asking her the same questions—name, date of birth, next of kin. Alex swallows hard and only realizes she had made a tight fist with her right hand when she feels her fingernails digging into her palms.

Dismissed. I just got dismissed again.

She suppresses the urge to give the lieutenant a good slap to the side of the head. It's one thing to get sidelined by Corporal Doran, who has known her since she was twelve, but another matter entirely to have it done by this Fleet lieutenant she just met two minutes ago, someone who doesn't know her at all, doesn't know anything about life in the Vault or any of the people in it.

Val must be sensing her emotional state because even while her friend is busy answering the lieutenant's questions, she puts her hand on Alex's thigh underneath the table and gives it a light squeeze.

Alex takes a slow, deliberate breath. She knows what the squeeze says because Val is Val, and Alex knows her better than anyone else alive.

Easy there, it says. *We'll sort it out later. Just don't get us both thrown in the brig.*

—

A few hours into their stay on the carrier, Alex concludes that the military really loves making people stand in line, because it feels like she's been doing almost nothing else since they came on board. After waiting for their turns for medical checkups in sick bay, they spend a good while in yet another queue of colonists while the Fleet officers assign them temporary quarters in an empty berthing section deep inside the ship. Finally, she gets to claim a two-person berth with Val, and she's glad to have a door again that can be closed to lock the world out.

"This is like old times," Alex says when they stow their bags and claim their bunks. When they shared a pod together, Val got the upper bunk because she's tiny, half a head shorter than Alex, and they assume the same arrangement in this berth automatically. The berth is tiny as well, much smaller than the pod they shared in the Vault for years, but Alex doesn't mind the tight quarters. After the flight deck and its overwhelming assault on her senses, she's happy to have a room that wraps around her like a comforting blanket.

"How long do you think it will take them to get the Lankies off the planet?" Val asks her from the upper bunk.

"I have no idea," Alex says. "I mean, they wiped out two dozen of them in a heartbeat when they arrived. But there's thousands of Lankies down there. Maybe tens of thousands. And most of them hide out underground."

"So *not anytime soon* is what I'm hearing."

Alex reaches up and touches the bottom of the top bunk with her fingertips. It's so low above her head that she doesn't even have to extend her arm all the way.

"I wish they could get it done in a week or two, Val. But think about it. Even if they could kill all the Lankies right now, it'll take ages to rebuild all those terraformers."

"I know, I know." Val dangles one leg over the edge of her bunk. "We're never going back to the Vault, are we?"

"I don't think so," Alex admits.

"So that's it, then," Val says after a brief silence. "No more Misfit Cove."

"No more farm chores either, though. And no cleanup duties."

"Don't tell the others, but there were days when I didn't mind those too much."

"I know what you mean," Alex says. "Sewage patrol can fuck right off, though."

"Yeah, not gonna miss that one either."

They listen to the sounds of the ship all around them for a while. There's a steady, low, humming vibration that's not unlike the constant background noise in the Vault. In the semidarkness of their berth, Alex could almost imagine they're back in their old living pod if it wasn't for the completely different smell. The warship has a particular scent to it that has been in her nose since she stepped out of the drop ship, a smell that's a mix of floor cleaner, new plastics airing out, and the ozone scent of warm electronics. Her jumpsuit still smells like the Vault, though, and she wraps one arm across her face and buries her nose in the fabric.

"What do you think is going to happen to the Vault?" Val asks.

"I think they'll use it for the military, as a command center. That's what it was built for in the first place."

"Makes sense. It feels wrong, though, doesn't it? The thought of all those strange soldiers down there. Going through our stuff. Sleeping in our pods. Hanging out in our places. Eating the veggies we planted."

"Finding our old alcohol stash in the Cove," Alex says, and Val chuckles.

"They'll have no idea what went on in there over the years."

"If they did, they'd cleanse the place with fire and fill it with concrete to seal it forever."

The laugh they share is interrupted by a loud alert tone outside in the passageway, followed by an announcement.

"General Quarters, General Quarters. All hands to combat stations. Set material condition Zebra throughout the ship. This is not a drill."

Alex sits up with a jolt and hits her head on the bottom of Val's bunk.

"*Ow*. Shit."

"That sounds serious," Val says and jumps off her bunk. "What are we supposed to do? Where are our combat stations?"

Alex swings her legs over the edge of the bunk.

"I have no idea. Check outside in the corridor. Maybe there's someone there who can tell us where to go."

Val walks the two steps to the door and tries to turn the handle, which doesn't budge. She tries again with the same result.

"It's locked. That's just great."

"Guess our combat station is going to be right here," Alex says and rubs the top of her head.

"I suppose so," Val replies. Instead of climbing back into her bunk, she sits down next to Alex. Outside, the sounds of the ship have changed to a much busier cadence. They hear the pounding of boots on the decks around them, hatches slamming shut, and shouted commands.

"I really hope that's just a security thing to keep us out of the way," Val says. "I'd hate to be locked in and miss the ride out of here if they call to abandon ship."

"They wouldn't have come this far out to pick a fight if they weren't pretty sure they can hold their own," Alex replies. "I hope. Or this will be a very short rescue mission."

"I'm sure you're right," Val says. "I'm still going to freak out a little if you don't mind."

—

Sitting in the semidarkness of their tiny compartment with nothing to do at all except listen to whatever is unfolding feels scarier to Alex than even the Lanky assault against the Vault's airlock a few hours ago. She doesn't know the nature of the threat that made the ship go on alert, and the lack of awareness makes the anxiety much more potent somehow. Val exchanges worried looks with her every time there's a new unfamiliar sound.

Alex has lost track of the time they've spent in the berth since the general quarters alarm sounded when a low rumble goes through the hull that makes the deck under their feet vibrate. The rumbling is followed by a thump that travels through the ship from somewhere deep below.

"What the hell was that?" Val demands.

"Beats me," Alex replies. "Sounded big, though."

The long rumbling sound repeats, followed by the same concussive thumping noise. Then there's a much louder rumble, and the entire ship shudders for a moment. Val looks at the ceiling as if she expects the deck above to fall on her head or disappear into space any second. Alex reaches over and squeezes her hand. For a long while, they sit silently, waiting for some clue to figure out what just happened.

Outside in the passageway, the alert blares again, and the sound makes Alex jump a little.

"Cancel General Quarters. I repeat, cancel General Quarters. All hands, stand down from combat stations. All departments, resume operations."

Over by the door, there's the faint electric sound of a lock retracting. Val gets up and tries the door handle. She pulls the door open and looks outside. The lights in the passageway switch from the red combat stations lighting to normal illumination.

"Guess we won," Alex says. "Whatever we just fought. I'm pretty sure that was a missile launch we heard."

Val closes the door again, then changes her mind and opens it once more. She leaves it slightly ajar as she walks back to the bunks and climbs up into hers, where she lies down on the mattress with a shaky little groan. The light from the passageway spills into their berth in a narrow strip that runs across the floor and splashes against the bulkhead to their right.

"Well, shit. How am I supposed to go to sleep after *that*?" Val says from above.

"You could go see someone in medbay for some sleep aids," Alex suggests. "Or focus on your breathing. You know the trick."

"That shit never works for me," Val replies. But Alex hears her starting to take deep, slow breaths anyway. After a while, her friend's breaths turn shallower and more regular, and she can tell that Val has drifted off to sleep despite her protestation.

Outside in the passageway, there's the sound of boots on the deck as people walk past the open door. Alex stands up and goes to close it quietly. She stretches out on her own mattress and puts her arm across her face again to take in the scent of her jumpsuit.

It's just like being back in the Vault, she thinks. *Val and I are sharing a pod. The world is pretty okay, and tomorrow morning I get to have breakfast with my friends before we head out to do our chores.*

Above her head, Val's slow breaths turn into soft little snores, and even as Alex starts to drift off herself, she smiles at the realization that she finds the sounds soothing instead of annoying.

CHAPTER 24

"I haven't been marched around this much since kindergarten," Val says when they walk into the mess hall the next morning, again chaperoned by two Fleet officers at the front and the back of the line.

"They really want to make sure we don't stray into places we're not supposed to be," Alex replies as they queue up for breakfast trays. The escorting officers had peeled off from the group when they entered the mess, and now they're hanging out by the door again to keep an eye on everything.

"Well, it is a warship. I'm sure there aren't really any places we're *supposed* to be." Val is a little bleary-eyed, and her wavy, shoulder-length hair is tied up in a loose ponytail. She loads up a plate with scrambled eggs and a few strips of soy bacon, then picks up a ketchup bottle and squirts a lattice pattern of messy red lines across the eggs. Alex makes up her own plate and follows Val to a free table.

"Mind if I join you?" Gina Velasco walks up behind them with her breakfast tray. Val's mom looks even more tired than her daughter, and when she sits down, she lets out a hearty yawn.

"You look like you haven't slept in days," Alex observes.

"I haven't," Administrator Velasco says. "I may have nodded off a few times last night. But this place is just so noisy all the time. All these announcements and signals. I don't know how anyone can sleep on this thing." She takes a sip of her coffee and looks at Alex and Val over the rim of her cup. "How are you two doing?"

"Fine," Val replies. "Not much to do up here other than sit on our butts, though."

"Where are Administrator Conley and Constable Morrissey?" Alex asks. "I haven't seen them around yet."

"They're still down in the Vault," Velasco replies, confirming Alex's suspicions from yesterday. "Conley's not going to leave without a full copy of the data modules. And those soldiers need to be shown how we run things down there. I'm sure they'll join us as soon as things are wrapped up."

"Did someone bring the burial capsules?" Alex asks.

"Of course we did. Those were our friends and family." Gina Velasco looks at her daughter when she says the word "family." "Your grandfather used to have a saying from the old country. He used to say 'that guy jumped off the devil's shovel' whenever he heard of someone getting out of a dangerous spot by a hair. Well, we really jumped off the devil's shovel yesterday, let me tell you."

"What are we going to do now?" Alex asks. "I mean, when we get to Earth."

Mrs. Velasco wraps her hands around her coffee cup and sighs.

"I have no idea, to be honest. I never made plans for that possibility. But we still have family on Earth. I suppose we'll go to where they are once everything is sorted out."

She looks at Alex. "What about you? Do you have people back home?"

The question throws Alex off for a second. She doesn't think of Earth as *home*. Home to her is the planet below, where she has spent almost all her life, and where her parents and so many of her friends died. But she knows what Mrs. Velasco means, of course, and she supposes she may as well start getting used to the idea.

"I don't really know," she says. "I have an uncle. My dad's brother. But I only know him from some pictures. My dad never really talked about him. I think they had a falling out before my parents left for the colony. I don't even know where he lives. Or whether he's even still alive."

"I'm sure they can find that out for you. All the information is instant on Earth. No waiting for a supply ship to deliver the mail."

There's movement at the front of the mess hall, and Alex looks past Mrs. Velasco to see more officers walking in. Alex is far more familiar with enlisted and NCO ranks because the Vault garrison never had an officer leading it, but she recognizes the insignia of a colonel on the oldest-looking of the group, a short and hard-faced fellow with a scar that crosses one side of his forehead diagonally and ends on the bridge of his nose.

"Good morning, everyone," he says to the room. He has the voice of someone who is used to talking to groups at an assertive volume. "No need to get up. Enjoy your breakfasts and please take your time."

The clattering of utensils on plates stops, and the conversations die down as everyone turns their head to listen.

"I'm Colonel Prescott. I'm the executive officer of this ship. Let me begin by saying that it's an honor to have you on board. What you all managed to accomplish in the face of extreme adversity is nothing short of awe inspiring. Our work here in 18 Scorpii has only begun, but being able to evacuate all of you means we've already been successful far beyond our most optimistic hopes."

He waits out the pleased reactions from the colonists for a few moments before he continues.

"That said, we don't have you all out of danger yet. As I mentioned, our work here has only begun. This system is an active combat zone now. I'm sure you all heard the combat stations alert a few hours ago. We got accosted by three enemy ships that objected to our presence in the neighborhood. We managed to, *uh*, sternly decline to cooperate with their attempt to evict us."

There's some chuckling in the crowd, and Colonel Prescott smiles briefly.

"But while missiles are flying, you're not safe. And they'll be flying for a while yet, I'm afraid. The task force is in the middle of a full-scale planetary assault. This battlecarrier is going to be in the middle of the fighting, and it's a major target for the enemy. It's not a place for civilians. Therefore, we have decided to get you out of here and back to Earth as quickly as possible."

He checks his wrist computer.

"The frigate *Concordia* is currently commencing docking operations with this ship. We are detaching her from the task force with the sole assignment to bring you home safely. She'll be escorted by a battlecruiser all the way back to the Alcubierre point, where she will make the transition back to the solar system. She's one of the fastest ships in the Fleet, so you'll all be home in six days."

There's that word again, Alex thinks. *Home.*

After breakfast, their officer minders lead the colonists back to their quarters, and for the second time in just two days, Alex packs up her few belongings and leaves without knowing where she'll be sleeping next.

The passage from the carrier to the frigate is a large docking collar made out of telescoping segments that move slightly as the colonists walk through it in single file. Just like the drop ship and the carrier, the collar has no windows to allow Alex one last view of her home planet as she shuffles through the flexible connection to the other ship. When she passes through the airlock of the frigate, she's greeted by another array of smiling faces and thumbs-up gestures, and she returns the smiles politely even though she doesn't feel a reason to be upbeat right now. A new set of officers is standing ready to take over the escort duties, and their previous chaperones wish them well and head back to the transfer collar to return to their own ship.

Everything is smaller about the frigate than the carrier they just left. The passageways are narrower, the ceilings are lower, and the distances between the deck bulkheads much shorter. But if the carrier was new, this frigate just came out of a shipping crate, because Alex can tell that everything on board is being used for the first time. Even the paint on some of the doors and bulkheads smells fresh, as if it has been applied only very recently.

Their new escorts lead the colonists down several decks and to a berthing section that looks like it doesn't quite match the age of the rest of the ship. There's an open space at the front that has exercise equipment lined up along the bulkheads on either side, as if it has been moved in a hurry to clear the space. On the bulkhead, a big crest shows a stylized eagle holding bolts of lightning in his claws, diving toward the semicircular outline of a planet's hemisphere, the branch logo of the Spaceborne Infantry she knows well from the patches on the uniforms of the Vault garrison. Unlike the rest of the ship, this section looks and feels like it has been lived in before, and Alex hopes they didn't just evict a bunch of grunts from their shipboard homes to make space for the civilian passengers. When she asks one of the officers about it, he laughs and shakes his head.

"No, ma'am. This is the berthing module for the garrison companies we transfer out to the various colonies. They only stay in here for the ride. Not that we wouldn't kick out the grunts for you, mind."

The berths are on either side of two long passageways at the back of the module. They're even smaller than the ones on the carrier, and each of them has four bunks instead of two. For the next ten minutes, there's a great deal of discussion and reshuffling of bodies in line as people try to bunk up with their preferred podmates or partners. Val claims a berth for them, but with the limited space on the frigate, Alex has no illusions about the odds of keeping the four-person unit to themselves. When Athena and Luther pass by in the passageway, she pulls Athena into the berth to redirect them.

"We wanted to have our own," Athena says.

"I don't think that'll happen," Val replies. "There's a hundred and fifty of us squeezing in here. Count the doors. Nobody gets a private room. Now get your asses in here unless you want to bunk with some of the kids. Or maybe my mom."

The thought of having to bunk with Administrator Velasco or a pair of elementary-school children seems to horrify Athena sufficiently to obey Val. She drags Luther in behind her. With all four of them standing in the berth, it's too crowded for anyone to move around. Val climbs up on one of the top bunks and tosses her bag onto the mattress with her.

Athena inspects the beds.

"These are tiny," she says.

"So are you," Val replies. "You'll be fine. And you guys can sleep in separate bunks for a few days. *Please.* I'm not up to trying to go to sleep while you try to figure out how to do it in a shoebox."

They all stow their things in the drawers underneath each mattress. Alex is happy to see that the individual bunk nooks all have privacy curtains. She draws hers shut and lies down on her bed to try it out. With the curtain closed, it's a tight space, but surprisingly comfortable in its snugness, and the curtain seems to block at least half the volume from her friends' conversation on the other side.

"This isn't so bad," she proclaims when she opens the curtain again. Across the berth from her, Athena is trying out her own bed. She gives Alex a look that makes it clear she doesn't share her assessment.

"At least it's not six days in the back of a mule," Alex tells her. "Just think. You and four soldiers. Sharing one chemical toilet."

She laughs at the look of horror on her friend's face at the description of the scenario.

—

With her things stowed, Alex leaves the compartment to give her friends a bit more room to unpack their own gear. She walks into the open space at the head of the berthing module to check out her surroundings a little. There are small bathrooms on the ends of either of the two passageways, and a larger one in the middle, this one with two shower stalls. It's all sparse and utilitarian, but everything is clean and neat, and not much different from the facilities in the Vault.

There's nobody standing guard in front of the module's open door, and she steps across the threshold and ventures out into the passageway beyond. At the end of the passage, she sees the stairwell they used to come down to this deck. Alex walks up to it and decides to test her range of freedom by going up a deck.

At the top of the stairwell, a Fleet officer is standing near the door to the next deck, looking at a data pad in his hand. When he hears her coming up the stairs, he slips the pad into the side pocket of his uniform. She recognizes him as the one she asked whether they had to evict a bunch of SI troopers for them.

"Sorry, ma'am. I'm going to have to ask that you stick to the auxiliary berthing deck while you're on board. They're going to open the mess for you down there in about an hour if that's what you're looking for."

"I'm just snooping around a little," Alex says with a smile. "Probably not the best idea on a warship, is it?"

"No, ma'am," he says and returns her smile. "Too easy for you to get lost on the ship. Or open the wrong hatch somewhere and accidentally flush yourself out into space."

"Does that happen a lot? Seems like a safety flaw."

"Once or twice a week, tops," he says, and she laughs.

Overhead, an alert tone sounds, followed by an announcement.

"Prepare for undocking. Secure docking collar and all auxiliary support lines. Airlock chief, report readiness to CIC."

"Looks like we'll be on our way shortly," the officer says. "Bet you can't wait to get out of here."

She looks at his rank insignia and the name tag on his uniform.

"Lieutenant Morales, is it?"

"Yes, ma'am."

"I'm Alex," she says. "No rank."

"Nice to meet you, Alex, no rank," he says. After all these years in the Vault, she doesn't have any flirting skills that she's aware of, but she can sense by the way he's looking at her when she's talking that he doesn't mind her presence at all.

"This may sound stupid to you, but is there anyplace on this ship that has windows? Any place I'm allowed to go, that is."

He shakes his head.

"No windows on a warship. There's a heavy cruiser class that has an observation dome on the armor saddle. That's a good spot for stargazing. But this ship doesn't have one. Sorry."

She doesn't try to hide her disappointment.

"That's too bad. I really wanted to look at the planet one more time. I'll probably never get to see it again."

"Oh, you just want an outside view?"

Alex nods.

"That's easy enough," Lieutenant Morales says.

He gets his data pad out of his pocket again and taps the screen for a few moments. A screen projection materializes in the space between them, and he expands it with a gesture to increase the size of the frame.

"Let's see. External views—lateral array—starboard side. And here we go."

The screen fills with a view of the planet below the ship. Alex can't tell which part of her world she's seeing because the cloud cover conceals the features and shapes of the continent. She knows it's just a laser projection of a camera feed from the outside of the hull, photons filtered and transmitted through many layers instead of reaching her eyes directly, and that she isn't technically looking at the planet directly, but her breath catches in her throat for a moment anyway.

Morales puts the data pad on the deck in front of the bulkhead. He flicks the projection against it and enlarges the frame until the image fills as much of the wall as possible.

"How's that?" he asks.

"It's amazing. Thank you," she says.

On the bulkhead in front of her, the clouds are doing their perpetual dance, roiling and billowing, swirling in enormous patterns driven by the restless atmosphere. A quartet of drop ships appears in the frame and hurtles toward the maelstrom, their position lights disappearing one by one as they enter the tops of the clouds a few moments later. It's not a very exciting view, one she has seen many times from the other side of the layer, but she can't take her eyes off the screen.

"Do you mind if I look at it by myself for a minute?" she asks.

"Not at all," Lieutenant Morales says. "I'll be on the other side of the door. Take your time."

He steps across the threshold and closes the door behind him.

Alex slowly sits down on the deck next to the data pad. The square frame of the projected screen makes it look like there's a window in the hull after all, even if the lines are slightly distorted by the shape of the bulkhead.

She knows that the bodies of her parents are probably long gone, skeletal remains at best, and most likely collected and used by the Lankies for some awful purpose. But the molecules and atoms that made up those bodies are forever part of this world now, and this is the closest she will ever be to those echoes of their existence for the rest of her life.

Goodbye, Mommy. Goodbye, Daddy. Thank you for everything. I love you.

The tears she feels welling up are unwelcome, not because she is ashamed of the feelings that produced them, but because they blur her vision and obscure her last view of her home planet. She wipes her eyes with the sleeves of her jumpsuit, and the sob she can't suppress echoes in the confines of the stairwell.

CHAPTER 25

The image of the green-and-blue planet fills almost the entire screen projection on the galley bulkhead. It looks exactly like it did in the pictures in the school database, a beautiful orb of green and blue and brown covered in white swirls, gleaming in the darkness of space like a gemstone on a black cushion. But there's also something different about it, and it takes Alex a little while to figure out what it is.

It's not the planet, she decides. *It's everything around it.*

The pictures in her schoolbooks didn't convey how *busy* Earth is. There is movement everywhere she looks. Hundreds of spaceships are silently gliding across the screen in front of that tapestry of bright colors, lined up in various orbits with their position lights blinking. Smaller, faster dots of light are flitting around everywhere, satellites and atmospheric craft at high altitudes. There's a massive space station slowly crossing the planet's equatorial bulge, and Alex can see hundreds of spacecraft of all sizes docked on the station's many extensions like clusters of pods on a soybean plant.

The mess hall is crowded with Vault colonists. Almost everyone wants to get a good look at Earth as the frigate is approaching the planet. Alex feels the same wonder she sees on the faces of her friends, who are standing next to her in the crowd. Even the usually unflappable Val is stunned into silence by the view. From the camera's perspective, a third of the globe is shrouded in night, but that darkness is studded with millions of bright lights, big clusters of them connected to each other in a tightly knit web of streets and maglev lines.

This is it, Alex thinks. *This is where almost every human that ever existed has lived and died.*

Behind her, the older colonists are chatting and laughing, pointing out continents and geographical features to each other, talking about things that have changed since they left. She has no real memories of the day her family went up to orbit in a shuttle to get on a colony ship to 18 Scorpii. There's nothing on the screen in front of her that triggers any sort of association in her mind beyond the shapes of the continents she had to identify and label in Earth Studies class. But it's undeniably pretty—the snow-capped mountain ranges, the glint of sunlight on the oceans—and the thought of being able to go outside without a mask and see blue skies again makes her feel a tingle of anticipation.

"All departments, prepare for arrival. Commencing docking maneuvers in ten minutes."

"All right," Val says at the announcement. "Time to pack up. I can't wait to get off this thing."

The view on the screen is from a bow camera tracking the planet, so Alex doesn't see their destination move into their field of view until they're already on approach to the docking arm. The scale of the station is mind-boggling. There are dozens of docking arms extending in regularly spaced intervals from the central part of the station, many hundreds of berths for spaceships, and a lot of them are occupied by ships of all sizes. The frigate is larger than most of them, but next to the station, it looks insignificantly small, like a minnow swimming up next to a whale.

"Look," someone says in an excited voice. "Look at that."

Every ship in the camera's field of view, whether docked or floating freely, is flashing its running lights in unison as the frigate glides toward the station. In front of the ship, above the berth they're approaching, a large sign on the outer hull scrolls the words **WELCOME HOME, HEROES** in enormous letters. Several smaller craft are accompanying the frigate on a parallel course now, and Alex can see multiple optical arrays pointed in their direction, tracking the ship as it makes its way to its orbital parking spot.

"Guess word got out," Alex says.

"Welcome home, heroes," Val says next to her. "Do you feel like a hero? Because I don't."

Alex just shakes her head. The sentiment of the greeting feels a little overdone, granting them all a status that Alex feels she didn't ever come close to earning. If their group had heroes among them, they were the ones who died—Sergeant Frye, Administrator Blake, the soldiers and techs who were crushed or swept into a chasm many light-years from here—and they can't appreciate the message on the sign. All she did was hide in a cave behind a thick airlock and hope the monsters would go away.

"Maybe they use the word a little differently here," she says to Val.

The first time Alex feels genuine awe about anything having to do with Earth is the moment she steps from the frigate's airlock onto the space station.

The docking concourse on the other side is a long extension that juts out several hundred meters from the main part of the station. There are docking berths and airlocks on both sides of the concourse, each with a sign that displays the airlock number and the name of the docked ship. In between the airlocks, there are large polyplast windows that afford a spectacular view of the hulls of the ships and the planet below. It's an overwhelming panorama of technological prowess that shocks her senses and makes her feel like she just stepped into a place belonging to some advanced species. She moves out of the way of the people coming out of the airlock behind her and walks over to one of the large windows to put her hand on it. The material feels cool and smooth under her palm.

Not a screen, she marvels. *Just a clear window into space.*

Val walks up next to her and puts her hand on the window as well. They both stare out at the scene on the other side, all the ships arriving and leaving, and the planet spread out in front of them, a brilliant tapestry that's alive with light and movement.

"This isn't so bad," Val says. "Can't deny the view."

"No, you can't," Alex agrees. "It's the most beautiful thing I've ever seen."

They gaze at Earth in silence for a little while. The line where the day turns to night is nearly bisecting the planet now, the advancing night leaving a galaxy's worth of little points of light in its wake.

"Valeria," Mrs. Velasco calls out from the back of the line of people that's forming in the center of the concourse. Alex and Val turn their heads.

"Come on, you two. I want us to stick together. You have no idea how busy this place can be."

"It's like we're eight years old again," Val says in a low voice as they walk to catch up with her mother. "If she tries to hold my hand, I'll lose it."

—

As soon as they walk out of the docking section, Alex hears cheers and applause. Dozens of soldiers and civilian techs are standing out in the middle of the concourse to welcome the arriving colonists. A group of Fleet officers and important-looking people in civilian dress are waiting just outside the connector, and Administrator Velasco, as the ranking colonist in the group, makes her way to the front of the line to be the first to greet them. Alex can't make out what they're saying to each other because of the din from the crowd, but all the smiling and handshaking gives her a good idea. After a few minutes, the formalities seem to be finished, and the Fleet officers take the lead and usher them along the concourse. The applause and cheers follow the colonists as they make their way through the station. Alex sees several people with camera rigs in the crowd trying to keep up with them, wearing professional-looking setups mounted on steadying arms that are strapped to their bodies with harnesses. They're shouting questions that are all but drowned out in the general commotion. The sudden attention by so many people is almost overwhelming, and Alex is glad when the Fleet officers at the head of the line lead them off the main concourse and into another docking section. This one has been roped off with security tape strung across the connector's entrance, and several uniformed soldiers with white armbands are standing guard behind the barrier. They retract the tape to let the colonists through, giving them friendly nods and smiles as the group files past them into the docking section. Alex and Val are at the back of the line, and the soldiers on guard close the symbolic barrier behind them, locking out the handful of people with cameras who have managed to keep up with their group.

There's only a single airlock at the end of this docking concourse. The Fleet officers who escorted them line up on either side of it to see off the colonists as they go through the airlock and onto the ship beyond.

"Honor to have you here," one of them says to Alex, who is the last one to board. "Welcome back. Best of luck on Earth."

Val is right in front of her as they enter the ship. When her friend steps into the cabin, she looks around and flashes a grin back at Alex.

"It has windows," she says.

The craft they are boarding is much smaller than the frigate. The interior compartment is only a few meters wide, just enough space for two double rows of seats on either side of a center aisle. The windows on the side of the hull Val pointed out are small circular portholes, set into the flank of the ship in regular intervals that line up with each row of seats. They make their way past all the occupied seats until they get to the rear of the craft, where plenty of rows are still empty. Val dives into one and claims the seat by the porthole window. Instead of sitting down next to her friend, Alex ducks into the next row and slides over to the window seat behind Val.

"Do I smell bad or something?" Val sniffs her armpit.

"I wanted a scenic seat too. It's our first trip to Earth, you know. But yes, you do smell."

When all the colonists have stowed their things and settled in, a pair of crew members come down the aisle, stopping at every seat row for safety checks and tucking away loose gear quickly and efficiently. Not ten minutes after they stepped aboard, the craft's airlock closes, and the hull vibrates with the thrumming of propulsion systems coming to life.

The window seat turns out to be a redundancy because numerous screen projections appear on every bulkhead and divider in the cabin that begin cycling through exterior views of the craft. The imagery from the high-definition optics of the ship is much superior to the view Alex is getting from the porthole, whose transparent inset is so thick that the straight lines of the docking area's edge seem to curve at the corners of the window, but Alex turns her attention away from the projections after a few moments. She decides that she wants to experience the world outside with her own eyes rather than through yet another screen.

—

Alex vaguely remembers the puddle jumper rides she had to take back to the main spaceport on Scorpio with her parents every year for the medical annuals and school exams, and she recalls that they were bumpy and noisy every time. The descent into Earth's atmosphere is much more comfortable, a smooth and quiet ride that only gets a little dramatic when they enter the denser layers of the atmosphere, and the view from her window turns into a peek into the core of a fusion reactor, white-hot plasma streaming past the porthole and activating the automatic dimming feature of the glass, which turns gradually opaque until it's black. There are a few little jolts and rattles, but this ride is nothing like her puddle jumper flights, or the harrowing ascent in the drop ship that convinced Val they were going to fall out of the sky. When the craft levels off after the entry burn, the window next to Alex's seat turns clear again.

The view through the thick polyplast makes her gasp. In the seat in front of her, Val makes a similar involuntary expression of astonishment. The shuttle is high above a landmass that stretches from one end of the horizon to the other. The sky is a stunning gradation of colors, from the almost black near the edge of space to the cloud-streaked light-blue haze just above the surface. The craft is streaking through the sky much faster than any puddle jumper. Alex cranes her neck a little to peek past the bottom edge of the porthole to look at the ground underneath the shuttle's broad triangular wing. It's strange and a little disorienting to see a blue sky that isn't covered with dark clouds, and she knows that it will take a while before she is used to the sight again.

As they descend, the landscape comes into sharper relief, gradually resolving into lakes and rivers, snow-topped mountain ranges, and sprawling cities, huge grids of countless immense buildings that take minutes to cross even at the shuttle's dazzling speed. The scale of it is almost inconceivable to Alex. Every few moments, they are flying over a thousand times more buildings, a million times more people, than existed on her entire home planet when it was still a thriving colony.

The scenery below changes from the ordered geometry of cities to rough and unkempt landscape again, with smaller patches of urban sprawl that grow increasingly far apart as the shuttle gets closer to the ground. The craft has slowed its descent, and it banks into wide turns now, following some invisible traffic pattern, and Alex cranes her neck to look at the streets and buildings below, much easier to make out in detail at the slower speed and lower altitude, until they are so low that she can see individual vehicles and people down there and make out the words on the holographic signs that seem to be lighting up every intersection, even if the names and slogans on them hold no meaning for her.

She has been on an atmospheric craft before, so she knows the procedure of landing on a runway, but when they are barely above the ground, her brain still wants to convince her that the shuttle is about to plow into the ground and disintegrate. Then she sees blinking lights rushing past just below the belly of the ship, and a moment later the threshold of the runway appears, a second or two before the thumping from underneath signals that the shuttle's wheels have touched down safely. Outside, sensor masts and large, utilitarian buildings are lining the side of the runway, unfamiliar craft parked in long rows in front of them. She's surprised that the ground beyond the buildings is not all that different from the surface of her home planet just outside the Vault, a rugged landscape shaded in red and brown. In the distance, a low mountain ridge rises into a sky that shows patches of blue peeking through the gaps in the cloud cover.

The shuttle's engines reverse their thrust, and the craft slows rapidly until they are rolling along slowly enough that a mule on low throttle could keep pace with them. It turns off the runway and onto a large concrete apron that's crowded with drop ships, lined up in neat rows with precise spacing between them. People in uniform are everywhere, loading up the cargo holds of drop ships, pushing carts with equipment and ordnance, or driving small utility vehicles along traffic lanes marked on the apron with bright yellow paint.

Their orbital transport comes to a slow stop next to a pair of vehicles Alex has only ever seen in pictures, long and tall, with large windows that show rows of seats inside, a smaller Earthbound version of the shuttle that brought them down from the station. The Fleet officers that are accompanying them are out of their seats and in the aisle of the shuttle.

"Welcome back to Earth, everyone. When you leave through the airlock in a few moments, please mind your step on the air stairs, and proceed to the buses that are waiting for you on the apron next to us."

"Where are we going?" Alex asks one of the officers as he walks by her seat row.

"There's a facility set up for you here on base, ma'am," he replies. "They'll tell you everything you want to know when you get there."

The shuttle empties out gradually from front to back. Alex gets in line to exit the airlock at the front of the craft. When she turns the corner into the lock, she's unprepared for the air that is blowing in through the opening. On the other side, there is no docking collar, just a little platform with safety rails that juts out into the open air, and a staircase that leads down to the concrete apron. It's cold out there, much colder than any weather she has experienced back home. When Alex walks out onto the platform, the wind that blows across the tarmac seems to cut right through the fabric of her jumpsuit and makes her shiver involuntarily. In front of her, Val has the same reaction. She turns her face away from the breeze and looks at the officer standing behind them by the outer door of the airlock.

"Holy hell, that's cold. Is it always like this down here?"

The officer smiles and shakes his head.

"No, ma'am. But it's late November. The tail end of fall. It'll be winter next month. I'm sure they'll set you up with some warm clothing."

"Right," Val says. "I forgot about *seasons*."

Alex follows Val down the air stairs. When she is about to step onto the airfield, she hesitates briefly.

It's not like I'm here for the first time, she thinks. *I was born in this place, after all.*

Still, when she leaves that last metal step and walks out onto the rough concrete of the apron, the flood of unfamiliar sights and sounds and the sensation of the cold air on her face make it feel a little like she really is taking her first steps onto an alien planet.

CHAPTER 26

The colonists file into the waiting buses, where they are greeted and guided by more Fleet personnel. There's heated air coming out of the vents above the seats, and Alex holds her hands up against them for a few moments to warm up her cold fingers, marveling at how quickly the cold wind has drained the warmth from her.

The airfield is clearly part of a big military installation. They leave the apron behind and pass through several security gates before the buses turn onto a wide road and pick up speed. Every person she sees out here is wearing a uniform. They pass a formation of troops running at a brisk pace, dozens of fit young men and women whose sight reminds Alex sharply of her friends in the colony garrison. She hasn't seen any of them since they left the Vault, and the thought of never seeing them or Ash again sends a piercing little fear into her heart.

They drive along those wide streets for a while, then turn onto smaller streets and past rows of identical-looking buildings. Every time they pass a cluster of houses, Alex expects the buses to slow down and stop, but they keep rolling along swiftly and silently. Next to Alex, Val has started to snore softly, her head leaning back against the headrest of her seat. The sound of it makes Alex realize that she is bone-tired as well after days of sleeping in spaceship bunks, but she wants to stay awake to keep her bearings, even if the gentle motion of the bus on the smooth surface and the regular low humming from its electric drive do their best to try to lull her to sleep as well.

Finally, when it feels like they have driven out so far that it would have been justified to use a drop ship for the trip, the buses turn off the road and slow down. Alex gently shakes Val's shoulder.

"Huh?" Her friend sits up and looks around with bleary eyes. "Are we there?"

"Looks like it," Alex says. "Took long enough. This place is huge."

"We're on Earth now. My mother says we need to get used to thinking in bigger scales."

Their two-vehicle convoy comes to a stop in a courtyard between three large buildings. They're the first ones Alex has seen on this base that look different from the military structures, which all seem to have come from the same generic mold. The houses that form a U shape around the courtyard are asymmetrical designs made of steel and glass. They're only two floors tall, and the many large windows make them appear fragile and almost insubstantial to Alex, who is used to the sturdy, thick-walled and windowless dome shapes of standard colonial housing. These look like they would blow away in a stiff wind on Scorpio, but they're undeniably beautiful. Alex stares at their graceful lines through the window while the other colonists are preparing to get off the bus. Outside, the sun is setting, and in the gathering darkness, the light coming from those large glass panels makes it look as if the buildings are glowing from within.

Outside, it feels even colder than it did on the airfield apron. Alex is amazed to see that the soldiers coming out to assist them are all wearing fatigues with the sleeves rolled up, as if this temperature feels balmy to them. On the way to the entrance of the nearest building, she has to stop and look at the spectacular view to her right, where the sun is slowly disappearing below the tops of the mountains in the distance, bathing the cloudy sky above the horizon in brilliant hues of orange and red.

"I had almost forgotten what a sunset looks like," she says to Val.

"It's lovely," Val replies with chattering teeth. "But I think we should watch it from the inside. Come on."

The building has a large atrium behind the front entrance. It's a warmly lit space with high ceilings and artwork on the walls. The back of the room is a huge window that reaches from floor to ceiling and offers a stunning view of the darkening landscape outside. Once again, it strikes Alex how much it would look like Scorpio out there if it wasn't for the shrub vegetation sprouting up in various spots.

The military has set up tables along one side of the room, and soldiers are directing the colonists into lines marked on the floor with yellow tape. Two Fleet officers are sitting at each table with data terminals in front of them and signs that mark the tables by letter ranges: A–E, F–J, K–O, P–T, U–Z.

"This is where we part, then," Val says to her and wanders over to the line that has started to form in front of the last table in the row.

There are a few of Alex's fellow colonists in the A–E lines as well, and it doesn't seem to be moving at great speed, so she wanders off to the window and stands in front of it to look outside. The sun is now mostly below the mountains, with only the smallest sliver of bright orange still visible above the distant peaks. The air here is so clear that she can see for dozens of kilometers, with no fog or rain squalls in the way to limit her line of sight, and the view of all this space spread out in front of her makes her feel a little queasy after a while. She looks to her right and focuses on the texture of the nearby wall until the feeling passes.

Baby steps, she tells herself and gets in line in front of the desk marked with the A–E sign.

—

"Archer, Alexandra," she says to the smiling officer when she reaches the front of her line. He looks at his terminal and starts typing.

"Alexandra Archer," he repeats. "Let's have a look."

"Colonial ID number 17112013-A-31415," she recites.

He types the information into his terminal without pausing.

"There you are. Looks like we may have to update your picture in the data banks," he says with a smile and flips the screen around so she can see her entry. The face looking back at her is her own, of course, but it's an echo from the past, a relic of a different life. The girl in the picture is wearing her long auburn hair tied into a ponytail, and she's flashing an awkward little half smile at the camera. She's twelve, and someone is taking the routine annual headshot to keep her file in the colonial records up to date. She has no idea that the world as she knows it will end in less than three standard months. Nobody will make her sit for an official picture again, and she'll be frozen in the records at twelve years old. Alex knows that the officer is showing her the image because he thinks it will amuse her a little, so she flashes a smile that feels only slightly less awkward than the one she gave the camera eight years ago.

The Fleet officer flips the screen toward himself again and continues typing.

"We're going to set you up in unit 203, on the top floor if that's all right with you. More stairs to take, but you get a nice view."

"Sure," she says. "But if we can pick roommates, I'd like to stay with my friend. Valeria Velasco."

"Oh, they're all singles," the officer says. "We have plenty of space for all of you to have your privacy. If you find that you hate the view, come see one of us, and we'll assign you a different unit."

"What is this place, if you don't mind me asking? This doesn't really look like a military facility."

"It is," he replies. "This is called the Mills Center. It's a new medical unit. A place for treating soldiers with combat-related stress disorders. It's not due to open until next month. They decided to use the space for you all until then."

"I see. Thank you."

Alex shoulders her bag and turns to walk across the atrium toward the signs for the stairs and elevators.

A place for traumatized people, she thinks. *At least they're putting the place to the intended use.*

When she opens the door and walks into unit 203, her first thought is that her assignment was a mistake. It's roomier than her pod in the Vault, a large living space with a desk and a network terminal, a bathroom with a shower cabin, and a separate sleeping area with a bed that looks big enough for her to sleep in it sideways. The large window in the living area looks out over the square between the buildings instead of the mountains on the other side, but even with that limited line of sight, the transparent pane greatly amplifies the feeling of roominess. Alex puts her bag down on the floor and paces the room for a little while to look at everything until she feels a little unmoored in the middle of all that space and sits down on the bed. With the door closed, the room is almost eerily quiet. There's no background noise from an environmental system or the low-frequency hum of a starship's drive. Alex wouldn't have thought that a complete lack of sound could bother her, but after a few minutes of sitting in the room by herself, the silence feels like a physical thing against her eardrums. She gets up and checks the terminal on the desk, which comes alive as soon as she touches it. The interface looks more modern than the one on the terminals in the Vault, but the layout is roughly the same. She brings up the control screen for the room and selects White Noise from the audio menu. The option for Air-Conditioning doesn't sound exactly like the background noise in the Vault, but it's close enough, and she adjusts the volume until it's just a faint whisper.

Alex empties her bag on the bed. The few things she brought from home make a pitifully small pile. She lays out her last clean jumpsuit and underwear, then strips out of her clothes and walks into the bathroom to take a long shower, as hot as the control panel will let her turn up the water temperature, until the bathroom is filled with steam and the mirror above the sink is opaque with condensation.

The shower makes her feel a little more normal again. She slips into her familiar underwear and turns down the lights in the room before getting under the covers of her bed.

Even with the background noise, the room still doesn't feel right to Alex. Every time she shifts her head, the presence of the window forces itself to the forefront of her awareness. There are four walls around her, and the room is as private as any she has ever slept in, but the transparent pane to her left makes it feel too open, as if her bed is sitting out in the middle of the Vault's Downtown cave. The feeling doesn't subside when she closes her eyes, as if the open space exerts its own faint form of gravity on her subconscious. She gets out of bed again and finds the controls for the window on the terminal screen. There's an option for Blackout Blinds, and when she taps it, rows of interconnected polymer slats slowly descend from the top of the window frame. When they touch the bottom of the frame, they interlock as they stack on top of each other, and the little rows of gaps between the slats disappear one by one until the window is covered by a solid sheet of dark polymer that blocks out the light completely.

It still doesn't feel quite right when she gets back into bed. The berth in the spaceship was close enough to the inside of her pod that she had little trouble sleeping, cocooned as she was in the tight quarters of the bunk. This room is too big and open, the smells are strange, the bed is far too big, and the mattress layer is too soft. But the wall to her left at least appears solid again, and that calms the primitive part of her brain enough to let the faint white noise slowly lull her to sleep.

CHAPTER 27

The next few days feel as if they're all being put through boot camp, or at least the speculative version of it in Alex's head that is informed by the stories from the Vault's Spaceborne Infantry garrison. They stand in line for clothing issue, where they get measured by a swift and efficient laser-imaging device and supplied with new outfits suitable for the different seasons of Earth weather. The clothes are all military-issue utility wear, but without unit patches or name tags. One of the items Alex receives is a heavy coat with a hood and about twenty different pockets, and she's briefly in awe of the weight and thickness of it when she tries it on for fit, unable to imagine the climate conditions that would require such massively insulating outerwear.

Between meals and medical checkups, there are orientation sessions. The facility has several large meeting rooms where the colonists from Scorpio are broken up into age groups and made to attend what feel like school lessons to Alex, an impression she is happy to embrace by sitting through them in a cluster with her friends: Val, Athena, Luther, and Dallas. They went to colony school together in the Vault, spending months and years in the same classroom grinding through the same academic material at the same time, and this is a comforting echo of their common past. They're already several sessions into the orientations when Alex realizes that their little group even assumed the old seating order from their Vault school pod.

The lecturers are a mix of military and civilian, and the lessons are refreshers for the older colonists and new information for the younger ones, a wide variety of topics for which Val coins the umbrella term "How Earth Works 101": the history of the last eight years on Earth and in the NAC, the Exodus that happened when the Lankies were at Earth's doorstep, the political and social structure of the post-Exodus Commonwealth, and the military campaigns that have happened since then. To Alex and her friends, the most amazing fact they learn is that an NAC battlecarrier disappeared during a raid into Lanky-controlled space and returned almost three years later, with the crew having only experienced and aged six weeks in shipboard time. This story sparks excited discussions among the Misfits when they hang out together by the facility's pool in the evenings after dinner in an attempt to continue their social routines from the Vault.

There are orientations on how to use networks, and they're all given their own personal data pads, handheld devices that seem to have become ubiquitous on the planet in the almost twenty-five years since the founding settlers in their group left for Scorpio. Other lessons cover personal finances, safety, public services, transit and travel, and so many other aspects of life on Earth that Alex starts to find them more bewildering than informative after a week. The facility is very nice, and the personnel assigned to their welfare are helpful and patient, but everything seems to have been put together without much of a cohesive system, and Alex has the strong suspicion that the notice of their rescue threw the people here into a loop and forced them to improvise a program on very short notice. It solidifies her certainty that the military never expected to find survivors when they started their campaign to reclaim the lost colonies.

—

"Agoraphobia," Dallas says to Alex as they are walking their third lap around the path that snakes around the periphery of the Mills Center. They're at the spot where the walking path's loop is farthest away from the buildings, a little less than half a kilometer.

"What?" Alex says. She has been looking at the military base in the distance, a conglomeration of buildings and antenna clusters that makes the largest spaceport on Scorpio look like a handful of equipment shacks around a parking lot.

"That's what the shrink says we have," Dallas replies. "A fear of open spaces, and of leaving familiar surroundings. She says it's perfectly normal after what we've experienced."

The air is so cold that his breath is visible in little white puffs as he speaks. The beard he started to grow in the Vault has turned into a full growth that has just a few scraggly spots. The wind laps at their faces, but after a week of increasingly longer walks, Alex has mostly gotten used to the temperature.

"I wouldn't call it a phobia," Alex says. "I mean, I'm not *scared* of the outdoors. I'm just not used to seeing farther than I can run in a minute. But I wish my brain would let me go to sleep without making me roll down the blinds every night so it can pretend I'm still in my pod."

"We lived in a hole in the ground for almost a decade, Alex. That's not natural. And we still remembered what it looked like outside. Think about the younger kids. Pedro and Lilia have never been out of the Vault until now."

"I think they'll be used to it faster than the rest of us," she says. "I see Lilia and Malik running around on that courtyard every day. They don't seem to be bothered by all the sky above their heads."

"I think kids' brains are more pliable. Lucky for them."

He lets out a puff of breath and rubs his beard with a gloved hand.

"They said we can start leaving tomorrow. Those of us who want to, I mean."

She gives him a bewildered look.

"What do you mean, *leave*? To go where?"

"Some people still have family on Earth. I know Miss Buckler is going to head home to her parents. She was only twenty-one when she came out to Scorpio, you know."

"She told me. Back when I was doing the apprenticeship with her. They paid for her school. And then she gets us as her first job. Some shit luck, huh?"

Dallas smiles and shakes his head.

"We all got lucky, Alex. You know how unlikely all of this was from start to finish? The fact that we were close enough to the Vault that day. The fact that they went back to Scorpio first."

Too bad there wasn't any luck left in the bag for Blake and Sergeant Frye, or Cheryl and Andres, or Corporal Bayliss, she thinks. But the thought makes her tap into a pool of sadness and sorrow that seems bottomless these days, so she takes a deep breath and watches her exhalation streaming from her mouth and dissipating in the cool morning air.

"Have you had your talk with the counselor yet?" Dallas asks.

Alex shakes her head. "I have it on my schedule for this afternoon."

Dallas tucks his hands into the pockets of his oversized military coat and looks into the distance, where a pair of drop ships descend out of the sky above the base.

"I think we have some pull with them right now because we're the first. I don't think they really know what to do with us."

"You really think there'll be others after us?" she asks.

He shrugs. "We got lucky. Maybe someone else will too. I think that from now on they'll plan for the possibility."

The door to the counselor's office is open, and Alex knocks on the doorframe to announce her presence.

The counselor is sitting on a couch in the middle of the room. He's dressed in what Alex assumes is regular civilian fashion because it's the first outfit she has seen down here that isn't either utility fatigues or camouflage patterned, just a light-blue jacket with a stand-up collar and contrasting white stitching on the seams, and a matching pair of trousers. He looks up when Alex knocks and puts his data pad down on the low table in front of him.

"Ms. Archer?" he asks.

Alex nods.

"Do come in. Sit wherever you feel comfortable. Pleasure to meet you, Ms. Archer. I'm Deshawn Keys. I work in the Office of Colonial Affairs."

"Just 'Alex' is fine, sir. We don't call anyone by their last names in the colony. Just the soldiers and the administrators. And our friends when we want to rib them, maybe."

Deshawn Keys smiles. "That's what your friends said too. At least I assume they're your friends because they're roughly your age. But I always start with the last name because I work for the government. People down here don't like it when their public servants act too familiar with them."

Alex walks over to one of the chairs set up across the table from the couch and sits down in it.

"Alex it is," he says. "Call me Deshawn, please. How are you adjusting to Earth so far?"

"I haven't really seen much of Earth yet. Just this place and what's around it. But it's fine, I guess. It's nice not to have to wear a mask outside. I had forgotten what wind feels like on my face."

"I can't even imagine. I've never been out to the colonies. We do take our perks for granted here on Earth, I suppose."

"You work for the Colonial Affairs office, and you've never been on a colony planet?" Alex asks.

Deshawn responds with a little laugh. "It does sound wrong, doesn't it? But I'm with the Resettlement Department. When people need our services, they're already back home. I've never been farther out than Luna. I'd love to go out and see one of the colonies one day, though."

"The Resettlement Department," Alex repeats. "I didn't know there was such a thing. I thought colonists get to stay on their planets for good."

"Sometimes people can't handle the stress. We do our best to make sure everyone we send out is psychologically fit, but things happen out on the colonies. Humans are humans, after all. But it's not a common thing. We rarely need to deal with a hundred and fifty returnees all at once."

Deshawn picks up his data pad and looks at the screen. In the mirror image that's showing through the transparent back of the device, Alex sees her own picture again, that long-obsolete headshot from her personnel file.

"I'm very sorry about your parents," he says. "That must have been extremely difficult for you. I won't even pretend I have any idea what that would feel like."

Alex nods to acknowledge the sentiment.

"I'm afraid I don't have any good news regarding your next of kin," Deshawn continues. "We found your uncle in the public records. Unfortunately, he's deceased. He died two years ago, in one of the PRCs in the Philadelphia area. I'm sorry."

Alex doesn't remember ever meeting her uncle before her parents left for the colony. She knows there had been a falling out between her father and his older brother, but he never talked about it with her when he was still alive, and she never asked for details when she was a little kid. She had no emotional investment in a man she doesn't know at all. But the knowledge that she has no direct family left in the whole universe hits her harder than she had expected, even if she hadn't put much hope into the possibility.

"There's a picture of him on file. Do you want to see it?" Deshawn says in a gentle tone.

Alex nods and takes the offered data pad.

She's not prepared for just how much he looked like her dad. The man in the file image has more wrinkles and gray hair than her father did when she last saw him. He has the same full head of hair, the same sharp profile to his nose. The only thing that sets him immediately apart from his younger brother is the dimple on his chin. She has no idea what he was like as a person, whether he shared her father's quick wit and easygoing nature. But the finality of the knowledge that she'll never get to know him makes her feel a sense of loss that brings tears to her eyes. She wipes them away with her sleeve and looks at the information listed underneath the picture, the details the NAC government had on file for him.

ARCHER, MICHAEL DAVID, it says. DOB 25NOV2069. DOD 02APR2122. Alex looks at the date display on the lower edge of the data pad's screen: 01DEC2124.

Uncle Mike, she thinks. *He would have been fifty-five last week.*

"He was so young," she says. "Only fifty-three. Does it say why he died?"

"Let me see if it does." He holds out his hand for the data pad. Alex hands it back, and Deshawn flips through the data on the screen for a few moments before he finds the relevant entry.

"Cancer," he says. "It's still an all-too-common ailment in the PRCs. His capsule was buried in a public cemetery plot in PRC Philadelphia-33. I can get the exact location for you if you want to know. In case you ever want to visit it."

Alex takes a shaky breath and nods.

"Thank you," she says.

"Of course. Anything else I can do, let me know. And I am sorry for your loss. Your losses," he corrects himself.

"It's strange. I have no idea what to do next. It took us almost a week to get back to Earth. And I've been here for a week already. You'd think I would have figured it out by now."

"That's what I'm here to do," Deshawn says. "To talk with you about your options. Just keep in mind that whatever you decide, the basics will always be covered. The Commonwealth doesn't let anyone go hungry or without a roof over their head."

He consults his data pad again. Alex watches as he dismisses her uncle's file from the screen and calls up a different data set.

"We will settle you in a PRC—that's a Public Residence Cluster. It's where most NAC citizens live. The allocations usually go by place and region of birth. In your case, you can choose where you'd like to go, and we will do our best to find something suitable in that area. Beyond that, it's really up to you what you want to do."

"What can I do?" she asks.

"What do you know how to do? I already heard about your rotational system. That was a pretty smart setup. Was there anything you liked doing in particular? Something you were really good at?"

She doesn't have to think long about her answer.

"Teaching was kind of fun. Farming wasn't. I've had my fill of soybeans. But I would have done salvage any day over anything else, though. Whatever got me out with the dog."

"Tell me about salvage," he says.

"We'd go out and pick through what was left of the settlements and the terraformers. For spare parts, food, batteries, anything else we could find. I was one of the dog handlers. We have two dogs that learned how to alert to Lankies when they were heading our way."

"I see. That's interesting. I've never heard of something like that before. Using dogs as Lanky early-warning systems."

"There's not much of a need for that here on Earth, I suppose."

He flashes a smile. "No, thankfully not. But the Corps could use about a thousand of those dogs, I think."

"Is that something I could do? Be a dog trainer? I mean, I've done it for the last few years already."

"That is a job in the military," he says. "But you'd have to enlist in the NACDC. And from what I know, there's no guarantee to get any particular job. They assign occupational specialties after Basic Training. It's based on aptitude. So you may enlist trying to get into the working dog corps and end up in a maintenance unit. Or as infantry on a colony somewhere. The Corps recruiters will say what they think you want to hear to get you to sign up, but don't take their word to the bank. Once your signature is scanned on the enlistment form, they can assign you however they want. And the chance to get into a particular job is low."

Deshawn scrolls through the information on his data pad's screen.

"But there are other options for you. With your parents both deceased, you are eligible for survivors' benefits. You could use those to attend public college. A PC degree would open up more pathways for you. Civil service, Colonial Administration, that sort of thing. And you wouldn't have to decide on a career right away."

Even the limited choices put in front of her are confusing enough to make her head spin a little. What she wants to do right now is to be with her friends and wait for the world to start making sense again, not having to choose her life trajectory with this government bureaucrat. But at least she has a choice, and she knows that if she doesn't pick her path, someone else will.

"What would you do in my place?" Alex asks.

Deshawn shrugs.

"If I were in your shoes, I'd make use of those survivor benefits and attend school. Two years of privileged access to public services. That's plenty of time to decide what to do after graduation."

What would Mom and Dad want me to do? she thinks. They both went to public college, and even though they never got a chance to advise her on a career, she feels that they would have wanted her to go the same route. And if she must make a choice right now, it's probably best to pick the one that gives her the most options later, and two years to figure out how she can fit into this new and bewildering world.

"I guess that's what I should do, then," she says.

He smiles, seemingly pleased at her quick acceptance of his advice.

"I think that's a very smart choice. We'll set those gears in motion for you."

CHAPTER 28

When the sound of the electronic door chime pulls her out of her dream, Alex has forgotten what it was about as soon as she wakes. Only the lingering dread she feels tells her that it wasn't a pleasant dream. She sits up in her bed and tries to shake off the feeling.

The door chime keeps up its insistent rhythm. Then whoever has woken her up decides to add frantic knocks on the door to back up the electronic noise.

"Hang on," Alex shouts toward the door in a voice that's still thick with sleep. "Give me a minute."

"Hurry up, Archer," Val says from the other side of the door. Her friend's voice sounds excited rather than alarmed, so Alex takes a few extra moments to get out of bed and put on pants and an undershirt on the way to the door.

"This better be good," she says when she opens the door. The hallway outside is brightly lit, and she raises a hand in front of her eyes. Val pushes past her into the dark room.

"You sleep like a vampire," Val says. "Can't see shit in here."

"That's how I like it," Alex says. "Why are you so spun up this morning?"

"It's 0830 and you should be up anyway," Val replies. She walks over to the unit's desk and taps the screen with her finger to turn it on. "But you really don't want to miss this."

"Miss what?" Alex demands.

Val clicks her tongue and taps the screen again, and the blackout blinds in front of the window begin to rise with a faint electric humming. The light that floods the room hurts Alex's eyes, and she puts up her hand again to shield them.

"*Ow.* What the fuck, Velasco."

"Shhhh." Val walks over to the window and waves her hand at Alex in an impatient gesture. "Come here and look at this. *Look. At. This.*"

Her curiosity wins out over her bewilderment and mild irritation, and Alex crosses the room to join her friend at the window. When her eyes finally adjust to the light and she can see what has Val so excited, she can't suppress a gasp of surprise.

Outside, the courtyard between the buildings is blanketed in white. There's a layer of it on the roof of the building on the other side as well, and the air is full of thick, heavy flakes that descend leisurely like ash from a fire.

"It's *snow*," Val says in an awestruck voice. "Have you ever in your whole life seen anything this fucking pretty?"

Alex looks at the bright white world on the other side of her window. It looks like they went to sleep on one planet and woke up on a completely different one. Snow is another thing she knows only from a schoolbook, a meteorological condition unique to cold moons like New Svalbard, and planets like Earth with enough axial tilt to have seasons. Even before the Lankies came and turned Scorpio into a hot and humid greenhouse, it never snowed on the colony because the temperatures never got low enough to freeze water. If she ever saw any snow when she was a small child and living on Earth, she has no recollection of it, and she thinks she would remember something as beautiful as the sight in front of her. She can't see the far horizon or all the open space between here and there anymore, just swirls and bands of falling snow that shroud everything in brilliant white, as if the world has wrapped itself in a blanket.

"We should go outside and check it out," Val suggests.

"Can we?"

Her friend gives her an incredulous look.

"It's snow, Alex. It's frozen water, not hydrochloric acid. Come on. Get your clothes on and let's go."

—

As soon as she walks out of the building, Alex suddenly understands why the winter coats are as thick as they are, and she's glad she decided to test the garment this morning. It's much colder than it has been all week. The wind that is making the snow swirl as it slides off the rooftops stings her face and makes her cheeks feel numb. They walk out from underneath the front door's awning and out onto the courtyard, where the snow is already more than ankle deep. Val kicks at it and laughs in delight as the fine powder disperses in the wind in front of her only to be blown back at them and sprinkle their faces with cold crystals.

"*Gah*, that's cold," Alex says. Her heavy military coat has a hood on it, and she reaches back and pulls it onto her head. Val doesn't bother doing the same, and within a minute or two, her head is frosted with snow that sticks to her long curls in little white clumps.

They walk into the middle of the courtyard. It feels strange to walk in the snow, with every step cushioned and silenced even as her boot sinks into the white layer. Every time Alex lifts her feet, there's a small but noticeable resistance, enough that she knows she'd probably fall flat on her face if she tried to run in this. Val tries just that, plowing through the snow while trying to kick as much of it up as she can, and she tumbles to the ground within half a dozen steps, laughing brightly.

Alex grins and walks over to hold out her hand and help Val to her feet, only for her friend to pull her down to the ground as well.

"This is even colder than skinny-dipping in the cavern," Alex says.

Behind them, there's the sound of high-pitched voices chattering in excitement. They turn their heads to see several of the Vault children coming out of the building, with Miss Buckler shepherding them from the rear. They spill out from under the awning into the snow and start examining this new and unfamiliar environment.

"Guess they had the same idea," Val says. She gets up and brushes the snow from her pants. Then she scoops up a handful of it and presses it between her gloves.

"What are you doing?" Alex asks.

"Something you're supposed to do when it snows. Watch."

She opens her hands and shows Alex the snow she's compressed into a clump. Then she cocks her arm and hurls the clump at the nearest kid. It hits the back of their coat with a muffled thump, and they let out a surprised little squeak. The other kids understand the assignment immediately. They grab big handfuls of snow and start hurling it at each other. Miss Buckler wades into the middle of the fray and squats to scoop up a big handful of snow with both hands. She demonstrates how to make a proper snowball and throws the fluffy missile in Val's direction. Val swats it out of the air, and it disintegrates, spraying her face in the process and making her yelp. Behind Miss Buckler, the kids all gather more snow to emulate their teacher's manufacturing technique, and before too long, their group is a little flurry of limbs and snowballs as they engage in a free-for-all.

"Uh-oh," Alex says. "I think you started something."

"Look at them," Val says. "I haven't seen them have fun like this in ages. I don't think I've ever seen Irene laugh."

She turns toward Alex, and her expression turns serious.

"So, I haven't told you the news yet," she says.

"What news?"

"We're leaving tomorrow. Mom's going to refresher training for the Colonial Administration. I'm going with her."

"*What?* Where?" Alex says in disbelief.

"It's up in Alaska. Six months. I get to stay with her until she's finished. They just told us last night."

Alex feels like she has just been punched in the center of her stomach.

"You can't *leave*, Velasco. That's not acceptable. Request denied."

Val laughs, but there are tears in her eyes now, and Alex can feel her own welling up.

"We had to decide on the spot. If Mom's going back to the colonies, this is going to be the last time I am with her for a long time. God, you'd think we'd be sick of each other after all this time in the Vault, right?"

They both laugh through their tears, and Val hugs her fiercely.

"I'm so sorry, Alex. I'm going to miss the shit out of you. But hey, it's just six months. After that, who knows? Maybe they can find you a place near wherever I end up."

"They fucking better," Alex says. "Because I am not going to just let you bail on the best-friend position. It's a lifetime appointment."

After Val goes back inside, Alex stays behind to sort out her thoughts. The snow has mostly stopped falling since they came out, and the sun is peeking through gaps in the cloud cover occasionally. Whenever it does, the pristine snow in front of her sparkles in the sunlight as the ice crystals reflect the light in a thousand spots. It's one of the most beautiful things she has ever seen, but the pleasure of it is greatly tempered by the knowledge that her best friend is going to leave her. Val has been an integral part of her life for so long that the thought of not having her around feels like someone told her she'd have to get an essential limb removed tomorrow.

At the periphery of the courtyard, big autonomous machines with large scoop-like chutes are clearing the snow from the road, spinning augers biting into the smooth white blanket of crystals and carving clear swaths into it. The snow comes out at the top of the machine in a wide arc that glitters in the sun. A smaller version of the snow machine is busy cleaning the walking path that loops around the facility, cutting a neat trench through the knee-high snow. Alex follows the machine down the path at a slow pace. When she first felt the cold wind on her face earlier, she had thought she could never get used to temperatures like that, but after an hour outside, it doesn't bother her anymore.

The personal data pad in her pocket makes a trilling sound. She pulls off one of her gloves to fish the device out from underneath her three layers of clothes and looks at it to see a message on the screen.

> VALERIA VELASCO: Hurry back. You have a visitor at the main building.

Alex selects the reply function with rapidly numbing fingers.

> On my way. Tell them I'll be right there.

She turns around and strides back the way she came, her curiosity kindled.

At the building, there are two military vehicles parked on the courtyard in front of the main door's awning, and she quickens her pace, her heart beating faster with the anticipation.

Lopez, she thinks. *They finally let them rejoin the rest of us.*

She's twenty meters from the door when it opens. The soldier who steps out isn't Lopez. It's Private Clark, the Scorpio garrison's other dog handler. She holds the door open behind her, and a familiar low-slung shape appears in the opening.

"Ash!"

Clark lets go of Ash's leash, and the shepherd lopes toward the sound of Alex's voice with long, easy strides. She goes down on both knees, not even trying to stifle the sob that escapes her throat. When Ash reaches her, he does a little hop to put his front paws on her shoulder, and the weight and momentum are enough to make her topple over on knees that seem to have lost the ability to hold her upright. He's never been an affectionate dog, but he's wagging his tail now, and she laughs at the feeling of his muzzle under her chin. She uses his harness to pull herself up again and buries her hands in the ruff of his neck fur.

"Ash," she says. "I've missed you. Oh, buddy. I've missed you a lot."

She takes his face in her hands and looks into his expressive brown eyes. It occurs to her that this is the first time she has seen him under an open sky without his mask. He's wearing a vest harness, but it's not the one from the colony. It's a far sleeker one that looks like it was made to fit. On the side of the harness, a patch bears the words **MILITARY WORKING DOG—DO NOT PET.** She disregards the directive and ruffles the fur between his ears. He nuzzles up against her face again and gives her cheek a single brief lick.

"Holy shit, a kiss," Clark says. She has walked up behind Ash, and now she is watching their reunion with a little smile on her face. "He never kisses anyone. That's some high distinction."

Alex stands up and walks over to Clark to hug her. The older woman tenses up at the unexpected contact but returns the hug after a moment.

"I thought I'd never see any of you again," Alex says. "How are you, Private Clark?"

Clark nods at the rank sleeve on her shoulder, which now has three parallel diagonal bars on it.

"It's Sergeant Clark now. We all got promoted on schedule in absentia while we were MIA. Lopez made sergeant too."

"Congratulations on the promotion," Alex says. Ash flips her hand up with his nose, and she laughs and continues to stroke the top of his head.

"I get to wear the stripes, but I'll still have to go to NCO school. At least I get the pay as well," Clark says. "We got word that you were asking for your buddy here. I managed to talk my new CO into letting me take Ash out to see you."

"You have no idea how much I love you right now," Alex says.

"Hey, you earned your stripes too. Least I could do."

"Is everyone all right? They wouldn't let me go down to Grunt Country on the way home."

"Everyone's fine," Sergeant Clark says. "We all got scattered into the winds, though. Almost everyone ended up reassigned to a different unit. Slow-stepping stuff, mostly. They want to ease us back in, I guess. Lopez is already in NCO school. Doran got bumped all the way from corporal to staff sergeant. They're sending her off to drill-instructor school next month. Talk about a perfect assignment for her. I'm assisting the canine corps with Knucklehead here for a few more weeks." She nods at Ash. "Blitz is there too. They're really interested in our Lanky detection methods."

"They're going to take him out on missions?" Alex asks, alarmed at the thought of Ash going into danger again without her.

Sergeant Clark shakes her head. "Nah. He's just training now. He'll never go off-planet again. Once the canine corps is done with him and Blitz, they'll get to retire with Constable Morrissey. He's never going off-planet again either."

Ash pokes Alex's hand with his snout again, a little more insistent this time. She kneels next to him and rubs his ears with both hands.

"How long are you going to be here?" she asks.

"Just an hour or two. It's a three-hour flight back to Lackland once I get back to the airfield."

"You're flying six hours just so I could see Ash again?"

Clark shrugs. "Like I said, you earned your stripes too. I was just putting myself in your shoes. Thought about how I'd feel if I never got to see Blitz again."

"Thank you," Alex says. "I owe you, big time."

"You don't owe me a thing. You went out with the rest of us and kept our asses safe."

Alex hugs Ash again and breathes in the familiar scent of his fur.

"An hour or two," she says. "What are we going to do in an hour or two?"

She looks up at Clark.

"You think I could take him for one more walk? There's a path that goes out half a klick."

"He's a really important military asset," the sergeant replies. "I could barely convince them to let me take him up here. I'm not even supposed to let go of his lead while he's out of the kennel."

She flashes a curt smile.

"But you know what? Fuck it. He always listened to you better than he did to anyone else. And I'd feel like a total asshole if I said no."

It's amazing how quickly an hour can go by when it's the last one you get with someone, Alex thinks.

She's at the apex of the walking-path loop, almost half a kilometer from the Mills Center's little cluster of buildings. Ash is confined to the path by the snow on either side that's shoulder-high to him, but he doesn't seem to mind. They're far enough away from the facility that all she can hear is the wind and the occasional faint engine noise from drop ships landing at the spaceport in the far distance. The snow is falling again, this time in a lighter volume than before. The wind is blowing around the loose powder on top of the stuff that has already fallen, and the white haze obscures the distant buildings. If it wasn't for the difference in temperature and the snow on the ground everywhere, she could almost pretend they're both back on Scorpio, walking Lanky patrol while a salvage team is stripping the ruins of some shattered research station. Ash walks with her the way he always has, focused and attentive, completely sure of his place and purpose. She feels almost completely unmoored, and with Val and Ash about to be gone from her life, the last few ties holding her in place are coming undone. For the first time since they left the Vault, she finds herself wishing that the rescue had never arrived that day.

I'm alive, she chastises herself when she realizes where her thoughts have gone. *I'm alive, and he's alive, and we'll be fine even if we're not in the same place. We'll be fine, and that's enough right now. Everything else will sort itself out sooner or later.*

She only realizes she has stopped in the middle of the path when she sees Ash looking at her expectantly. She squats in front of him and cups his furry face with her hands. She doesn't know whether he has self-awareness, but she has no doubt that he's sentient, and when she looks into his eyes, she's almost certain there's a kind of sapience behind that unflinching gaze as well.

"We did some crazy stuff together, didn't we?" she says.

He responds with a single wag of his tail. Alex leans forward and kisses the spot between his ears.

"Come on, buddy. Let's head back before Clark sends a search party for us."

She stands up and tightens her grip on the leash, and he turns and starts walking with her, eager to keep going.

CHAPTER 29

PRC Pittsburgh-A5, North American Commonwealth
Planet Earth
20MAY2125, 0700h Eastern Standard Time
Six months and one day since the evacuation of Scorpio

So much for having one's fill of soybeans, Alex thinks when she opens the box from today's food delivery. There are only six variants of breakfast in the daily trays that get sent up to her kitchen's dumbwaiter node from the distribution station in the basement every morning, and four of them are soy based. It doesn't taste bad, the calories are plenty, and the processed food contains all the necessary vitamins and nutrients, but she found herself craving fistfuls of fresh soybean pods after just a month of PRC food.

She takes out the breakfast tray—scrambled eggs, soy bacon, chickpea-flour pancakes—and puts it in the processor to heat it up. The barley coffee in her cup is the only part of her breakfast that tastes close enough to its Vault equivalent to be a comfort flavor. She walks over to the window of her little kitchen nook and looks outside while the food is heating up.

Pittsburgh A-5 is considered a nice PRC, reserved for privileged-access citizens like public service workers and people on elevated benefits like Alex. She has never been to one of the bad PRCs, but she learned quickly that the biggest difference is that the nice PRCs have six- and ten-floor residence towers instead of ones with a hundred or two hundred floors. The view out of her kitchen window isn't terrible, even if there are more people living in the slice of the world she can see from that thirty-centimeter-wide sliver of unbreakable glass than ever lived on the entirety of Scorpio. But the buildings are not so tall that she can't see the sky, there's a river in her line of sight that's snaking through the low hills behind the PRC, and the small size of her one-person unit is cozy in a way because it's not much more space than she had in her Vault pod. The only thing that really bothered her in the beginning was all the noise—the PRC is infinitely louder than the Vault even when it's at its quietest in the middle of the night—but even that became tolerable after a few months, and now it's all just background noise to her. She picked Pittsburgh from the offered list because that's where she lived with her parents before they left for Scorpio, and telling herself that she was really just coming home and not moving to a strange place helped to calm her mind in the beginning.

The processor chimes to let her know that her breakfast is warmed up. She takes the tray out and puts it on her little kitchen table, then gets a fork from her utensils drawer and sits down to check the week's class schedule while she is eating.

In the unit next to hers, on the other side of her kitchen wall, her neighbor has his screen on and his preferred network news at a volume that's loud enough for her to hear the ten-second news bits of the day whether she wants to know them or not. She has only seen his face three times in the six months since she moved in, but she knows his taste in entertainment and his daily schedule without having exchanged more than ten words with him. Her own network screen, built into the back wall of her living space, stays dark most of the time. Getting used to the noise and the food is one thing, but tolerating the bombardment of inanity pouring from the screen is another matter entirely. The first few times she tried to sift meaningful information from the flood of content thrown at her, she got throbbing headaches, and now she only ever looks at the screen when it comes on automatically for public announcements.

Alex is almost finished with her breakfast and the school schedule when the two-tone sound of the door's intercom startles her. In the living nook, the network screen turns on to display the feed from the security camera above her door. When she sees who is standing outside, she leaps out of her chair so quickly that she knocks her data pad off the table and onto the floor. She pays it no mind and rushes to the door to unlock it. Her visitor starts to speak as soon as the door opens in front of him, but he doesn't get out more than two words before Alex has wrapped her arms around him in a rapacious hug.

"Oof," Lopez says under the weight of her assault. He returns the hug and squeezes her gently.

"Glad to see you too," he says.

Alex tries to suppress the joyful tears that are welling up.

"What are you doing here?"

"I'm on leave for a few days. Finished NCO school. Thought I'd come up and see you before I head out to my new unit."

"I thought I'd never see you again. They wouldn't let me come down to Grunt Country on the ship. And then they moved us to another one and you weren't with us anymore."

"We got back a few days after you."

Alex reluctantly loosens her embrace and takes half a step back to look at Lopez. He's wearing Spaceborne Infantry fatigues, the digital camouflage pattern she knows so well after all this time spent in the military section of the Vault. The rank insignia on his shoulders are the three diagonal bars of a sergeant. "Clark told me you made sergeant too."

He looks at his shoulder boards as if he's noticing the new rank sleeves for the first time.

"Yeah, they promoted us while we were MIA. Couldn't take it all back when we ended up being alive after all, I guess. You saw Clark? Here on Earth?"

"She came out to the place where they put us at first. Just so I could see Ash again."

"That's good," Lopez says. "I know it meant a lot."

"You have no idea. If I had known they wouldn't let me take him with me on the drop ship, I never would have left the kennel that morning."

Somewhere down the hall, a door opens, and two people come out of their unit and start walking down the hallway toward Alex and Lopez. They startle visibly when they see the soldier in uniform, and Alex nods toward her own door.

"Come inside. There's a security camera every three meters out here," she tells Lopez and pulls him into her unit. She closes the door and waits for the soft swishing sound of the electric dead bolt before she turns around. When she does, she has to pause for a moment to let her brain reconcile the sight of Lopez in his SI uniform with her new reality. He looks out of place in her crummy little PRC apartment, too vital and vibrant, as if he's standing in the middle of a washed-out computer-generated scene.

"Welcome to—whatever this is," she says and waves her hand in a vague circle.

"It's nicer than the pods back home," he says. "Isn't it?"

Alex shrugs.

"It's bigger. But my pod was cozier. I tried to do a few drawings on the walls, but the paint won't take any color."

She walks into the kitchen nook and takes her meal tray off the little table to put it in the recycler.

"I'd offer you some breakfast, but they only send up enough for one person," she says. "But I think I can get two more cups out of this instant coffee bag. Want some?"

"Sure," Lopez says. "And don't worry about breakfast. I had some at the chow hall back on base this morning."

"It's still morning," Alex says. "When did you get up?"

"At 0500," he replies. "I stayed in the guest quarters out at the Pittsburgh TA base last night. I got in late from Lejeune. Decided I didn't want to brave the PRC in the evening."

"That's smart. I don't brave it in the daytime on most days."

"This is a pretty nice one, though. Much better than the one I grew up in."

She turns on the water heater and gets out a clean cup for Lopez. Now that he's here and standing in the room just two meters away, she has to keep herself from staring at him. When the water has heated to a boil and she can fill Lopez's cup alongside her own, she turns to hand him his coffee and nods at one of the chairs by the kitchen table.

"Sit down, will you? You still stand like you're always at parade rest."

"Sorry." He smiles and takes off the small gear pack he had slung over one shoulder. Then he pulls out one of the chairs to sit on it. Alex takes her own cup and sits down across the table, glad to have a reason to look at him again without making things weird. He looks sharp, with a clean shave, a crisp military haircut, and a new uniform with perfectly rolled sleeves. His face has more color now, and it makes his cheekbones even more defined than they were before.

"So this is where you live now," Lopez says with a look around the apartment. "How are you getting along with it?"

Alex shrugs.

"It's fine, I guess. Food's okay. No sewage-line duties. And there are no Lankies walking around outside."

"What are you doing now?"

"Public college. Another year and a half and I get a civil degree. Survivor benefits," she replies.

"And after that?"

She shrugs again. “I have no idea yet. I guess I have some time to figure it out.”

She takes a sip of her coffee. Lopez does the same, and she watches for his reaction. He looks at her over the rim of his cup and purses his lips.

“It’s pretty good,” he says.

“You lying sack of shit,” she says with a smile, and he smiles back. It’s still disconcerting to see someone from her old life right here in the middle of her drab new life, two incongruent realities spliced together.

“What about you? Now that you’re done with NCO school, I mean.”

“I got a squad leader slot in one of the line regiments. Cashed in the reputation points we all got when we came back and everyone treated us like big damn heroes.”

“So you’re going back out there? To the colonies?”

“That’s what I know how to do,” Lopez says. “They’re keen on people with Lanky experience. There’s a major new offensive under way. Whatever they brought back with the ship that disappeared for three years, it really got R&D spinning. We have shiny new ships, new tech, all new weapons. Stuff I can’t even tell you about if I don’t want a drone strike on my head as soon as I leave this building.”

“You’re actually excited about jumping back in,” Alex says and shakes her head with a little smile.

“What am I going to do down here?” he asks. “Count ammo boxes in a logistics regiment somewhere until I can retire? Sit on my ass in some office and look at screens all day?”

“No,” Alex concedes. “That’s not you.”

“That’s not any of us,” he says. “The squad from Scorpio, I mean. You know that every single one of them signed reenlistment papers? We all had a golden ticket out if we wanted it. And nobody took it. Everyone went back into the line.”

He takes another sip of coffee and puts the cup on the table, then turns it slowly with his hands.

"We're not playing defense anymore. We're taking the fight to them. We have the tech to wipe these things off our colonies, and that's what we're doing right now, one by one. I want to be in on that because that's where I'm most useful. And, you know, there's a shitload of payback due. For Sergeant Frye and Corporal Bayliss. And all the others."

"Blake, Cheryl, Andres, Scott," Alex recites. Every name stings anew when she speaks it out loud.

Lopez nods. "I have a lot of names to write on warheads."

After all she has been through, she knows that the idea of going back to face the Lankies should terrify her. But when she thinks about all the Vault troopers heading into battle without her and Ash, she feels a sudden sense of deep sorrow and despair.

"I miss you," she says in a halting voice. "I miss all of you. Call me crazy, but there are days when I wish we were back in the Vault together. Lankies outside and all."

He chuckles and smiles at her.

"I'm not going to call you crazy. I've been there myself a few times since we got back."

Lopez glances down at the bag next to his chair.

"Oh, hey, I almost forgot. I brought you something."

He reaches down and opens the flap of his gear bag, then pulls out a familiar-looking box wrapped in olive-green plastic and hands it to her with a little smirk.

"Rations?" Alex laughs and turns the box in her hands. "You know, I thought I was sick of those for life. Until I had PRC food."

He nods at the box and grins. "Open it."

She cracks the seal and peels off the protective outer bag. When she opens the lid of the box, she laughs out loud. Instead of the usual variety of three meals and assorted condiments and snacks, there are about two dozen dessert bars in the box, stacked on their sides in two tidy rows. She knows what flavor they are, but she pulls one out of the stack anyway to read the label.

"Lemon," she says. "Of course."

"Those are a lot easier to come by on a big base like Lejeune," Lopez says. "They should last you a little while. Can you believe that's one of the least-popular flavors in the Corps right now?"

"Yeah, well, some people don't know what's good," Alex says. She doesn't realize she has tears in her eyes until she reflexively wipes them away with the back of her hand.

"Some people are idiots," he replies.

Alex puts the bar back into the box and picks up the whole thing to hug it to her chest.

"Thank you, Lopez," she says.

He nods with a smile.

"How long can you stay?" she asks, suddenly worried that he's on a short timer for his visit just like Clark was when she brought Ash to her.

"I'll have to head back to the station before it gets dark," he says. "Unless I'm keeping you from something. You can kick me out anytime you want. I mean, I did show up unannounced."

Alex scoffs at the notion.

"There's absolutely nothing I wouldn't skip out on for this," she tells him.

A few hours into Lopez's visit, Alex realizes that she hasn't talked this much to a person face-to-face since she left the Mills Center and moved into this PRC. They talk all morning, catching up on what happened since the rescue from Scorpio. When it's time for lunch, she heats up her ration's lunch tray and splits it with him, and they eat several bars from her new dessert stash to supplement the meal and end it on a positive flavor note. As much as the time seems to drip by in viscous and slow-moving seconds whenever she's alone in her unit with nothing to do, the clock seems to positively race now that she doesn't want the day to progress. Lopez is sitting in the living nook with her, just an arm's length away, and he's as good-looking and kind and quietly funny as he has always been, and the sight and smell of him makes her drab little apartment feel more real and alive than it has since the day she moved in.

They're so engrossed in each other's company that she only realizes how far the day has progressed when the automatic LEDs in the ceiling turn on to compensate for the fading daylight coming through the windows. Alex gets up and walks over to the kitchen window to look outside, where the shadows of the people out on the street are getting long.

"Well, shit," Lopez says. "I need to head back to the station if I want to get out of here before it gets dark."

He gets up from her spartan little couch and straightens out his fatigues. Then he walks into the kitchen and stands next to her to look outside as well. Alex feels a wild sort of panic at the thought of him walking out in the next minute or two and maybe leaving her life forever, and that feeling combines with his sudden proximity to make her throw caution to the wind. She turns toward him and pulls him close to her by the front of his jacket. Then she kisses him before her brain can override the impulse. He stiffens a little in obvious surprise, but he doesn't recoil from her or push her away, and then she can tell with certainty that her move isn't exactly unwelcome.

They stay entangled like this in front of the kitchen window for a long moment. When their lips part again, he looks a little dazed.

"Was that weird?" Alex asks.

Lopez shakes his head. "I thought it would be. But it really wasn't. Makes me think we should have done that ages ago already."

She clears her throat.

"Look, you don't have to try and beat the dark," she tells him. "You can just stay here and take the first train in the morning. Public transit starts up again at 0600."

He looks at her with a little smile, still looking a bit like he just woke up from a restful nap.

"First shuttle out leaves at 0700," he says. "I may not make it to the base on time. But you know what?"

This time he's the one pulling her close. This kiss lasts longer than the first one, and now it's Alex's turn to feel a little dazed in the aftermath.

"What are they going to do, send me to a Lanky world?" he says.

Alex laughs with relief and pulls him close again.

So much living to make up and so little time, she thinks. *But at least I'll get these few hours.*

CHAPTER 30

When Alex's alarm wakes her up in the morning, the spot on the bed next to her is empty. Only a depression in the mattress and the faint scent of whatever soap Lopez uses serve as evidence that last night wasn't just a very pleasant dream.

She silences the alarm and sits up on the edge of her bed. The door to the bathroom is open, and the room beyond is dark, so she knows Lopez isn't just using the bathroom. She checks the time projection on the ceiling above her sleeping nook: 0700 hours.

The kitchen is dark and empty as well. She turns on the ceiling lights and opens the dumbwaiter flap to collect the day's meal tray. The two cups they used yesterday until they ran out of barley coffee powder are still sitting on the kitchen table. Between them, her data pad is placed faceup, with a new quick note in the center of the screen. She picks up the data pad to read it.

> HAD TO HURRY TO CATCH THE 0600 TRAIN. YOU WERE SOUND ASLEEP SO I DECIDED NOT TO WAKE YOU. (ALSO BECAUSE I'D JUST STAY ANOTHER DAY AND THEY'D LIST ME AS AWOL.)
>
> I PICKED ONE HELL OF A TIME TO LET THEM DEPLOY ME AGAIN, HUH?

MY .MIL NODE ADDRESS IS AT THE BOTTOM. STAY IN TOUCH, PLEASE. I'M BOUND TO BE BACK ON LEAVE AT SOME POINT, AND I WANT TO DRINK SOME MORE SHITTY COFFEE WITH YOU.

Alex smiles as she taps the note and saves it to the data pad. A schedule warning pops up on the screen just a second later, reminding her that she needs to be at the college at 0900 for the week's physical presence classes.

Back to real life, she thinks, even as she realizes that yesterday felt more like real life than all of the last six months in this place put together.

—

It's a warm May morning, and the moisture in the air outside after last night's rain makes her think of the heat and humidity on Scorpio. She leaves the vestibule of her residence tower and walks down the street toward the transit station, past the street-level shops and services that cater to the residents of the A-class PRCs, who have a slightly easier time getting their hands on real currency than the people in the crowded megaclusters that ring the outskirts of the city. Nobody she passes on the street spares her a second glance as she walks by. It was strange in the beginning, when she felt an urge to acknowledge everyone, but now she has adopted the Earth habit of pretending nobody else exists because she learned that it's so much easier in a place with so many people in it.

She's still thinking about last night, remembering all the details so she can commit them to long-term memory like emotional emergency rations, and her attention isn't fully on her surroundings like it usually is whenever she leaves her building. When she rounds the corner one block away from the transit station, she almost collides with someone standing on the sidewalk, a stocky man with a dark buzzcut. He's wearing a camouflage jacket in a familiar pattern—she has seen the same one on the garrison uniforms at the Vault—and when he addresses her, she almost stops to listen to his pitch before thinking better of it.

"Got some spare credits for a veteran?" he asks as she walks past him. "A voucher maybe? C'mon."

Alex pretends she can't hear him. She hears him trotting after her as she walks off.

"Hey, wait up. You lost something," he says. She knows good and well that she didn't lose anything—her school bag is still on her shoulder, and her few valuables are buried deep inside her front pockets—so she keeps up her pace. Three months ago, that trick may have worked on her, but not now, dozens of panhandlers and street hustlers later.

Keeping her pace instead of speeding up was a mistake, and she realizes it when the man in the camouflage jacket is almost next to her and grabs her elbow from behind. She yanks her arm away to shake him off, but he snatches her forearm and wraps his fingers around it with a strength she didn't anticipate. He nudges her sideways with the smoothness of a long-practiced move. She stumbles, but he holds her up by her arm before she can fall. To their left, there's a gap in the line of narrow storefronts and closed-up food stalls, and he shoves her into it. It's an alley with trash chutes every ten meters, and as the man follows her, two more people step out from behind the nearest chute. They don't look surprised at the intrusion, and she knows she just got yanked into a well-prepared little ambush.

The man behind Alex puts his other hand between her shoulder blades and pushes her forward toward the others. She thinks about the knife in her right front pocket, but her right forearm is still locked down by a strong hand.

"Sorry about that," he says. "Folks gotta eat, you know. Please don't make a racket."

The welcoming committee steps in front of her. There's no hate or glee in their expressions, just a sort of detached focus, professionals at work.

"What do you have in here?" the man in the camouflage jacket says and yanks the school bag off her shoulder before she can react. He tosses it to one of his comrades, who snatches it out of the air and steps back to open it out of her reach.

"School stuff," she says. "Data pad and a few hard-copy printouts."

The other man, who has thinned blond hair and a wiry build, takes the pad out of the bag and dumps the rest of the contents on the ground.

"You really know how to pick 'em," he says to his friend behind Alex. "Just school shit."

"Pad's gonna sell," the stocky man replies.

"It looks like it's from last decade, man. And it's got a school sticker. Locked down tight."

She looks back at the man in the camouflage jacket. They're just a few meters inside the alley, and if she yanks her arm free, she can dash back out onto the sidewalk. She felt no fear at first because everything happened in the blink of an eye, but now that she's surrounded by three people who look at her like she's just an object, a thing to be stripped bare of useful things, she feels the panic welling up inside her with an intensity that makes her nauseated.

"Don't," the man behind her says when he sees where she is looking. "You're not strong enough or fast enough. Just fucking hand it over and we can all be on our way."

"I don't have anything to hand over," she says, her voice strangely hoarse in her own ears.

"Time," one of the other men says.

The man in the camouflage jacket lets go of her forearm and punches her in the face with the same hand. His fist crashes into her cheekbone before she can do so much as flinch. Alex is on the ground in an instant. She hits the pavement with the back of her head, and the impact makes her teeth slam together hard enough to send a sharp spike of pain through her jaw.

"Why does it always have to be the hard way," the stocky man says. His voice sounds like it's coming from the other side of the street. Alex feels two pairs of hands grabbing her underneath her armpits and dragging her backward. Then the man in the camo jacket stands over her. He reaches into her left front pocket and pulls out the credit chip and ID card she keeps in there.

"Got nothing to hand over, huh?" he says with gentle mockery in his voice. He puts his hand on her right thigh and pats down her other front pocket.

"Bonus item," he says when he feels the pocketknife. "Let's see what the mystery prize is."

When he starts to put his fingers into her pocket, Alex feels a swell of hot anger flaring up in her chest that burns the fear away in an instant. She pulls back her leg and kicks it out as hard as she can, then follows it up with the other leg. The stocky man takes the first kick to his belly, and he doubles over with a muffled shout. Her second kick catches him square in the face, right on the bridge of the nose. The muffled shout turns into a scream as he scrambles backward and stumbles. He falls over on his back and holds his nose with both hands.

Alex feels the grip of the hands on her arms loosening a bit. She yanks her shoulder away and reaches into her pocket. Someone grabs the collar of her jacket from behind and pulls her back, but her hand grasps the knife and deploys the blade from muscle memory, and the man behind her lets go with a curse when she jabs backward and slices the blade across the back of his hand.

The adrenaline flooding her system makes her feel as if someone electrified her from head to toe, making every nerve in her body vibrate with the rage she is feeling.

"That's my dad's," she shouts. The sight of the blade in her hand causes the two men who are still on their feet to recoil a little. They immediately move away from each other, and even though she has never been in a fight, she understands instinctively that they're preparing to

tackle her from two directions. The man in the camouflage jacket is sitting up on the ground, still holding his nose, blood pouring out between the fingers of his hand. She feels a wild sense of satisfaction at the sight. The left side of her face feels like it's on fire, and her eye is already starting to swell shut, but she repaid him in kind for the pain.

"Fuck me," the stocky man sitting on the ground says in a voice that sounds more irritated than anything else, as if he just dropped a bag of groceries instead of getting his nose broken by a woman he's trying to mug. He spits out a mouthful of blood as he slowly gets back to his feet and stands on shaky legs. He bends over and lets out a groan, and more blood spills onto the pavement in front of him.

"Fuck me," he says again. Then he reaches under his camouflage coat and pulls a gun out of the waistband at the small of his back. It looks nothing like the military sidearms Alex has seen all her life on the colony garrison troops. It's small and it looks battered to hell, with lots of scuffs and rust spots, but the sight of it makes her blood run cold.

"All right, playtime's done."

He brings up his hand and points the weapon at her. The muzzle looks small, too inconsequential for something that can end her life at the press of a finger.

The shot that thunders in the alley is much louder than she had expected out of such a small weapon. The stocky man in the camouflage jacket flinches and drops the gun. He coughs, a wet sound that ends in a gurgle when he falls forward and crashes to the ground face-first. There's a hole in the back of his jacket that's as large as her fist.

In the mouth of the alley to her left, an armored figure is aiming a gun at them. It looks a lot larger than the weapon that is now on the ground next to the body of the mugger. In the early-morning shadows of the alley, Alex sees a green targeting beam hovering in the air. She looks at the men in front of her to see the green dot at the end of the beam wandering from one man to the other and back.

"POLICE. DO NOT MOVE," an amplified voice booms. *"GET ON THE GROUND AND SPREAD OUT YOUR HANDS IN FRONT OF YOU OR I WILL SHOOT YOU."*

The two remaining muggers get down on their knees in almost perfect synchrony, as if they've performed that maneuver many times before. Alex drops her hand with the knife in it and takes a step back. Then her legs give out underneath her, and she stumbles backward until she hits the wall behind her. She slides down into a sitting position and puts the back of her head against the cool concrete. She folds her knife closed against her leg and sticks it back into her pocket with shaking fingers.

There's noisy movement in the alley to her left, but her eye on that side is now swollen shut, and she turns her head to bring the other eye to bear. Two armored men are tromping toward them, guns aimed at the men on the ground. They stop next to the motionless man in the camouflage jacket. One of the officers trains his weapon on him while the other takes out a set of flexible cuffs and ties up the stocky man's wrists with a quick and practiced motion even though he is clearly dead. They repeat the same process for each of the other men, who are not making a sound or moving a muscle as they get trussed up by the officers.

When they have finished searching the cuffed men, one of the officers walks over to Alex. In his bulky armor, he towers over her in a way that makes her think of a Lanky.

"Get a medical unit," he says to the other policeman. "They roughed her up pretty good."

He squats in front of her and raises the visor of his helmet.

"Are you all right, ma'am?"

Alex coughs, and the sudden motion sends a stab of pain through her head.

"No, sir. I am very much not all right," she says. Her voice sounds thick and mumbly to her own ears. She raises her hand and gingerly touches the left side of her face, and a new, sharper sort of pain flares up and makes her cry out softly.

"Medics are on the way. Just sit still for a few minutes."

"I wasn't really planning to do anything else right now," she says. The officer chuckles and flashes a smile.

"You got real lucky. Someone came out of the transit station and saw them push you into the alley. We were pretty much around the corner."

"Thanks," Alex says. "And here I thought I used up my lifetime luck already."

"They beat you up like this, and you were still standing when we got here. Looks like they picked the wrong mark today."

"I don't know about that. I'm pretty sure they had the upper hand all the way through."

He chuckles again.

"One of the guys I cuffed has a nice deep cut on his hand. Did I see a knife in your hand just as I turned the corner?"

She slowly pats her pocket. "My dad's old pocketknife. It's all I have left of him. They tried to take it and I didn't want to let them have it."

"Can I see it?"

Alex pulls the knife out of her pocket and hands it to the police officer. He turns it over in his hand and folds out the blade.

"That is a well-loved knife," he says. "It has a locking blade, though. You're not really supposed to carry that in public. It's illegal."

She has to restrain herself from snatching the knife back from his hand.

"Please don't take that away from me. I'll stow away on a ship back to Scorpio before I give that up. I've got nothing else left."

"Scorpio?" he repeats. Then realization dawns on his face. "You're one of the colonists they brought back? The Scorpio one hundred and fifty?"

"You know about that?"

"It was on all the networks. *Hey, Caleb,*" he shouts at his fellow officer. "She's one of the Scorpio settlers."

"No shit," Officer Caleb replies from the mouth of the alley.

He closes the knife again. Then he gives it back to her and wraps her hand around it.

"My mistake. That's clearly not a locking blade. Put it away and keep it safe."

The medics arrive just a little while later. They walk Alex out of the alley while the police officers are cleaning up the scene. There's an ambulance parked just outside the mouth of the alley, and they lead her to the back of it and help her into the rear of the vehicle. Outside, a small crowd has gathered to observe the entertainment, and Alex is glad when the medics close the door and shield her from the curious eyes.

Whatever they put on her face takes the pain away almost immediately. One of the medics gives her a full-body scan while the other works on her injury.

"You're tough," the medic working the scanner says. "Your cheekbone's only bruised. I thought for sure it was broken, the way your face looked. Must have been a pretty good punch."

"It felt like a pretty good punch," she says. "Do I need to be taken to the medbay or something?"

"Medbay," the other medic says. "Are you in the Fleet?"

She shakes her head. "Colonist. I'm from Scorpio."

The medic lets out a low whistle. "Scorpio. Holy shit. You folks are kind of famous."

"Someone forgot to tell the guy who punched me in the face," she says.

"Have you ever seen a Lanky?" the medic on the scanner asks.

"Yeah," Alex replies. "You could say that."

"That is pretty awesome."

She just smiles curtly in response, unwilling to douse the medic's excitement by explaining in detail just how very much not awesome it is to come face-to-face with a twenty-meter extraterrestrial that weighs as much as a small building. "We're going to fix you up right here," the medic by her side says. "No big deal. By the end of the week, you'll barely have a bruise."

"That's good to know," Alex says.

There's a knock on the back door of the ambulance. The medic on the scanner walks over and opens it. Outside, the police officer who spoke to her in the alley is carrying her school bag. He climbs into the ambulance and holds it up in front of her.

"This was your stuff, right? I think I got everything they dumped out."

She takes it from him and looks inside. The school data pad is in there, along with her printouts for Biology 101.

"Thank you, Officer. I'm pretty sure I'm going to be late for school, though."

He laughs. "Hey, if you need an excuse note, I can write you a really good one."

CHAPTER 31

A week after the mugging, Alex still can't sleep through the night.

Every night, she wakes up at three in the morning with her heart racing, convinced that something terrible is about to happen. Every time, she gets out of bed to check the status of the security lock on the door of her unit, only to repeat the process when she tries to go back to sleep and can't. Every noise in the building turns into a portent of impending doom in her head. She hasn't left her unit since the attack, skipping two test days back at the academic center. After so little sleep, she stops attending the remote classes as well because it feels like her brain is operating on emergency power only, just like their mule on Scorpio after the power cell got fried by the Lanky. It doesn't seem to matter because nobody from the school sends her so much as an automated message to check on her and find out why she hasn't been able to turn in any work or come in for proctored exams.

A week and a half in, not even the fear of another mugging can override the boredom of her days, and she dresses in street clothes for the first time since the attack to go outside.

—

It's the middle of the day on a Saturday, and the streets are comfortingly crowded, the first time she has put those two words together in her head. Even with all the people on the sidewalks, she still gives alleyways a wide berth when she passes them. If she had felt that she was getting used to the PRC before, all that comfort has been blown out of her brain by the punch from the stocky man in the camouflage jacket. When she passes the transit station, she keeps walking. She knows it's an irrational fear response, but she is suddenly unwilling to walk through the narrow confines of the station tunnels, even though there are hundreds of people moving through those same tunnels at the same time.

Alex has no idea how long she has been walking when she passes a familiar transit stop and realizes she's gone all the way to Government Center, the big plaza in the middle of the PRC where the academic center takes up a few floors in one of the tall buildings looming over the square. For a moment, she considers going up to her public college and checking on all the work she has missed. Her brain vetoes the idea almost immediately, and she doesn't try to push through the sense of resignation she feels when she thinks about her math and physics classes right now. If she needs all the focus she can muster just to put on clothes and go outside, she concedes that she probably wouldn't be turning in any coherent work on Rotational Kinematics or Momentum and Collisions.

She realizes that she has never really explored the area around the central square. Every time she has been here, she has made a beeline from the transit stop to the academic center because she had to get to class on time. Now that she isn't on a timer, she wanders down some of the streets that branch off from the square, hoping that walking herself tired will make her go to sleep and keep her down all night.

In one of the streets near the central square, a holographic sign catches her eye. The street is dotted with them, advertising everything from cheap haircuts to subsidized data pads, but this one sticks out to her as soon as she spots it. There's a soldier on it, a handsome dark-haired and dark-eyed young man in Spaceborne Infantry fatigues who looks a little bit like Lopez. His uniform is crisply ironed, with the sleeves rolled up in perfectly even folds that have sharp and precise edges. Above the soldier's head, a scrolling text says **COMMONWEALTH DEFENSE CORPS—JOIN TODAY TO DEFEND OUR TOMORROW**.

Alex walks down the street until she is in front of the place the sign is advertising. It has the seals of all the services on the windows—Spaceborne Infantry, Fleet, and Homeworld Defense. Inside, there are several desks and informational displays set up in the room. A handful of soldiers in uniform are sitting around one of the desks and talking to each other, and the sight makes Alex instantly homesick for the squad room back at the Vault, where the soldiers would gather after missions or during downtime to blow off steam or share laughs. It was a different world from the rest of the Vault, a special place where not even the administrators of the colony dared to trespass.

She loiters in front of the office for a little while, trying to be inconspicuous while she watches the soldiers inside having an animated conversation about something. After a few minutes, one of the soldiers catches her eye through the window, and he gives her a friendly nod before returning his attention to the group.

Oh, this would be a terrible idea, she thinks.

—

Alex only realizes that she has been hanging out in front of the recruiting office for a long while when the shadows are starting to become pronounced. She checks the time to see that it's past 1700 hours. Sunset is a little over an hour away, and she does not want to be out in the PRC when it gets dark. But the thought of going back to her unit and spending another restless night is almost as unappealing right now as the possibility of getting mugged again.

What the hell, she decides. *I just want to talk. Doesn't mean I need to sign anything.*

When she opens the door and walks into the office, the soldiers all turn their heads to look at her.

"Hello there," one of them says, a broad-shouldered gunnery sergeant. "Do come in. We don't bite."

"Good afternoon," the female staff sergeant says with a smile. "Any questions we can answer for you?"

"Yeah. What's in those mugs?" Alex asks.

The gunnery sergeant looks down at the coffee mug in his hand.

"Fleet sludge," he says. "It's sort of like coffee, only much worse."

"Got any left? I haven't had a cup of fleet sludge in months."

The gunny raises an eyebrow and looks at the others.

"The young lady likes fleet sludge. Get her a cup, Corporal. We aim to please."

"Aye, sir," the corporal at the table says and gets up from his chair. He walks over to the kitchen nook and takes a cup out of an overhead cabinet.

"Are you prior service?" the female staff sergeant asks.

"No, ma'am."

"Didn't think so. You look a bit too young for that."

"So how the hell are you familiar with our terrible coffee?" the gunny asks.

Alex smiles at the memory. "It's a long story. I was with an SI squad for a while."

"As a civilian," the staff sergeant says, skepticism in her voice.

"I was a dog handler."

"Dog handler? Where was this?"

"Out in the colonies," Alex replies. "In the 18 Scorpii system. That's where I lived until six months ago."

The gunnery sergeant does a double take and almost spits out the sip of coffee he just took from his mug.

"You're one of the colonists from *Scorpio*?"

Alex nods.

The gunny puts his mug on the table and gets up from his chair. He walks to the adjacent empty table and snatches a chair by the backrest. He carries it to his own desk, puts it down, and nods at it.

"Do have a seat. This is a story that I absolutely want to hear. I'm Gunnery Sergeant Phelps. This is Staff Sergeant Shea. Corporal Grady, get a move on with that coffee."

—

Twenty minutes into the conversation and two cups of coffee later, Alex realizes just how much she has missed talking to people who understand what she is telling them, who have a common ground with her when it comes to the things she has seen and done. Once the soldiers in the recruiting office figure out that she isn't making up her story, the questions fly thick and fast. At some point, the young corporal gets up to lock the door and lower the blinds of the office.

It's long dark outside when she has gotten to the end of her tale, the evacuation from Scorpio and the trip back to Earth. When she is finished, it feels like a great weight that she didn't even notice for six months has been lifted from her shoulders.

"That is the wildest shit I have heard in a long time," Gunny Phelps says.

"I'm pretty sure it's the wildest shit I'll ever hear," Staff Sergeant Shea concurs. "Hanging on for that long, with so little. One freaking understrength squad, with two mules and no support."

"You've had close calls with more Lankies than most SI troopers have ever seen with their own eyes." Gunny Phelps had finished his coffee a while ago, but he's still holding his mug, turning it slowly in his hands.

"So what on earth are you doing here in our lovely PRC Pittsburgh A-5?" Shea asks.

"That's where I asked them to place me. I lived in the area with my parents when I was little. Figured it was as good a place as any. But now that I'm here, I just want to get on the next ship back to Scorpio. Lankies or not."

The staff sergeant lets out a throaty chuckle.

"Yeah, that sounds about right."

Gunny Phelps finally puts aside his empty mug. He rubs his face and exhales slowly into his palms.

"You didn't go to Basic or take the oath, and you didn't wear a rank," he says. "But the shit you went through? That's more war than any five soldiers I know have experienced in total. And I include myself in that. We had guys coming home from just three weeks of fighting on Mars who had to get medical retirements because of combat stress. You were in the line for *years*. It's freaking appalling that the civvie administration just gave you a week's worth of how-to lectures and sent you out into this shithole to fend for yourself."

"I didn't know what to do," Alex says. "I still don't. I walk around in this place and it's like I'm the only real person on the street. I talk to people, and they don't listen to what I'm saying. The medic asked me if I had ever seen a Lanky. He thought it was the most exciting thing."

Staff Sergeant Shea exchanges a look with the gunny. She shakes her head and smiles at Alex.

"You know the number one reason why people reenlist?"

Alex shakes her head.

"It's not money. Can't buy shit for that these days anyway. It's because they feel they don't fit in at home anymore. Their old friends spending their days getting spun up about pointless shit, watching network shows, getting wasted, fighting each other over the dumbest stuff. You come back to that after a tour in the infantry, you feel like you belong to a different species."

The relief Alex feels almost makes her want to cry. Everything the staff sergeant just said rings true. She feels like she has been wandering a foreign country for the last six months, one where the customs are inscrutable and the language is completely different even though it sounds the same as hers, and she wasn't able to make sense of anything until she walked into this office a few hours ago. It feels like the first real conversation she's had since she came here.

"What would you do in my place?" she asks, repeating the question she had asked the resettlement bureaucrat almost six months ago, starting the chain of decisions that got her to this place and point in time.

"What would I do?" Staff Sergeant Shea laughs and folds her arms across her chest. "I'd get the fuck out of this place. I know I'm a recruiter, and that's the sort of shit you'd expect me to say to sign up these PRC kids out there."

She leans forward and locks eyes with Alex.

"But you're not one of those PRC kids. Like the gunny said, you may not have the dog tags or the rank, but you're a grunt. You don't belong in this place, and you know it. If I found myself in your boots, I'd sign enlistment papers so fast that the stylus would leave a contrail. And that's the grunt speaking, not the recruiter."

Gunnery Sergeant Phelps shakes his head and chuckles.

"Damn, Shea. You got me reaching for the forms, and I've been in for fourteen years."

Alex doesn't want to decide now because she doesn't want to commit to anything on the spot. That's what got her into the PRC and into this situation in the first place. But something seems to click into place in her head that has been out of alignment and jamming up the gears from the day she left Scorpio until this moment.

"I know they select by aptitude, but could you get me a slot in the Spaceborne Infantry if I decide to join?"

There's a moment of silence in the room, and then Staff Sergeant Shea laughs out loud.

"It's ranked choice now, honey. You list your preferred service and they take it into account. I'll tell you that if you put SI as your top pick, you're going to get SI. Hardly anyone picks infantry as their first choice. But even if they still selected by aptitude, you wouldn't have anything to worry about. You've got that in spades."

CHAPTER 32

When Val answers the connection request for their weekly face-to-face talk over the network, she recoils visibly when she sees Alex's image on her screen.

"Holy shit. What happened to your face? You look like you went a few rounds with a Lanky."

Alex touches the side of her face. Even the light pressure from her fingertips still hurts, and she grimaces.

"Yeah, the medic lied. He said I'd have nothing but a bruise left by the weekend."

"What the hell happened?" Val demands.

"I got jumped. Out on the street. Some asshole pretending to be a vet. I wasn't paying attention for a moment, and *pow*."

"Shit. Are you all right?"

"Yeah," Alex says. "Mostly. Except for the face. Caught a punch when I didn't want to give up my knife. If I'd had Ash with me, he would have torn the arm off that son of a bitch."

"I hope you stabbed the shit out of him."

Alex shakes her head. "He had friends. And a gun. But so did the cops that showed up. I'm not going to have to worry about him again."

"That's good. Wish I could have been there."

"You don't want to be anywhere near this place," Alex says. "But let's not talk about that. It'll just make me anxious again for the rest of the day. What's going on with you?"

"Oh, it's all peachy here. Mom's almost done with her training. She already has a colony assignment," Val says.

"Really? Where is she going?"

"Arcadia. In the Leonidas system. She'll be chief administrator. What used to be Blake's job."

"She'll be great," Alex says. "God help the slacker teenagers on that colony."

"She wants me to come with her," Val says. "It's a loophole. I won't be twenty-one for another few months, so I'm still a dependent. I can start training out there. I'm not sure I want to, though. It's a long way to that system. More than twice the distance to Scorpio. I'll probably see Lankies around every corner."

"I hear Arcadia is the nicest of the colonies," Alex says. "The most fortified too. I don't think you have to worry about Lankies there anytime soon. Lopez said the military started a new offensive to take the old colonies back."

"You heard from Lopez?"

Alex feels her cheeks flush. "You could say that. He came to visit two weeks ago."

"He did *not*," Val says, and for a moment, the old version of her friend pokes through, the Val who was always on top of all the social news in the Vault.

"Yeah. It was great to see him. Felt a bit like old times."

"And?" Val looks at her expectantly. "Don't make me drag it out of you, Archer."

"He stayed over," Alex admits. Val pumps her fist and lets out a triumphant little hiss.

"Fucking *finally*. You'll have to fill me in on all the details the next time we get together in person."

"I most certainly will *not*," Alex says, and they smile at each other.

"I don't want to be a hundred friggin' light-years away from my best friend," Val says. "We won't even be able to do live calls. Just canned messages."

Six months ago, the news would have cut Alex much deeper. But they've been apart for half a year now, and even though they are talking over vid chat every week, there's a distance between them now that goes beyond the physical space between Pittsburgh and Alaska, and Alex knows that it will widen a little more with every passing month. All the pieces of her old life have drifted apart since she left the Vault, and she knows that she won't be able to pull them back together no matter how hard she tries.

"You need to go," she tells Val. "Don't stay just because of me. I'll be gone soon anyway."

"What are you going to do?" Val asks with a tinge of alarm in her expression.

"I think I'm going to join the Corps," Alex says. "I went to a recruiting office today."

She expects her friend to laugh her statement off as a joke. But to her surprise, Val only smiles a little, as if she had expected this development.

"Good for you," she says. "I mean, I think all soldiers are a little bit nuts, don't get me wrong. But you've always been down in the military section when we were in the Vault. They sort of adopted you. It makes total sense."

"I don't feel like I belong here," Alex says. "I never did. You want to know the hardest part of living in this place?"

Val nods.

"The hardest part is not the food or the noise," Alex continues. "Not even the crowds of people. I never would have guessed it before I came here, but the hardest part is all the time on my hands. And nothing worthwhile to do to fill it."

"You need to go," Val returns Alex's earlier advice to her without any indication of humor or sarcasm.

"You think so?"

Her friend leans closer to the camera, and Alex is sure that Val would cup her face with her hands if they were in the same room together to hold her gaze while she's imparting some important wisdom.

"I've never seen you more together than when you returned with the salvage team. I don't know if it made you happy to be out there risking your neck. But I know it made you content. Go do what makes you content. I don't have to be there with you to know that the place you're in right now is draining the life out of you."

Alex feels the familiar tickling in her nose that tells her she's about to tear up.

"You can be pretty deep when you want to be, Velasco," she says.

"Don't fucking tell anyone," Val says. "I have a carefree reputation to protect."

"I'll miss you."

"I'll miss you too. But there's always this." Val taps the frame of her network screen. "This world just turned out too big for us, I think. It was much easier when our pods were just eighty meters and a flight of stairs apart, wasn't it?"

Alex nods with a soft sniffle. "Love you, friend," she says.

"I love you too, Alex. Now get off your ass and get the hell out of there."

EPILOGUE

The bus hums across the causeway in near silence. It's nighttime, and Alex hasn't slept since she left PRC Pittsburgh A-5 sixteen hours ago in similar darkness, but she's too wound up to even think about going to sleep. Outside, the landscape is mysterious and exotic, swamps and mangrove trees, and they haven't passed a house or any other human-made structure in almost an hour. Gunny Phelps told her that they always cross the causeway at night, to enhance the feeling of making a transition from one life to another, and she has to admit that it's effective stagecraft.

The bus is full to the last seat. Nobody else in here is sleeping either, as far as she can tell, and there's no chatter between the seats anymore. Her neighbor is a redheaded kid with freckles who reminds her a little of her friend Dallas, or at least the way he looked before he grew his beard. She can smell the anxiety in the recycled air, but she isn't feeling particularly anxious herself even though she knows from her squad's stories what kind of artificial stressors the drill instructors have in store for them all. She knows that nothing that boot camp can serve up will be anywhere near as stress-inducing as facing a Lanky with nothing but a pocketknife.

The first sign of their arrival is a lighted wire-mesh fence. The bus rolls to a stop in front of it, and a gate opens to admit the vehicle.

Stern-faced soldiers in camouflage fatigues are watching the bus as it rolls past the gate.

When the bus stops again a few minutes later, they're in front of a large one-story building that is lit up by light fixtures in front of every corner. The front door of the bus opens, and a Spaceborne Infantry soldier in battle dress fatigues leaps up the stairs in two effortless steps. He squares off at the front of the bus, his expression stern and focused.

"Now," he says. The way he inflects it makes it sound like an invocation, as if he wants to make sure everyone on the bus is in the present and giving this new timeline their undivided attention.

"You will step off my bus in single file. There are yellow footprints on the concrete outside. Each of you will step onto a pair of those footprints. You will not talk, fidget, or scratch yourselves. Anything in your mouth right now will come out and be left in the trash receptacle by your seat. *Execute,*" he says. Then he turns and leaves the bus without another word.

Alex gets up and grabs her bag from the overhead storage. The people in front of her file out in good order, and she takes her spot at the back of the queue and shuffles along the aisle until she reaches the stairs. Outside, the rows of yellow footprints begin just a few meters next to the bus, and she follows the recruit in front of her and takes her spot on the prints next to his.

When they are all lined up in uneven rows, the doors of the building in front of them fly open, and three SI sergeants in campaign hats briskly stride out and line up in front of the rows of recruits with perfectly even spacing. Behind them, another soldier follows at a slightly weightier pace. When the figure passes underneath one of the lights, Alex makes out the rank insignia of a staff sergeant. Then the staff sergeant lifts her head to look at the assembled group of recruits, and the excitement of recognition gives Alex a little jolt.

"Welcome to NACRD Charleston," the staff sergeant says. "I am Staff Sergeant Doran, your senior drill instructor. You will now enter the receiving building to be processed for the start of your training to become members of the Commonwealth Defense Corps. The first row will follow Sergeant Kearns and line up single file to the left side of the door. The second row will follow Sergeant Flint to the right side of the door. The third and fourth row will stay put until the first two lines are inside the building. *Execute.*"

Alex is in the fourth row, so she stays put as ordered and watches the flustered new recruits follow their assigned sergeants while trying not to trip over their feet. It takes a little while for the first batch to make it into the building despite—or maybe because of—the instructors hurrying them along with shouted commands as soon as the doors open for them.

Then it's her turn to line up with her row. She passes within five meters of Staff Sergeant Doran, the woman who was the last NCO in charge of the Scorpio garrison. Doran looks ahead with the same stern expression she put on when she left the building to greet this batch of recruits, and Alex has no idea whether she recognized her in the rush and the semidark parking lot.

But as she stands at the back of her line and waits for the door to open and a pair of sergeants to shout at them, Doran walks past the line on the left. She pauses when she reaches Alex's spot and leans close until the rim of her campaign hat almost touches the side of Alex's head.

"Don't think for a second I'll be going easy on you," Doran murmurs in a low voice that's barely above a whisper. She gives Alex an almost imperceptible little wink and continues up the line.

Alex can't avoid a smile even as the doors fly open again and the assistant drill instructors rush out to herd them all into the building.

Now it's finally starting to feel like home, she thinks as she follows the other recruits, shouts from the sergeants propelling them along and through the waiting open doors.

ACKNOWLEDGMENTS

When I first sat down to write the acknowledgments, I wanted to start with "This was not an easy book to write." Then I realized that it would be trite and redundant because the sentiment applies to every book that has ever been written, including the ones their authors dashed off in two weeks in a blaze of brilliance. *All* novels are hard to write. Some, however, come easier than others. Some of my drafts took just three months to write, others took most of a year.

This one fell somewhere in between, at least as far as time spent writing goes. I started it in earnest in the early summer of 2022 and turned in the finished draft in February of 2023. In that respect, it's about average. What wasn't part of the metrics, however, was all the time I *didn't* spend writing. I planned to write the draft in three months or so, plus or minus a few weeks, and it ended up taking nine. Part of the reason for that was the need to come up with a new narrative, main character, and tone of voice. All of those had to be unique enough to be interesting, but they also had to dovetail with the existing Frontlines universe in a compelling way. That task was more difficult than I had anticipated. Add to that a case of professional exhaustion that hit me in the second half of the year like a pallet of bricks dropping on my head from a great height, and I can now confidently say that this was the most difficult draft I've ever produced. It didn't feel like it during those days last year when I only managed to get a few sentences written, but it turned out to be a good story. I think it's a solid jumping-off point for the new series (now officially called Frontlines: Evolution).

That said, this novel wouldn't be in your hands right now without the steadfast support of my personal and professional networks of family, friends, and colleagues, and it would be a grave oversight to omit the thanks they are due.

Thank you first and foremost to my wife, Robin. The book is dedicated to her (as most of my books are), but she deserves to have her thank-you doubled because she went above and beyond for this one. I am certain that this book wouldn't exist without her keeping me on track, nudging me along, and assuring me that it was just a phase that would pass. (She was right, of course, and it did pass.)

Thank you to my editor, Adrienne Procaccini, who probably pulled out a fair amount of her hair while accommodating my continued overshooting of the deadline.

Thank you to my agent, Evan Gregory, for his continued good advice and support.

Thank you to my friends, in particular Tracie, Monica, Tamara, Stacy, and Paul, who were (and are) part of my emotional-support scaffolding.

Thank you to my friends and colleagues, especially Delilah S. Dawson, Chuck Wendig, and Kevin Hearne, the first writer friends of mine I got to see in person again since the start of the COVID pandemic. Our get-together provided a much-needed reminder that we're all working by ourselves but not alone.

And thank you to my readers, who have waited patiently for whatever was to come next in the Frontlines universe. This book is the start of a new adventure, and I am grateful you're on board for it.

Marko Kloos
Enfield, May 2023

ABOUT THE AUTHOR

Marko Kloos is the author of two military science fiction series: The Palladium Wars, which includes *Aftershocks* and *Ballistic*, and the Frontlines series, which includes *Orders of Battle* and *Centers of Gravity*. Born in Germany and raised in and around the city of Münster, Marko was previously a soldier, bookseller, freight dockworker, and corporate IT administrator before deciding that he wasn't cut out for anything except making stuff up for fun and profit. A member of George R. R. Martin's Wild Cards consortium, Marko writes primarily science fiction and fantasy—his first genre loves ever since his youth, when he spent his allowance on German SF pulp serials. He likes bookstores, kind people, October in New England, fountain pens, and wristwatches. Marko resides at Castle Frostbite in New Hampshire with his wife, two children, and roving pack of voracious dachshunds. For more information, visit www.markokloos.com.